The author was born in Scotland and after serving in the army embarked on a career in industry and commerce.

He has worked in several different sectors of business mostly in senior roles and latterly as CEO of a large international data capture company.

He retired for the first time in 1995 but continued to work as a consultant helping new businesses become established.

In 2018, he finally retired from business life to become a full-time author.

John lives in the UK and Portugal with his wife and they have two grown-up sons.

To my wife, Liz, for her patience and support during the hours spent in writing this novel.

Also to my friends Guy, Mike and Jimbo together with their wives for their encouragement and good humour throughout the writing process.

John Reid

THE FORGOTTEN GUN

A DCI Steve Burt Mystery

AUSTIN MACAULEY PUBLISHERS™

LONDON * CAMBRIDGE * NEW YORK * SHARJAH

A CIP catalogue record for this title is available from the British Library.

ISBN 9781398417946 (Paperback)
ISBN 9781398417953 (Hardback)
ISBN 9781398417960 (ePub e-book)

www.austinmacauley.com

First Published (2021)
Austin Macauley Publishers Ltd
25 Canada Square
Canary Wharf
London
E14 5LQ

Chapter One

The killer sat on an ordinary high-backed dining chair, looking out the window at nothing in particular. His mind was calm, but adrenaline pumped through his veins. He was looking forward to the kill he knew was coming. He absently noted that the window was an old-fashioned, sash-corded type with two frames. One frame was above the other, which meant both frames could slide up and down. For no reason, he noted each frame had six panes of glass.

He'd previously lifted the bottom frame, so it now stood open and raised about nine inches. To his left sat his machine. His very own killing machine. He thought it a work of art with its advanced engineering and revolutionary basic computer system. The high-power optics were unbelievable and controlled the whole machine. There was nothing like it in the world. He was very proud of this present from his father. There was no other weapon that could kill from such long ranges and hit the target every time. Using the machine meant killing remotely. The killer preferred this. He didn't like the sight of blood.

The only drawback to the killing machine was its size and weight. This didn't worry the killer too much. He was a planner. He knew the importance of good planning. It was what he did best. Everything was planned down to the last detail, including having enough time to assemble his machine once he had it at the kill spot.

He knew everything he needed to about his victim. He knew where he would be today. He knew he was a creature of habit. He knew every Friday was the same. He knew that between 12 noon and 2.30pm, he met with two business associates in the upmarket 'La Jola' restaurant. The killer had no idea who the other two men were nor what they discussed. He didn't care. He knew after their lunch, the three men always stood on the pavement outside the restaurant chatting and waiting for a taxi that took the target from the restaurant. He knew this Friday would be his victim's last lunch. He knew exactly what time his victim would die.

Sitting looking out the window, the killer thought back to how his plan had come together and how he was now just hours away from getting justice for his father.

He had staked out the restaurant each Friday for a month and knew the routine was always the same. He knew the spot he had chosen was the best place to get to the victim. He only needed a clear shot. He knew he would get one.

He'd acquired planning maps from the town hall and had walked the area trying to find the best kill spot to set up his killing machine. He also had a copy of the local electoral roll so knew who lived where and how many people were in each household in the area he planned to shoot from. He knew he was looking for somewhere he could take the shot without any outside interference. He was looking for a location, probably an apartment or rooftop with a clear field of vision. If he decided to shoot from an apartment, then he would prefer it to be occupied by only one person. He couldn't leave any witnesses.

He had scoured the streets armed with the electoral roll and his maps. He soon realised a block of apartments, known as Sedgwick Close, was ideal for his purpose if he could gain access to one on the third floor with a clear distant view of the restaurant. He would dress in a police uniform. This always helped.

He knew people with nothing to hide trusted authority. His plan had come together. All he had to do was execute it.

He thought of yesterday. How he had started putting his plan in operation. There was a part of his plan he didn't like. He had decided the apartment on the third floor, owned by a Mrs Jemima Boyd, was perfect as his kill site. He knew Mrs Boyd was a widow aged 78 and when she had answered the door to the killer at 3pm the previous day—Thursday, 2 April—it was obvious she weighed no more than 100 pounds. The killer, dressed as a police sergeant, said he was there to carry out a security inspection of the flat. In reality, he was confirming his research that the view from the living room window of this flat gave exactly the view he needed. Mrs Boyd had been welcoming and had invited the sergeant in.

The killer confirmed what he already knew from the electoral roll that Mrs Boyd lived alone. She told him she received almost no visitors, didn't have meals on wheels and her family was living in Scotland.

He wouldn't be disturbed. This was a perfect choice. As Mrs Boyd was explaining that she saw no one from one day to the next, the killer put his hands around her throat and squeezed the life from Mrs Jemima Boyd. He needed her apartment and could leave no witnesses.

He felt physically sick as he carried the body into the bathroom and placed it in the bath. He knew if he filled the bath, the smell of the corpse would be reduced. It could take days before the body was discovered. Once the bath was full, he sat in one of Mrs Boyd's living room armchairs and wept. He told himself over and over that this wasn't who he was. He wasn't a murderer. He was a caring individual who'd been forced into this course of action to avenge his father. He wasn't a coldblooded killer. People like Mrs Boyd were necessary collateral damage. It was unavoidable.

After about half an hour, he recovered his composure. Wiping his eyes, he got to work.

The killing machine was in the back of his white Ford van that was parked just around the corner from Mrs Boyd's apartment. The road was reasonably quiet. He walked to the van and drove it to the entrance of Sedgwick Close. There was no one about so he unloaded three heavy, large suitcases from the back of the van. He had a sack barrow and loaded all three cases onto the L-shaped foot of the barrow and wheeled them into the lift and up to Mrs Boyd's apartment. The killer then went back to the van and drove it to a 24-hour garage, where he parked it.

It was after 7pm when the killer got back to Mrs Boyd's. His kill day was tomorrow: Friday, 3 April. He could feel the thrill of finally getting the revenge he was seeking for his father. Like a slow flame, the anger inside him had built and built and now he was close to releasing all his pent-up frustrations and anger. This was to be the first of three revenge killings.

He stayed the night in Mrs Boyd's flat. This was part of his plan. He couldn't afford to be seen by any stray passer-by. Better to be in position and ready early. He was high on nervous tension and knew he couldn't eat. It would soon be morning and then he would set up his killing machine.

By 11 o'clock on Friday, 3 April, the killer was ready. He'd set the computer, double-checked the data for trajectory, distance, wind speed, direction and velocity of the projectile and confirmed the primer charge was ready. He checked everything every 15 minutes. He marvelled at the quality of the optics on the combined range and viewfinder as he made small adjustments.

He knew his target was due to get into his taxi at 2.30pm and would say goodbye to his colleagues for three minutes, meaning the kill shot should be made between 2.27 and 2.29pm. The killer would have to time the introduction of the projectile into the breach of the killing machine very precisely. He had practiced with the killing machine and knew how important it was to place the projectile into the breach at the right time. As the clock turned towards 2.30, the killer made his final preparations. The machine was set so he could do no more other than make final adjustments to the aim, load it and press the fire button. He was having difficulty controlling his emotions. The high-backed dining chair was not very comfortable and he wished he had a cushion.

The countdown to the killing began.

2.26. The killer put on a thick, insulated industrial glove and unscrewed the top of an electric flask that he'd plugged in the previous evening. As soon as the lid was removed, a stream of smoke appeared as the killer lifted out the projectile. The flask contained liquid nitrogen. The killer didn't know how cold it was inside the flask, but he knew not to go anywhere near it without the protection of the glove.

2.27. He placed the projectile into the chamber using his gloved hand. With his other hand, he placed the charge behind the projectile and closed the breach. He took one final check of the settings and placed his eye on the range and viewfinder. He waited.

2.28. As expected, three men—all wearing overcoats and carrying briefcases—appeared from the restaurant. Through the viewfinder, the killer picked out his target and adjusted the killing machine to bear down on this one individual. The killer noticed the target carried his briefcase in his left hand. A small point but a detail. It meant he wouldn't change hands when shaking goodbye with his fellow diners. He would be stationary longer. This was good. The killer waited.

2.29. The taxi hadn't arrived. It was late. The men were shuffling their feet, obviously ready to go. The killer had to decide. He did. With a final, small adjustment, the target was firmly locked and in the centre of the sights. The killer pushed the button on the side of the killing machine. The machine gave a small lurch. Through the viewfinder, the killer watched the scene.

2.31. The victim was lying on the pavement and blood from the side of his head began to stain the cobbles a bright pink colour.

2.32. The killer was crying floods of tears and couldn't stop. He didn't know if they were tears of joy or despair. He knew he was crying in part for Mrs Boyd.

She was an innocent victim, but he also knew he was crying for himself. He was now a double murderer and he knew there was no redemption for him.

2.47. The killer had composed himself enough and started to plan his escape. He knew the police would never find him and that he could take his time. He returned to the 24-hour carpark and drove back to Sedgwick Close. He then disassembled his killing machine and placed the parts back inside the three suitcases he'd used earlier. It was an easy job to close the apartment door, return to the van pushing the three suitcases on the sack barrow and drive off. He was safe in the knowledge he was getting away with murder. His weekend would be all the sweeter knowing he'd had his revenge on the first of the swindlers. Only two more to go.

Chapter Two

Monday, 6 April

The detective inspector woke with a start. By now, he knew the routine. After three months spending his evenings in the pub and trying to drink it dry, he knew how this worked. He opened his eyes slowly. Very slowly! His first thought was, *Where am I?* Followed by, *How did I get here?* There was a television playing. He remembered there always was when consciousness called him. He tried to focus on the television without success but realised it was showing an old black and white film.

With relief, he recognised the overly large TV screen as his. He was in his own apartment, in his own armchair. He also now knew without looking that he was still dressed in his suit. He figured it must have been another successful night at the pub!

He knew instinctively that beside his chair, which had been doubling up as his part-time bed for three months, would be a side table and on it would be what was left of his whisky from the previous night. He usually had a tipple after a night at the pub. Last night wouldn't have been any different.

Slowly, he came to as he always did. His mouth was dry, and his brain was beginning to tell his eyes to focus. He knew he needed a few more minutes to surface. Apart from his TV, he recognised this room. His room. Probably not too tidy but adequate for a soon-to-be ex-detective inspector.

Since his suspension exactly three months ago, his routine had been the same. Now it was all too familiar. He spent most of his daylight hours in this apartment, sleeping and watching television. Evenings were spent in the Bush Public House where he was now a regular. He knew he was becoming something of a sad figure. He wasn't proud of what he'd become over the past three months, but he couldn't find the enthusiasm to do anything about it.

This was his life now. Apathy plus booze with the occasional female thrown in. He was on the slippery slope to a future of Alcoholics Anonymous meetings and liver failure. He was really down and feeling sorry for himself. This feeling was also normal now.

As he gathered his senses, the soon-to-be ex-detective inspector congratulated himself. At least there was no evidence he'd brought back one of the scrubbers from the pub last night. He knew he'd done it in the past and knew he'd recently started going for quantity over quality when it came to female companionship. He remembered his father had once told him that alcohol could make ugly women better-looking. This was a truism he had experienced in the recent past. He shuddered at the memories and his skull rattled inside his head. He didn't feel well.

Last night he must have avoided the three or four regular ladies who were always available. He'd obviously concentrated instead on drinking as much beer and whisky as he could. He still felt miserable but was surfacing slowly. He was going through 'a never again' moment. As with most of his awakenings, he had had a total blackout and had no idea how he'd made it home. At least he wasn't driving, mainly due to the fact that his car had been repossessed by the finance company last month.

As he continued to slowly surface, he looked at the clock on the mantle shelf. It was showing 3.35am. Between 3am and 4am had become his normal time to return to consciousness after a night at the Bush. He was becoming a creature of habit but not one he was proud of.

He eventually felt sufficiently human to consider going to bed but only after he had the last drink left in the whisky bottle beside his chair. He was always amazed at the medicinal power of single malt. Keep the blood out of your alcohol stream. That was the mantra of the drunks at the Bush Public House. He thought it was good advice.

He reluctantly pushed himself off the chair and shuffled out of his living room, leaving the television still switched on. He was always full of good intentions at this point in his now regular routine, but he knew his clothes would be in a heap beside his bed in the morning. A shower before bed wouldn't happen tonight, again.

Chapter Three

Monday, 6 April

The detective inspector again woke with a start. Something in the far distance was making a horrible noise that threatened to give him an even more serious headache than he knew was awaiting him when he returned to the land of the living. After several attempts to ignore this noise, he came out of his alcoholic coma and reluctantly returned to consciousness. He realised it was the telephone beside his bed that was calling him.

He stretched out and somehow managed to grab the receiver the right way up.

"Yes?" was all the detective inspector could manage in a croaky voice. His mouth was furred up and his head was full of stones bouncing around as though his head were a washing machine on a spin cycle. He was impressed he even managed this basic greeting.

There was a pause on the other end of the phone as though whoever was there may have been expecting a more formal greeting.

"Is this Inspector Burt?" Without waiting for a reply, the female voice continued, "This is Miss Hawkins. I am the personal assistant to Chief Superintendent Charles, head of Human Resources at Scotland Yard." The voice sounded very impressed with her position.

The inspector had the phone to his ear and his head on the pillow with his eyes tightly shut. He was only semi-conscious and was ready for either more sleep or a quick single malt. He thought he preferred more sleep.

Without pausing for breath or any confirmation from the inspector, the woman continued, "This is to remind you that you have an interview with Chief Superintendent Charles this morning at 11 o'clock. I'm sure I do not have to remind you that this interview is to advise you of the decision of the disciplinary board that was established three months ago. The Chief Superintendent has asked me to remind you that you may be accompanied by a police officer of your own rank. Is this clear, Detective Inspector?" The voice was very correct. The Queen's English was being drilled at the detective inspector like bullets from a machine gun.

The soon-to-be ex-detective inspector grunted another "Yes". Anything to get this woman to go away. She must have hung up. The receiver was unceremoniously buried under the duvet and he turned over for more sleep.

Once again, he woke with a start; there was a strange noise he couldn't place. This was becoming tedious. What was going on? Why was his recovery from last night being interrupted? After a few minutes, he realised the telephone receiver was still in his bed and was screaming to be reunited with the body of the phone. With a great effort, he got the handset back onto its cradle and lay back, closing his eyes. He dozed off again. His hangover was demanding more sleep time; he lapsed into a dream in which he'd received a phone call from some snotty-sounding female. For a few minutes, he dreamed on oblivious of everything around him, then awoke with a start but this time with an "Oh shit". His memory bank had kicked in. He hadn't dreamt the phone call.

He looked at his watch. It said 08.54am. He remembered the voice had said he should be at Scotland Yard at 11am. As he lay looking at the ceiling, he realised there was no rush. If he were late, it would only delay his dismissal from the police service. It was a certainty this was his last day as a cop. Being on time would change nothing. The soon-to-be ex-Detective Inspector Steve Burt calculated the time he would need and thought if he started getting ready soon then he might just make it.

He realised pretty quickly there was no hot water as he stood naked in the bathroom. So, no shower this morning. Again! He couldn't clearly remember when he had last had a hot shower. He looked at the face in the mirror above the sink. He knew it was him, but he wasn't impressed. He stood staring at himself, and his mind drifted back to other, happier times. This was the beginning of his last day in the police force and as his mind drifted, he began to wonder what might have been.

The face in the mirror wasn't one he really knew. In his mind, he saw an athletic, fairly handsome young devil with clear eyes and a ready smile. What he saw looking back at him was none of these things. His daydream took him back to leaving school and going straight to the army aged 18. Sandhurst had been a good experience and he had been a good soldier. He reminisced about various escapades he and his fellow officer cadets had gotten involved in. He recalled the dances and the parties. The girls and life with his mates. He remembered the hard, physical training and the route marches. He recalled the drill sergeants and their colourful language. Happy days.

He'd been a good cadet and had won the sword of honour for his intake year. He smiled at himself in the mirror just thinking of these happier times. He had been welcomed into the Parachute Regiment as a 2nd Lieutenant. He had a solid career in front of him and his fellow officers were all good friends. He loved the camaraderie of service life. He found he was a good officer and was promoted temporary captain aged 24. Looking in the mirror, this wasn't the face of the man he was reminiscing about.

Then, by age 26, his glittering army career was over, and he was a civilian. All over a woman, and a punch at a senior officer. He asked the face in the mirror what had gone wrong. He was feeling sorry for himself. He knew it. He knew it very well. It was always like this the morning after.

Tomorrow didn't matter when you were young and had never met a woman like his second-in-command's wife. She was the sexiest thing he had ever seen, and she had made it plain she was available. He was told of her reputation with men and warned off by his mates, but he didn't listen. He went on to make a complete fool of himself over this temptress but when her husband had accused him of 'having it off with her', he'd over-reacted and finished up breaking the second-in-command's jaw. With that punch, he also broke his promising army career. The 26-year-old captain who'd won the sword of honour at Sandhurst was forced to resign his commission and become a civilian all because of a moment of madness and a large chest. The face in the mirror shook its head and mumbled, "What a waste."

He decided he'd better shave and look reasonably smart for his interview with human resources if this was to be his last day as a police officer. Unfortunately, he knew this would be a difficult if not impossible task. The disposable razor he was using had struggled the last time he used it and he now had at least a seven-day growth to get rid of. And he was shaving in cold water. After a valiant attempt and with his face covered in nicks and open wounds, he decided this was the best he could do. He told himself the odd tuft or two of facial hair was nothing to worry about.

He thought about his wardrobe and concluded this could be a problem. He hadn't been too concerned about his appearance over the past few months and knew formal or even smart casual was beyond his available bits of clothing, even if by some miracle they might be clean. He had spent the last three months living and sleeping in what he regarded as his best suit. He knew he had another but also knew it looked worse than his lived-in one. Still, at least he would be suited and booted for his final interview even though he might look a bit rough around the edges.

He realised he hadn't been near a laundromat in weeks and thought it was just as long since he had last used his washing machine. Still, he could only make the most of what he had. After all, it was the Metropolitan Police Force who had sent him home three months ago so what could they expect. It didn't matter how he presented himself. The sack was still the sack and he thought that after his sacking, the landlord of the Bush would still welcome him no matter how scruffily turned out he was.

Now ready to step out and meet his fate, the soon-to-be ex-detective inspector surveyed himself in his long wall mirror and had to admit the results of his efforts had not been too successful. The only smart thing about him was his tie. It had been a present from one of his lady admirers from the Bush Public House who for some reason had thought he was ready for a long-term relationship. How wrong she had been and anyway, a cheap tie was no incentive to get involved. As he stood admiring his efforts at sartorial elegance, he again drifted back and remembered the lady in question. He smiled thinking of her body that had bumps in all the right places. This was probably the first time he'd thought of her in the past few months. Facing the prospect of unemployment must be therapeutic. He was feeling happy and relaxed but didn't know why.

He looked at himself one last time and decided apart from needing to wash his hair and having it cut, this was the best he could do. He thought he'd made a good attempt at tidying himself up. He knew he was deluding himself; he looked a mess. Chief Superintendent Charles and Miss Hawkins would have to lump it. There were no photographs on a P45 and there would be worse-dressed patrons of the DSS when he went to sign on.

The current Detective Inspector Steve Burt left his flat for the last time as a serving police officer. Or so he thought! Never make assumptions.

Chapter Four

Monday, 6 April

Detective Inspector Burt arrived at New Scotland Yard at 10.55. The reception area looked more like an upmarket hotel than a police headquarters, although it was referred to as the Headquarters Building. The civilian receptionist looked at him sideways and gave him a look that suggested she thought he was a rough sleeper rather than a police officer. The fact he was headed for Human Resources seemed to amuse her and with some reluctance she handed over a plastic wallet on the end of a loop of tape.

"Please wear this at all times when in the building," she stated with her superior air. "You must return it to this desk when you leave. The pass is valid for today only. Is that clear?"

Burt held his tongue and realised this day was going to be worse than he'd expected. Even the civilians seemed hostile. He was given access to the waiting area and told that someone from HR would be down to collect him shortly.

He had just sat down and picked up an old *Police News* when he heard footsteps approaching. As he looked up, his previous thought that today would be bad was confirmed. Although he had never met the woman who had called him this morning, he knew instinctively that the middle-aged skeleton bearing down on him must be Miss Hawkins, also known as the personal assistant to the head of Human Resources. This had to be her. He recalled a high-pitched voice that talked too fast on the phone. Examining the body of the female walking towards him, he could see how the voice matched the woman. She stopped about three feet from him and in her high-pitched squeak, said, "Mister Burt. Chief Superintendent Charles is waiting for you. Will you please follow me?" If she had a view as to his appearance, she hid it well. Her own appearance as a forty-something plain Jane was all tweed and sensible shoes. He noted the use of Mister instead of Inspector and wondered if he was already a civilian in this woman's eyes. She probably knew his fate and was perhaps trying to let him down gradually, although he doubted it.

Neither said anything in the elevator that whisked them up to the 11th floor. The elevator doors opened onto what had to be HR country. There was an immediate air of peace and tranquillity. This probably meant no one did much real work here except shuffle paper all day. Nice work if you wanted it.

The soon-to-be ex-detective inspector was shown into what was obviously a conference room. Miss Hawkins said nothing and left, closing the door behind her. The room wasn't big and had no windows except for a few glass panels that fronted the corridor. There was a whiteboard screwed to the wall and the harsh neon lighting gave the room a depressing feel. Just right for the execution that was coming.

With nothing to do but wait, the still-detective inspector took a seat and again allowed his mind to wander.

He was back to feeling sorry for himself and pondered for the hundredth time how things had gotten to this state. He reminisced about his army career and how stupid he'd been. If only he could turn the clock back. His commanding officer, a career Lieutenant Colonel, had taken pity on him and allowed him to resign his commission so his service record was clean. If anyone asked, he said he resigned because his elderly parents were having difficulty coping on their own. This was only half true but sounded good.

He thought back to the days after he had left the service and the succession of odd jobs he'd taken just to keep body and soul together. He'd driven mini cabs, worked in a supermarket stacking shelves and best of all, in a bar as a barman.

In those days, he didn't drink to excess.

He remembered some of the shady characters he'd come across. The wide boys selling knocked-off gear down the markets. Some very easy women and ordinary people trying to do their best. Looking back, he felt he was more worldly wise as a result of his time mixing with these real people. He'd made some good friends and had been happy for a while. He remembered one of his mates, Big Solly, telling him to get a proper job. Big Solly was a part-time bouncer. He stood well over six-foot-tall, weighed more than twenty stone and was the salt of the earth. Steve thought fondly of his giant friend. The last time he had seen him, he was being arrested for headbutting a minor crook. Steve smiled at the scene. Deep down, he knew his style of odd job living couldn't last but it paid the rent and gave him pocket money.

He thought back to the day he saw the advert asking for young men to join the police service. He'd never been sure why he'd applied but recalled the interviews, the selection process and his first day at Hendon Police College. He had loved every minute of it. He had revelled in the training, the physical exercise and like Sandhurst, had excelled to the point where he was classed as best cadet of his intake.

He allowed his thoughts to wander to some of his initial experiences on the beat. Good times doing something useful. He remembered being picked out for accelerated promotion and the pride he had felt. They had said his selection was mainly due to his performance at Hendon plus his previous army career. Like the army, he had learned the top brass never told the whole truth. They didn't say they were short of uniformed sergeants, but he didn't care. His second career was up and running.

He went back to his first day as a newly promoted uniformed sergeant. He felt life couldn't get any better. But it did. He was quickly promoted to Detective Sergeant working in serious crimes. He thought of his time there and remembered the officers he regarded as friends and how much he liked catching real crooks. He remembered the rough and tumble of some arrests. The punch ups when prisoners didn't want to be prisoners. He remembered them as good times. He'd been a good police officer. He remembered the intellectual challenge of solving cases. He thought, *Happy days*. With a sigh, he was back in the present. Here he was waiting to be told his career was over and he was unemployed. All the hard work washed away and counting for nothing. He would soon be just another government statistic.

He wanted his thoughts to return to the past. He was comfortable and warm with his memories, but he forced himself to return to the present. His first career had ended when he was 26. His second career was about to end at age 39. He wondered if he would have a third career. He began to see a pattern develop. For the third time today, a slight smile appeared on his face. This was déjà vu. His first career gone with a punch. His second career also going with a punch. What of his third career? He would speculate later what it might be.

He was still daydreaming and didn't hear the door open and close. He realised someone had entered the room and looked up. On inspection, he realised the newcomer was more like a tailor's dummy pretending to be a policeman than the obvious policeman he was. His uniform was immaculate, his shirt sparkling white and his shoes polished to parade-ground standard. His haircut was a traditional short back and sides and he had rimless glasses perched on the end of a very large and sharp-looking nose. The newcomer wore the badges of rank of a Chief Superintendent. Even a poor detective could work out this was Miss Hawkins' boss. Chief Superintendent Charles, head of Human Resources.

The Chief Superintendent asked the now clearly soon-to-be ex-DI Burt to be seated at the far end of the table. He said this was protocol in cases like this. Burt took an instant dislike to his executioner. He rose slowly and moved chairs.

"Mr Burt," the chief superintendent began. His tone was very formal and official. Not a good sign if Mr Burt had been hoping for a miracle. "You're aware why you are here today. You have been suspended from duty on full pay for the past three months awaiting the result of a disciplinary board hearing into your recent conduct. The disciplinary board was set up on the 6th of January this year." A slight pause for effect. "We are here today to advise you of the board's conclusions and recommendations" The voice was high-pitched, very nasal, and the chief superintendent sounded like a real nerd lecturing a room full of other nerds. "I note you do not have a fellow officer with you. For the record, is this of your free choice?"

"Yes." Mr Burt had become a bit surly since the shopfront dummy had arrived. He wasn't going to help this pen-pusher.

The tailor's dummy continued. He was reading from a file that he had placed precisely in front of him. All the corners matched. "The board of enquiry was established on the 6th of January to investigate the circumstances that led to you engaging in an altercation with Detective Chief Inspector Derek Rose of the Metropolitan Police at a Police New Year's Gala Ball being held in the Universal Hotel on the 4th of January this year. You gave a statement to the investigating officers and acknowledged you punched Chief Inspector Rose twice on the face, causing him to sustain a broken nose plus a broken jaw and a dislocated shoulder. Medical records have been provided confirming these injuries that you admit were caused by you."

Mr Burt remained silent although the chief superintendent looked as though he expected confirmation. The condemned man shrugged his shoulders.

"Mr Burt. Can you please confirm that I have stated the facts as you gave them in your statement? I require your acknowledgment for the record."

"Yes, I suppose so."

The tailor's dummy stopped to turn a page. He actually licked the tip of his finger. He rearranged his papers into an even neater pile in front of him. He continued in the same monotone, nerdy voice.

"Having considered the evidence, the review panel is satisfied that you are guilty of bringing the police service into disrepute and that you exhibited conduct not becoming of a serving police officer."

At last, the chief superintendent paused for breath, perhaps expecting a response. The condemned man said nothing, letting the silence fill the room.

The room was oppressive and too warm; he knew he needed a drink and soon. After another pressing of his papers into another neat stack, the head of HR continued, "This file"—pointing to the stack of papers— "has been forwarded to senior management and regrettably, they cannot find any mitigating circumstances that might allow for a degree of leniency. It is therefore my sad duty to inform you…" At this point, the head of HR opened a second file that was under the first and produced a sealed envelope. Steve Burt knew the envelope was poison for him. The chief superintendent was about to pass the envelope over to the now certainly ex-Detective Inspector Burt when the door opened and another tailor's dummy entered. This one was—in the opinion of the civilian Mr Burt—a bit more frayed around the edges and not quite so well turned out. He was a bit older than either man in the room, and heavier built.

Without introductions, the second tailor's dummy handed the head of HR a folded piece of paper. No one spoke. It was clear to Steve Burt that the newcomer was of a more senior rank than the head of HR. In fact, he could see the new man was a full commander of police. He also recognised the commander as his old boss, so maybe not so much of a shop dummy as the chief superintendent. Feeling the need for a beer as a minimum, the condemned man tried to take no interest in what was obviously some administrative issue that probably had nothing to do with him. His mind was back in the Bush Public House and the release he would get from this nightmare by downing a few beers.

The head of HR, having read the note, grunted and tidied his papers yet again. He rolled his eyes, stood up and made a quick exit, saying only "excuse me" to the commander. He took the envelope he had been about to hand to Steve with him.

Once the door had been closed, the commander—who had previously been known to Steve as Detective Chief Inspector Malcolm Clark—took the seat previously occupied by the head of HR. The commander studied the accused with a look of disgust on his face. Neither man spoke for what seemed like minutes but was in reality less than 30 seconds. The commander spoke first, "Well, Steve. Long time no see." The newcomer sighed. "It seems you're in the brown stuff. A bit of a mess, wouldn't you say?" The commander's voice was pure London. He waved an arm in the direction of the civilian now called Steve. "Jesus. Just look at you, man. I've seen better dressed and healthier looking scarecrows. Christ Almighty, how've you been living!" The commander raised his voice. He was obviously concerned about the appearance of his ex-colleague.

"I heard about the disciplinary and your suspension, but I never thought I'd walk in here today and find you looking like this."

Steve slipped lower into his chair just as a schoolboy might when being given a reprimand about a poor school report.

The commander continued, "And you stink of booze and sweat. When did you last have a shower?" The commander paused again just long enough for Steve to get a word in.

"Well, Malcolm, you're doing a great job of cheering me up." Yet another slight smile appeared on the Steve's face. "After the disciplinary, I suppose I just don't care anymore. That excuse for a police officer Rose got what he deserved. I'd do it again; only next time, he wouldn't get up."

The commander just looked on. He was calmer now. His tone was more pleasant and conversational. "I read the reports, but I didn't get a sense of why you did it. Christ, Steve," the commander's voice had a pleading sound to it, "when you worked for me, you were one of the best. I can't believe you're the same guy. What really happened? Try to help me understand, for old times' sake. At least help me understand why you have thrown away your career."

Steve Burt considered how to answer. He was out on his ear so did it really matter if he told the commander the truth? He decided to come clean. After all, there was nothing more they could do to him and Malcolm had been a good boss. By telling the whole story, it might also help him get some sense of closure.

"OK." Steve allowed his mind to go back, remembering the events that had led to his being here today. "About six months ago, I was seconded to Chief Inspector Rose's team operating out of Camden. They were on multiple drug operations that involved surveillance on an Eastern European gang operating out of the East End. Rose's squad was short of manpower and needed more boots on the ground. They got my boots along with a lot of others. We'd been at it for a couple of months. We had some good intelligence that a big deal was in progress and we should keep an extra watch on an apartment above a bookmakers on the High Road. I was keeping watch with my sergeant at the time. I think you know him, Plodder Barry Grace. Good man but not an original thinker."

"Yes, I remember Plodder. Always had an excuse for everything. Nothing was ever his fault." The atmosphere in the room lightened a little at this remark by the commander.

"That's him. Anyway, Barry decides he needs a leak and disappears to find a quiet spot. No sooner had Plodder left than a fancy Audi turns up and out gets a guy I recognise from the briefings. One Joseph Blinks. Blinks had already been identified as middle-ranking muscle for the gang although it was suspected he'd moved up in the organisation. He went straight up to the apartment. He barely had enough time to climb the stairs when a woman started screaming and calling for help. Plodder wasn't back so I got out of the car and ran across the road to the apartment." Steve paused to gather his thoughts.

"Once I got inside, this Joseph Blinks was knocking three bells out of some woman. She was on the ground and looked like she'd taken a real beating. Blinks is a big guy. We had a set to and eventually I got the cuffs on him. I read him his rights and then searched him.

"He was wearing one of those large anoraks with big patch pockets. I was looking for a weapon but in both anorak pockets, there was enough smack to feed the habits of all the junkies in London. It was far more than he could claim was for his own use. A result. A ranking member of one of the biggest London narcotics gangs bang to rights.

"We had him for GBH and dealing with intent to supply. Everybody was happy, so down to the pub for a celebration."

The commander just sat and listened but didn't take notes, although a lot of this was new to him. "OK. So that explains the background and it sounds like a solid collar. So why the hell did you thump Chief Inspector Rose?"

Steve carried on, "Joseph Blinks was charged and held on remand. These gangs all use this new breed of London criminal lawyer. You know the type. Flash cars and even flashier offices. They don't get out of bed for less than five grand an hour. Their version of the law is to win at all costs, even if it means getting into areas of the law that may not be too ethical. Blinks' solicitor was Cedric Black."

"I've heard the name. I know he's not liked too much by the Crown Prosecution Service, but he seems to get results."

"Oh! Yes, he gets results alright. He's also the mob's go-to lawyer and thinks a lot of himself. So, Cedric became Joseph Blinks' solicitor and where Cedric goes, his brief of choice—one James Robeshire QC—is sure to follow. We knew the mob would bring in their A-team and they did." Steve paused again. He was debating how much to tell Malcolm Clark.

"About a week before the trial was due to start, our DCI Derek Rose suddenly wanted to be the face of the case. As senior investigating officer, he claimed it as his right. He was front and centre and monopolised all the press briefings. It was my collar, but he didn't want me near the case. He was even interviewed on TV and local radio as the copper who was busting the drug gangs of London. What was a good routine collar was becoming the Derek Rose 15 minutes of fame show." Steve gave a shrug of his shoulders.

"The teams all thought it was hilarious until he started to broadcast some of the facts of the case. He seemed to be believing his own publicity as the great drug gangbuster. He would be down at the pub talking to anyone who would listen, making up events and citing them as facts. I told him he could be endangering the case, but he just said I was talking rubbish. Said I was miffed because he was getting all the plaudits. We had words but he was my senior officer so what could I do?"

"OK, Steve. Did you put anything on the record?"

"No. I knew we had a good case so anything Rose did wouldn't matter. How wrong I was."

Steve was warming to his tale now. "Then came the trial. With their highly paid lawyers, we knew the defence would try and take our case to bits, but we were solid. Everything had been done by the book and the evidence was overwhelming. That was until Mr James Robeshire QC got into his stride. He started to refer to some of the statements Rose had made to the press and in the pub. The defence called a series of drinkers who contradicted the facts of the case and claimed Rose had told them a different story."

Steve paused for breath and in his mind's eye could see the bar at the Bush. He really needed a drink. He realised his hands were beginning to shake.

"The judge allowed the defence a lot of leeway in presenting hearsay evidence, and this, plus Rose's apparent contradictory statements, planted doubt in the minds of the jury. In the end, there was enough doubt and Blinks walked free, but no action was taken against Rose. He'd blown our case."

The commander sat back and intertwined his fingers behind his head. He closed his eyes and looked to be asleep. "So, is that the reason you broke his jaw? Because you lost a case?"

Steve stood up. He badly needed a drink and wanted to stretch his legs. He knew the next part of his story was going to be difficult.

"Look, Malcolm. What I'm going to tell you now is unsubstantiated and doesn't put me in a very good light. Not that that matters now." Steve heaved a big sigh.

"Go on."

"Blinks was free, and I knew a serious villain had been put back on the streets. I don't really know why but I wanted to say something to him, so I followed him from the Old Bailey. I guess I just wanted to let him know we'd get him next time. I can't explain it. I know it makes no sense, but something got to me.

"The whole gang went on a bender to celebrate Blinks' good fortune. They finished up in a Mexican joint on Chattel Street and seemed to be in for the night. It was obvious that Blinks as the guest of honour wasn't coming out any time soon. I figured this Mex place must be a regular haunt for the gang. After a while hanging around outside, I think I realised I was being stupid and went home. I had other cases on the go and lost interest in Blinks."

The commander was focussed on Steve.

"It was around 7 o'clock on the night of the New Year Ball. I was off duty and found myself in Chattel Street. Don't ask why, I just was. I saw Blinks come out the front door of the same Mexican. He turned right and started walking away from the restaurant. I realised I hadn't thought about Blinks for weeks but here he was. He was alone and on foot. He seemed to be in a hurry and was walking fast. I almost had to run to keep up with him. His direction was familiar and I realised he was headed for the apartment above the bookies in the High Road." Steve looked at the commander, trying to gauge his reaction to his confession. The commander was expressionless.

"There were too many people around for me to try and challenge him so I just carried on following. Sure enough, he skipped across the road and disappeared into the entrance that was the way up to the apartment. I didn't think too much about what I was doing and just carried on and followed him into the apartment. I suppose I was about four minutes behind him by the time I crossed through the traffic." Steve pulled another big sigh and still the commander just stared at him.

"When I entered the apartment, the same girl I'd seen before was lying on the floor, clearly dead. She had a great lump missing from her skull. Blinks was standing over her holding a baseball bat with what looked like brain tissue spread over the end." Steve stopped. He could see the scene in his mind's eye.

"You can imagine what happened next. I told him he was under arrest for murder and we had a set to. I got the baseball bat from him and we kicked and clawed each other but eventually, I got him cuffed and read him his rights." Steve remembered the brawl and the enjoyment he had felt when he had landed a massive punch onto this criminal's jaw. "Then I called in the whole murder circus to attend and put Blinks into a chair while we waited." The ex-inspector realised how badly he needed a drink, but he carried on.

"Blinks didn't deny murder. He said he would never be convicted so I was wasting my time. He said he had 'that stupid bent copper on his side and he would get off again'. I asked what he meant. He boasted that his last trial for GBH and drug possession had been a fix. He said the plan to have Rose give out conflicting messages had been deliberate and thought up by Robeshire as a way of planting doubt in the minds of the jury. He said Robeshire said if the police could be shown to be incompetent and the facts could be muddled then there was a good chance of an acquittal. All he had to do was pay off a copper to circulate false information."

The commander still said nothing. Steve drew breath but his hands were still shaking.

"Blinks said Rose was the stupid cop they'd paid off. He said Robeshire had him in his pocket. Told him what false information to circulate and where to do it. He said again things were changing and that now smart lawyers could always get not-guilty verdicts. He said coppers were now throwing trials for money. Jury tampering and threats to witnesses was old hat. There were smarter ways to get acquitted." Steve took a breath and carried on.

"When we got him back to Camden, he denied everything, said he wasn't guilty. I had no corroboration. Nothing of his admission could be included in his or my statement. I didn't want to admit that I'd technically stalked him just in case his lawyers might make something of it at his trial. So I kept quiet. I knew we had him for murder. The other stuff about Rose was something else."

For the first time, the commander spoke. His voice was just above a whisper.

"What happened next?"

"After Blinks had been processed, I went to the hotel where the ball was being held. I was fairly certain Rose would be there. I saw him dressed in his fine dinner jacket, holding court with the great and the good, drinking champagne. I pulled him to one side and told him I knew he was bent and that his corrupt performance in the first Blinks trial had just caused a woman to lose her life. He pushed me away and told me not to get hysterical. He said we should discuss everything next week when I was calmer. He had a stupid grin on his face. I don't think he was sober so when he turned his back on me, I must have seen red. I remember pulling his shoulder around and letting go a left hook. All my anger was in that punch, so I knew I'd hurt him. I turned and walked away. People said later I hit him twice, but I can't remember the second one." Steve sat down, feeling exhausted, and looked at the commander. "As they say, the rest is history and here I am. A civilian because I punched out a bent copper."

Commander Malcolm Clark said nothing but looked straight at his ex-colleague. After more than a few minutes of reflection time, he stood and walked around the table and put his hands on Steve's shoulders from behind. His voice was gentle. "I read the reports but if you'd included Blinks' statement about Rose, the disciplinary panel might have taken a different view.

"For what it's worth, most officers would have acted as you did but maybe would've thought twice before punching Rose's lights out in public."

The commander became more formal in his tone. "The fact remains you hit a senior officer in a public place. Christ, now I understand your reasons, but you know yourself you shouldn't have done it." The commander paused again. He let a silence settle in the room.

"Just so you know. There have been doubts about Rose for some time. The top floor knows about the fiasco of the Blinks trial. When he gets back from sick leave, DCI Rose is going to be offered early retirement or a disciplinary hearing. Either way, he's finished."

Steve Burt was about to say something, but the commander beat him to it. Holding up his left hand. "I know. We would rather see that son of a bitch publicly thrown out of the Force and probably straight into a cell. He gets a walk and you get a P45. It doesn't seem fair. But given the present sensitivity around policing, this isn't the time for us to wash our dirty linen in public. It's been decided it's best if he just vanished. No fanfare and no ceremony."

The commander started to walk towards the door. "Come on. Let's get out of here. I'll buy you a coffee in the executive canteen."

As the two men walked out of the room, Steve suggested a beer might be better. The commander laughed but said nothing.

Chapter Five

Monday, 6 April

The canteen was split into two. One half with plastic tables and chairs for normal people and tables with white tablecloths and upholstered chairs for senior personnel. The commander and Steve were sitting at a table with a tablecloth. Steve felt honoured but wondered why.

The coffee arrived and Steve admitted to himself that it tasted good. Malcom Clark leaned forward and in a low conspiratorial voice said, "Steve. There's something I want you to know. First, you were a good cop and a very fair detective. You made me look good when I was your governor in Serious Crimes. It's no bullshit but I believe I'm here today partly thanks to you." The commander broke off his speech to sip his coffee.

"You look like a tramp and you're a bit of a loose cannon, but I feel somehow I owe you. You got results that reflected well on me. I really don't like seeing you like this." The commander looked directly at Steve. "You know I was never a great thief-taker. I'm more of a political animal than a street cop. I know I couldn't do what you do. I've found my place here crawling to the higher-ups, telling them what they want to hear and shuffling paper. Who knows, it could be the way of modern policing." Malcolm Clark paused and cracked a smile. Out of politeness, Steve also gave a slight smile but had no idea why.

"Anyway. That's what I want to talk to you about. I've been put in charge of yet another Force reorganisation to show our political masters that we can save money. It's all rubbish, of course. Our budgets are already so stretched we're barely able to buy enough toilet rolls." The commander took another sip of his coffee. Steve stayed quiet. "But it's politics. My job is to present the commissioner with a plan that'll satisfy the Commons Select Committee on London policing. It's total balls, of course, but we have to play the game."

Steve interrupted the commander's flow. "Why are you telling me? I'm a civilian."

"I'm coming to that. Like I said, Steve, I feel I owe you. What you did can't be undone but maybe I can do you a favour." The commander looked around the canteen.

"In any reorganisation, there's always scope to do things you couldn't do in normal times. Like, bend the rules a little, clear out dead wood. Officers who are a pain to work with or are stupid or just bloody useless. Not usually grounds to sack them in normal times. But in a reorganisation…"

The commander arched his left eyebrow in a 'you know what I mean' gesture. He paused for effect and to allow Steve to confirm his understanding. Steve said nothing. "The rules for getting rid of people these days are strict but can be manipulated when we have redundancies. We can clear out the dead wood without fear of being sued for wrongful dismissal and all that other political crap."

The commander again paused. Steve interrupted this time and threw up his hands. The call of the Bush Bar was getting stronger. "Look, Malcolm. This is all very interesting, but I have a date with a pint of IPA. Is there a point to this?"

Malcolm smiled and carried on as if civilian Steve hadn't spoken. "It's my job to put something together that'll look good to our political overseers. I'm setting up new fictitious units now and staffing them with the dead wood we want shot of. The commissioner has to report to the Commons Committee in six months. So in six months, we'll just say we've closed and merged units as a way of streamlining the service. Nothing will have changed, and the only closures and redundancies will be these new fictitious departments I'm setting up now. In one stroke, we'll have cleared out some of our dead wood and appeared to have cut costs. Job done. We'll look good."

The commander sat back and smiled a self-satisfied smile.

Steve stared at Malcolm and shook his head. "That all sounds very devious, cunning and clever. But unless you want me to leak your plan to the newspapers, I still don't see why you're telling me all this."

"Simple. Like I said, I'm a political cop and know how to play the system. For some reason, I feel I owe you, although looking at you now I'm not so sure. Anyway, I've persuaded the powers above to keep you on for six months and suspend your disciplinary."

Steve couldn't believe what he'd just heard. "What!"

"If you want, I can have you posted to one of these new temporary units. It means that instead of you leaving today with no pension, no salary and no

31

references, you'll have six months more service and can leave with your pension intact, a wedge of redundancy cash and glowing testimonials. I'd see to that."

Steve just stared at Malcolm in total confusion while the commander stared right back. Before Steve could ask a question, the commander carried on, "But listen. No matter what. You're finished as a police officer in six months. Even I couldn't change that. This is only a stay of execution. It's the best I could get for you."

The commander became more serious and pointed a figure straight at Steve Burt.

"I'm only offering you this if you promise to keep your nose clean for the next six months. I don't want to hear any reports about you. I've put my good name on the line so don't screw things up and make me regret trying to do you a favour."

"Just a minute." The maybe not so civilian Steve was becoming interested but also a little confused and animated. "This means you see me as a screw up alongside the dead wood you want shot of?" Steve looked down at the table. "I suppose I'd have to agree with you on that, but the Force is already shot of me. I'm a civilian as of today."

"You haven't been listening. I can stop your dismissal now. You get another six months in the job and leave with everything intact. Pension, redundancy and every chance of getting another job on the outside. In six months, you'll automatically be made redundant. Steve, there's no way back for you on a permanent basis. I can arrange for you to be posted to a new fake unit not as a screw up but as a favour."

"Well, thanks, I think."

"You'll head one of these new fake units called Special Resolutions. I've set it up so in theory, this unit will only handle cases other serious crime units have found too difficult to solve." The commander shrugged. "You know and I know no unit commander will ever admit he can't solve a case. So, for six months, you'll have nothing to do but report in and fill your day as you want. Do your knitting. Do crossword puzzles. Anything you fancy."

Steve was trying to take this all in. Out on his ear an hour ago. Now a six-month reprieve.

"I've done you another favour. Department heads are usually chief inspectors. As head of the Special Resolutions unit, you'll automatically be promoted. Everything has to look as though this fake unit is legitimate. If nothing else, it will give you a better pension and more redundancy money together with a higher salary for the next six months." The commander sat back.

There was a brief pause whilst both men drew breath. The commander spoke first, "So that's it. If you want to take it, it's yours. But remember, don't rock the boat for the duration. Keep a low profile and don't punch any senior officers." The last remark brought a smile to Steve's face. "So, what do you think. Is it to be DCI Steve Burt or Mr Steve Burt?"

The one-time detective inspector was in a state of shock and confusion, but not enough to turn down the offer of promotion to detective chief inspector and a six-month stay of execution.

"Well, Malcolm, sir, I don't know what to say but thank you. And yes, it's Chief Inspector."

The two men stood, shook hands and sat down again.

"OK, Chief Inspector," Malcolm Clark was once again the police commander, "if you see the lovely Miss Hawkins on your way out, she'll give you all your credentials. New warrant card, mobile phone and so on."

The commander appeared to have dismissed the new DCI. Steve stood and feeling awkward was just about to say thank you again when the commander interrupted, "Oh! By the way, I almost forgot. You've been assigned room 205 on the second floor and you'll operate out of headquarters. The other thing is you have two members of staff already posted to you. Miss Hawkins will give you their files. They know nothing of the six-month chop but are good examples of people we can afford to lose. I'll leave it to you to decide how much to tell them. Good luck, and please get a haircut and a decent shave. A bath and a visit to a tailor would also not be out of order; remember, you're now a DCI." The commander seemed in a jovial mood as he picked up a lunch menu and waved away the new detective chief inspector.

Chapter Six

Monday, 6 April

The new DCI thought he should at least look at his new office. Room 205 was on the second floor and seemed to be about the 3rd door on the left at the start of a nondescript corridor. The door was open and on entering, the DCI saw the room was about 20 feet square and in the middle of the room, three tables had been pushed together to form a square. Some cheap white plastic chairs were arranged around the square. He also noted that a man and a woman were seated around the tables. They both looked up but said nothing. Against the back wall was a grey metal desk that seemed to date from the 1960s with an old typist's chair on wheels sitting inside the knee hole. On one wall was a whiteboard about six feet by three feet and a cheap photographic print of a bunch of flowers on the opposite wall. The only office equipment on display were two telephones and a filing cabinet. The whole room had a neglected and rundown feel that wasn't helped by the floor that was covered by a cheap, institutionalised but serviceable grey carpet.

Drawing a deep breath, the DCI entered, nodded to the man and woman and went over to sit down at the grey metal desk. He assumed that as the man in charge, this was his desk. The woman was the first to speak. "Sir, I'm Detective Constable Florance Rough and this is Detective Sergeant Abul Ishmal. We were told to report to a DCI Burt by 2 o'clock this afternoon." She looked at her watch, noting it was well past 2 o'clock. "We presume you're DCI Burt?"

"You presume correctly, DC Rough. I don't know what you've been told but welcome to Special Resolutions. I hope you'll both be very happy here and find this to be the easiest duty you've ever had." He gave his staff time to look him over. "Right, I'm off to see my tailor and have a haircut. I'll see you both here tomorrow some time before noon. The rest of the day is yours."

With that, the DCI stood up and left. The sergeant and constable looked at each other. "What was that about and who is that guy?" asked Florance. "He looks as though he's working undercover tracking a gang of refugees."

"I think it means we're not going to like working here. How long do you have to be in post before you can apply for a transfer?" Abul waited for an answer but got none. "If that's an example of a modern-day DCI, then the force is in a worse state than we think." The DS allowed himself to smile at his own wit.

"He seems a bit rough around the edges, but you never know. He might—"

Before she could continue, Abul pushed his chair back and almost shouted, "Rough around the edges; did you smell him, woman? He hasn't washed in days and that suit could stand by itself. We're working for a loser. What does that say about us?" Abul picked up his briefcase from the table. "He said to look after ourselves, so I'm going home. See you tomorrow." Abul walked straight out without another word.

The DC sat looking at her hands. She knew she wasn't popular and suspected this posting to Special Resolutions was not a great career move. She asked herself what Special Resolutions was for. Maybe the DCI would tell her in the morning. Then she too left.

The DCI decided to walk to his flat. It should take about an hour and a half. On the way, he stopped at a barber. Well, not really a barber. It was a hair salon and was unisex. He was offered Mandy as his hairstylist. He didn't mind as Mandy was easy on the eye and displayed a more than adequate cleavage.

Unfortunately, her grammar was a bit primitive. Every sentence started with the word 'like' and the letter 'T' was completely missing from her vocabulary. "Just a good haircut and shave please, Mandy, and maybe you can wash my hair first." Mandy obliged but said she didn't do shaves. She got to work on Steve's head. The DCI kept conversation to a minimum. He would rather look at Mandy than talk with her.

He left the unisex hair salon £87 poorer than when he had gone in. Still, Mandy had a skill and he had to admit he looked and felt better. Next stop was Primark for a new suit and a couple of shirts. As he left Primark, he mused that his hair wash and haircut had cost more than his new wardrobe.

Having stashed his new clothes in his flat and put a new pack of disposable razors in his bathroom cabinet, the DCI visited the Bush Public House but vowed to only stay for a few beers and something to eat. After all, he now had additional responsibilities. He laughed to himself as he sank his fourth beer.

Responsibilities. What responsibilities? Do nothing, keep your head down and don't rock the boat. The new DCI thought he could manage that for the next six months.

Chapter Seven

Tuesday, 7 April

The newly promoted detective chief inspector woke again with a start. This time, he acclimatised to his surroundings more quickly. His mouth was dry but not furred up and his head seemed calm. He noted there was no whisky bottle on the side table beside his chair. He took this as a positive sign. The television was as usual still on but a glance at the clock showed it was only 01.05. More evidence he might be getting his act together. With some pride, he could remember returning to his flat from the pub last night. As he stumbled towards his bedroom, he flipped the switch for the immersion heater. He would have a hot shower and a shave tomorrow morning. He also stripped off before getting under the duvet and placed his clothes on a chair. This was a first in a long time. Maybe things were changing? He slept a deep dreamless sleep.

Dressed in his new suit and shirt but with the same tie, Detective Chief Inspector Burt proudly signed in at headquarters at 11.37 and headed for his office. The DS and the DC from yesterday were there and were seated in the same chairs. The DS was reading the *Daily Mail* and the DC had a book on rapid weight loss. The new DCI had to admit she could do with losing a few pounds or stones! She wasn't a small lady.

Before he could speak to his team, DC Rough said under her breath, "He looks a bit cleaner than yesterday."

Abul just carried on reading.

"Good morning both." Steve tried to sound upbeat as he sat at his desk. "Now, what do I call you?" Looking at DS Abul Ishmal, the DCI estimated he weighed around 180 pounds and that he probably worked out and could look after himself. He was clearly from an Asian background but was probably second or third generation. Steve detected a bit of animosity judging by the DS's body language. To break the ice, he asked, "Do you prefer Abul, Ishmal or something else?"

"I prefer Detective Sergeant, sir."

Not a very welcoming start.

"Ah well. There you go. You see, I'm not too good at real names and prefer to know my officers by a nickname. That way, when I'm in trouble and call out their nickname, they know it's me and can come running to my rescue." The DCI tried to keep his voice light and gentle with no seniority overtones. "How about I call you Ahab or better still, Captain after the Moby Dick character? He was a tough nut and you look as though you can handle yourself in a fight."

"Anything you say, sir, you're the boss."

Still not going very well.

"Yes, I am, but don't let that stand in the way if you've something to say."

The detective sergeant, now known as the Captain, bit his tongue.

"What about me?" asked Florance. "Do you have a funny nickname for me or don't you give female colleagues funny names? Especially female colleagues who don't have a clue why they're here or what Special-bloody-Resolutions is all about. I looked you up last night, sir. You've just come back from a three-month suspension for chinning a senior officer. Not only that but you were promoted to this new job only yesterday. What's going on and why have we been drafted into this department?" The DC was a bit red in the face and had started to sweat halfway into her rant. The DCI put the sweating down to her bulk.

Steve chose to ignore Florance for the time being. "We'll get to that later. But now, DC Rough. Do you have an existing nickname or shall I give you one?"

"Do what you want, why should I care?" was the response.

Still not going too well, thought Steve.

Florance looked to be in her early thirties, fairly well dressed and wearing a flowing gown-like frock. She was obviously not stupid. She had a strangely pretty face. However, even the flowing dress couldn't hide the fact she was the size of an elephant, probably over 200 pounds. She couldn't actually sit fully in her plastic chair. Instead, she had to perch on the front lip. Her arms were as thick as a rainwater down pipe and she had so many chins it was impossible to count them. The DCI wondered how she had ever passed the police medical.

"Right. If you don't already answer to a nickname, I'll call you Twiggy." Steve expected an avalanche of abuse from Florance but simply got a small smile.

"Oh! That's original. I've never been called that before. Ha. Ha." Just a bit overly sarcastic but who could blame her.

Steve thought things couldn't get more difficult. He would have to see these two for the next six months. He had to try and find a way of getting them on side.

"You can call me Steve when it's just us or boss or guv when there's others about." He pointed at the detective sergeant "So you, Captain, and you..." — pointing at the detective constable— "Twiggy, me, Steve. All clear!" He didn't wait for an answer.

"Let's go to the nearest pub to celebrate our new-found union. I'm buying. Then we can all go home and meet up again tomorrow morning." The DCI stood up and waved his arm for them to follow. "Are you coming?" With that, he left. Neither the Captain nor Twiggy followed.

Chapter Eight

Wednesday, 8 April

Next morning, and to his surprise, Steve was in the office just before 10.00. His nightly visit to replenish his blood alcohol level had been a quiet affair. He had left the Bush around 9 o'clock and had been in bed by 11 o'clock. He put it down to not wanting to crease his new suit, which had been hung up the night before. He thought he looked sharp in his £45 bargain.

There was no sign of the Captain or Twiggy. For something to do, he opened the envelope Miss Hawkins had given him with copies of the personal records for Detective Sergeant Ishmal and Detective Constable Rough. Seated at his desk, he opened the Captain's file first.

Detective Sergeant Abul Ishmal had been a police officer for 18 years. He was aged 41, married and—from the file—he still lived with his wife. There was a surprise in the file. The Captain had once been known as uniformed Inspector Abul Ishmal. He'd had a disciplinary three years before and had been reduced in rank but put into CID. The file was a bit vague on detail, but it appeared that the ex-inspector had received a few goodies from some gangland villains. It looked as though he had reported some of the bribes but not all. His job had only been saved because he gave evidence against the generous soul who had given him the goodies and had helped secure a conviction. The rest of the file was general stuff. His annual reviews up to his demotion had been above average but the last one described him as non-cooperative, surly and lazy. Not a good report. Steve could hear the commander's words about a chance to clear out 'those we don't want'.

He was about to open Twiggy's file when she arrived in the office.

"Good morning, sir. After your exit yesterday, I'm surprised to see you here and looking almost normal." Steve thought, *cheeky cow,* but let it pass.

"Good morning to you, Twiggy. Just a word to the wise. Don't push your luck. Now why don't you go and get me a coffee? Black with no sugar. Get one for yourself while you're there. Once the Captain arrives, we'll have a nice little chat, OK?"

Twiggy shrugged and before setting off in search of a coffee machine, she took a chance and said, "Nice suit. Better than the one you were wearing yesterday, sir."

Whilst she was gone, the DCI opened the file on Detective Constable Florance Rough. She was 33 years old, listed as single and appeared to live alone. She had been a police officer for ten years and her career was unremarkable. Her annual reports described her as smart but opinionated. Not afraid to speak her mind even to senior officers. There was a note that five years ago, she'd been referred to the Force doctor. She'd begun to put on even more weight and her superiors were finding her size an embarrassment. She was removed from frontline duties and given a desk. It seemed the doctors could do nothing and she continued to get bigger. The medical explanation was she had a thyroid and glandular problem and there was nothing that could be done. Her last report described her as highly intelligent, belligerent, not a team player and incapable of regular police work due to her size. She'd been offered a discharge on medical grounds but had refused. The file admitted it was easier to keep her than force her through a medical discharge. Again, the commander's words came back to the DCI.

Chapter Nine

Wednesday, 8 April

The killer was looking at the second name on his list. This was his next victim. The target was standing on the rail platform waiting for a train to take him into central London and his office. The killer was only ten feet away. He thought about pushing his next victim off the platform and under a train. However, satisfying it might be, he was likely to be seen and he couldn't afford that. He had to be free to complete his mission.

The killer had been following target number two for several days now. He knew that planning was everything as he had proved when disposing of the first name on his list. Number two was proving to be a bit more of a challenge.

The first victim had been a real social animal and spent time out of the office mixing with clients and friends. Number two was less sociable. So far, each day had been a repeat of the previous one. He left his Wimbledon house on foot at more or less 9 o'clock, late enough to miss a lot of the early commuter traffic but early enough to show willing by getting to the office before 10 o'clock. He walked for 12 minutes to the station where he caught the 09.20 tube train into central London. His office was located above the station and he never left it until he finished work for the day. This was usually around 6.30 but could be later. His journey home was the reverse of his journey in.

The killer couldn't see a satisfactory kill point. He'd acquired the borough planning maps and electoral roll for the area. Unfortunately, given the target's strict and boring schedule, this information wasn't helpful.

The killer decided to let the target take his train. He would go back over name number two's movements again and look for his weak spot. He just needed the target to be stationary for less than a minute. That, together with a kill site, was all it would take to remove the second name on the list.

Next morning, the killer—as on previous mornings—was seated on a bench beside park gates located on the opposite side of the road from the target's house.

The house was a grand mansion with an ugly extension to one side. It was built of red brick, probably within the past 20 years. There was a drive leading to a detached double garage. The killer concluded that ripping old folk off seemed to pay well. The thought of revenge gripped him as he looked at the grand manor. His lust for revenge nearly spilt over and he knew he wanted to kill this excuse for a human being now. He could easily shoot him as he left his house but that was not what he planned. His father deserved better. He told himself to keep faith with his planning. After a few deep breaths, he was calm again. This crook would certainly die. The killer just didn't know where. Yet!

The target left his house at exactly 09.01. The killer followed. The route to the station was exactly as it had been each morning. At one point, the target had to cross a main road by a pedestrian crossing controlled by lights. The killer noted that the target was stationary until the green man appeared and told the waiting pedestrians it was safe to cross.

This was the killer's eureka moment. How could he have missed it? Apart from waiting on the station platform, this was the only time his target was stationary when the killer might be able to bring his killing machine to bear. He noted it had taken the target four minutes to reach the crossing.

He pinpointed the crossing on his map and over a cup of coffee taken in a local greasy spoon, he drew sight lines to see if there was a suitable kill site. He started walking the area, following his lines of sight and looking for a place from where he would kill target number two.

After 20 minutes walking, the killer had another eureka moment. *Not bad*, he thought. Two in one day! Right on one of his sight lines stood a Holiday Inn Hotel. The second-floor windows looked to be perfectly located. He entered the hotel and charmed the receptionist into showing him rooms on the second floor facing the road. He made up a story that he wanted to film an upcoming procession and thought one of these rooms would be perfect. He would, of course, be staying in the hotel overnight.

Room 228 was perfect. The window opened by sliding up and there was a clear view of the crossing if you knew where to look. The killer had his kill site.

The killer now knew how and where the second name on his list was going to die. He felt elated. Revenge would be sweet. He refined the kill in his head. He knew the kill location. He knew the time. He surmised traffic had priority at nine in the morning so the green man should hold the pedestrians longer. The target would be stationary just long enough. He had his kill site. His plan was complete. Name number two was as good as dead.

Chapter Ten

Wednesday, 8 April

Twiggy arrived with the coffee. She had met the Captain in the corridor and bought him a coffee. All three now sat around the three tables that formed a square and drank their coffee. Twiggy, as seemed to be developing as the norm, was the first to speak. "Right, sir, I got you your coffee and you said we would have a chat once Abul arrived." The DCI noted she had not used the Captain's given nickname. "Abul is here now so is there anything you want to tell us?"

The DCI remembered the comments in her file. Belligerent and outspoken. He sat back and drew a deep breath.

"What I have to tell you will not be easy for you to hear. I was briefed on why this unit has been set up and told I could give you the full picture if I thought it appropriate. I think it is." The DCI paused for effect. He was glad he had had a fairly sober night last night. His head was reasonably clear.

"There's no easy way of saying this but the three of us in differing ways are not wanted by the police service. We're cast-offs." Twiggy was about to speak but Steve held up a hand, silencing her. "Just look at us. I was on the verge of being kicked out for hitting a senior officer a few days ago, the Captain has a demotion and a disciplinary on his record and Twiggy can't operate as a frontline PC because of her size." Steve looked at Florance. "Sorry Twiggy, but you know it's true."

Steve again held up a hand to silence any comments. He continued, "There's a reorganisation being planned that will be implemented in six months' time. This unit's been set up now so it can be closed down in six months. It's all smoke and mirrors. You know, be seen to close departments that never really existed.

"Show the politicians that cuts to the budgets have been made without actually cutting anything except a few rejects like us. I hear there are another four ghost departments that have been set up so that they can be closed at the same time."

Steve looked at the two grave faces in front of him. "We're here because the Force doesn't want us but, apart from me, they can't just sack you two without cause. It's not legal in a reorganisation anymore to pick and choose who should be sacked. The rules say if you take out entire departments then everyone employed in that department must be made redundant. No exceptions."

Steve saw his message was getting through to his colleagues.

"So, the plan is to create a department like this, staff it with waifs and strays like us then shut the whole thing down in six months. They get rid of us and look like they've made a saving."

The Captain put his hand up to get Steve's attention. "So, effectively, we're working our notice for six months."

"That's about it. The upside is in six months, you leave with a full pension, a cash sum in redundancy payments and your record sealed, meaning you'll get a reference that makes no mention of your past. If you think about it, it's not a bad deal."

The DCI could see a tear in Twiggy's left eye. She quickly brushed it away.

"What are we expected to do for the next six months?"

"Good point, Twiggy. Special Resolutions is, in theory, a unit set up to investigate serious crimes that other units can't solve. We all know that no senior officer is going to say he can't get a result given time especially when it comes to murder or gangs. So, we'll never be asked to do anything in the next six months. Like I said, smoke and mirrors. All we do is sign in each day and do nothing. We've been instructed to keep our noses clean and not to rock the boat. If we do that, then we'll all return to the streets as civilians with redundancy cash in our back pockets."

"Is this final or is there an appeal, and how come you're here instead of being marched out after the disciplinary result?"

"Twiggy…" Steve remembered again the comments in her file. "All I can say is there's no appeal, and it's only thanks to my old boss that I'm here now. But make no mistake, I'm swimming in the same pool as you."

All three sat in silence. Then, in a repeat of yesterday, the DCI stood. "Let's go to the other office. The one I found yesterday is just around the corner. It's called The Waterman. Not too bad and they serve a very acceptable pint. Come on, let's go." With a wave of his arm, the DCI was gone. The two remaining detectives looked at each other but they said nothing. The shrug of their shoulders said, 'might as well'. The Captain and Twiggy followed their boss to The Waterman.

The three found a corner table and the DCI went to the bar to order. A pint of IPA and a whisky chaser for him, a half of lager for the Captain and a diet coke for Twiggy. She said she was watching her weight. At least she was showing a sense of humour.

After an hour or so and a few rounds of falling down water the atmosphere that had at first been a bit strained began to lighten up. To Steve's surprise, both his sergeant and constable seemed to be enjoying themselves.

Each began to explain their route to Special Resolutions.

"I have to admit that after I punched DCI Rose, I regretted it." Steve was on his fourth pint and was mellowing. He needed to tell his story. It seemed important that these two understood him. "I wasn't expecting to be suspended, but looking back I suppose it was inevitable. I think I let myself go during the suspension." He took a large draft of his beer. "And developed a likeness for the local pub. You know, I didn't used to drink much at all. In the pub, I could drink and eat and not have to think. Not a good move in hindsight but what the hell, I didn't care, or so I thought." Steve was beginning to show pity for himself and slightly slur his words. He suddenly changed the subject.

"Don't ask me why I wasn't thrown out, I don't know. Malcolm Clark said he owed me a favour for making him look good in the past. Personally, I think it's a load of rubbish but what the hell." The DCI's speech was getting louder. "I'm now a Detective Chief Inspector with six months to go. I don't care what's behind Malcolm Clark's favour, I'll bloody well take it."

Rising from the table with a slight stumble, the DCI headed for the bar and shouted over his shoulder, "My round; same again?"

Both Twiggy and the Captain sat in silence until the DCI returned with a tray of drinks, most of which had been spilt. The DCI wasn't too steady.

"Abul, what's your story? I've read the file but there must be more to it." Surprisingly, the DCI now seemed more focussed and less drunk.

"It's simple." Abul, or the Captain, started, "Young family, ambitious parents-in-law and a wife who'd been brought up on the finer things in life. My glittering police career wasn't enough and an inspector's wage certainly didn't pay enough for private schools, new cars and a large mortgage. All to impress my wife's parents. When the offer of easy money came along just for turning a blind eye, I was tempted and yes, I was stupid and took the cash. It didn't seem like I was doing anything wrong." The Captain took a sip of his lager and carried on in his educated voice, "Then the gang leader turned up at our house, saying to my wife that he was a friend of mine. He put a brown envelope on the living room coffee table, told me of a job going down the next day and to make sure no beat officers or patrol cars were in the area. There was more money on the table than I had ever seen in cash before." The Captain was getting a little emotional at this point in his story and drained his half-pint glass. "I did as he said but during the robbery, at a high-end jeweller's in the High Road, the shop assistant was shot. I'd no idea this gang would be armed."

There was a pause. No one spoke, so the Captain continued, "Well, I realised I was in over my head. I didn't know what to do so I told my wife what I'd done. She went ballistic, saying she needed a husband at home, not in prison, and that the big house and fancy cars didn't matter to her. I'd gotten us into debt unnecessarily. My wife's a sensible woman. We agreed I should come clean and report everything and so I did. The gang was rounded up and sent down for 15 years. I turned in every penny of the bribe money, but the amount didn't tally with what the gang boss said I'd received. As God is my witness, Steve, I didn't keep a penny. It was only after my disciplinary board that I was told the exhibit's sergeant at Mile End nick had a reputation for having sticky fingers. We couldn't prove anything. He'd made out a receipt but hadn't given me a copy, so I had no evidence and had to let it go. I should have insisted on a copy, but I suppose I was in a state of shock. The board found me guilty of bringing the service into disrepute and other charges were proven. The rest you know."

Before anyone could draw breath, Twiggy had gotten up and returned with another order of drinks. Unlike Steve's previous effort, each glass was as it had left the bar with no spillages. She had steadier hands. The three sat in silence and started on their next drink. They were digesting Abul's story.

As the drinks were being consumed, Twiggy realised the DCI was on his sixth pint. She had to confess he could drink! Steve spoke up.

"Well, Captain, bad luck." He was slurring his words again but only slightly. "Twiggy, what about you? It's confession time. The Captain and I have had our go." The DCI sank most of his beer in one swallow.

"Well, my story isn't as colourful as yours, thank goodness. I always wanted to be a copper. I was always a bit on the big side." The DCI ungallantly and with slurred speech agreed.

Twiggy stared daggers and ignored the comment. "I just passed the entrance medical and no more and at Hendon, the physical instructors had a good laugh every time they took a PE class. I was good at the exam stuff but not so good at the physical, especially having to run a mile in less than five minutes. I just couldn't do it. Anyway, one of the instructors took pity on me and during my final PE test before graduation, he must have stopped the watch before I finished because he gave me a time of just under five minutes. An impossible time for me but it got me through."

"My first few years on the beat were ordinary except that none of my colleagues wanted to work with me. They viewed me as a liability if we ever got into anything physical. Of course, they were right, but it was hard to take. I tried going to the gym. I tried personal trainers. I tried diets. I tried starving myself. Apart from making myself ill, nothing worked. I am what I am. Big, overweight and defensive about it." Twiggy took a sip of her coke and tried not to show how emotional she felt telling her story.

"I suppose the last straw was being referred to the Force doctor and restricted to desk duty. No! Hang on, that's not true. The real last straw was being posted to CID." The Captain's jaw dropped.

"CID's usually a promotion. Some uniforms would give their eye teeth for an opportunity. Why was it the last straw?"

"Hear me out and you'll understand. I was called into the divisional commander's office one day. My inspector was there with the commander. They said I was not a good role model for the force and that the Force doctor could do nothing for me. The doctor had said my weight and shape would continue to increase. He had recommended discharge on medical grounds." Twiggy was beginning to show the emotion she had worked hard to keep hidden. She took out a handkerchief and dabbed her eyes.

"I told them I didn't want to be discharged. I pleaded, said I would go on a strict diet. Go back to the gym. Anything to stay in the Force. They said the paperwork involved in getting me a medical discharge wasn't worth it and I had some use. You can imagine how that made me feel! They said that as there wasn't a uniform big enough to fit me, it would be best if I wore my own civilian clothes to work. I was told to look upon it as a promotion but that I shouldn't tell anyone what had been said nor the real reasons for my transfer to CID. The pair said anything repeated outside the office would be denied and my record would show a normal transfer."

She looked at Steve. "A bit like your Commander Clark, they told me the truth. They kept me on the Force but knew they had broken all the HR guidelines. They were doing me a favour. If I did say anything, it would be my word against theirs and my police career would be over."

Twiggy dabbed her eyes and sat back. She looked exhausted as if telling her story had been a gigantic effort.

A not too sober DCI tried to lighten the atmosphere. "Let's have one for the road, and it's your round, Captain." Steve had in reality begun to sober up during Twiggy's tale and was ready for another beer.

They drank in silence until the DCI got to his feet. He was none too steady. "Well, it's been an interesting meeting. I'll see you both tomorrow for what promises to be a quiet hour or so in the office followed by our individual playtimes. See you sometime before 12 noon."

The DCI decided to walk to his flat. It would give him time to sober up. He ran through his mind the last couple of hours and what had been said. He was sorry for them both and felt that in different circumstances, he could get to like them. He let his mind wander and thought they could form a team given the chance. They all had different experiences and skills and were keen to show those in authority that they were proper police officers.

Ah well, he thought, nothing was going to change despite their newly found camaraderie.

How wrong could one detective chief inspector be!

Chapter Eleven

Thursday, 9 April

The next day, all three arrived within ten minutes of each other. The DCI was the last in. He had returned to his flat after his previous afternoon's drinking session with his staff. Slept for a few hours, changed out of his now not-so-new suit in favour of his old drinking suit and wandered down to the Bush for something to eat and a few more beers. As usual, he couldn't resist the final beer and although he now looked presentable in his suit, shirt, tie and almost polished shoes, his head and mouth were telling him something else.

All three were in their, by now, usual positions around the three tables that formed a square. The coffee was good and badly needed by the DCI. Conversation was ongoing, mainly between the Captain and Twiggy with the odd grunt from Steve. Life was forming some sort of pattern for the three. Arrive before 11.00. Coffee between 11.00 and noon followed by the afternoon to do what they wanted.

The DCI was about to call time and head for the door when there was a quick tap on the door, which was then opened with a flourish. Commander Malcolm Clark—all six foot two and 220 pounds—filled the door. He pointed at Steve. "A word please, Inspector."

Standing in the corridor with the door to room 205 closed, Malcolm handed Steve a thin file. "Don't think this is a favour, it's not. I'm just protecting my back and the reorganisation strategy. What I said about keeping your nose clean and staying out of sight still stands. However, you can't run a unit given over to solving impossible crimes without an impossible crime. It wouldn't stand scrutiny if one of those busybody politicians stuck their nose in and started asking questions." The commander stared at Steve. The DCI stared straight back and said nothing.

"I was at a case conference with the murder squad this morning. This case came up and the chief super in charge is genuinely stumped. None of his team has any ideas on how the killing took place. I told them I would pass it on to the Special Resolutions Unit for their input. The DCS didn't like it, but he couldn't do anything about it. So, your unit now looks legitimate. You have a case on paper, at least, that fits your department's brief. But don't forget, it's my brief that counts. Head down and don't rock the boat. Are we clear?"

"Crystal, but what do you want me to do with this if I'm to do nothing?" Steve waved the file around.

"Exactly that, do nothing. I don't want your name coming up with senior management. Remember, this is all for show. Just keep a low profile and everything'll be fine. Oh! I suppose you could maybe scratch the surface. You've never managed a murder investigation before so no one'll complain or be surprised if you don't know how to conduct a murder inquiry. If you must do something, just do enough to get your name in the file. That's all. If you do that, everyone will be very happy, and you get to keep your pension." With that, the commander patted Steve on the shoulder and strode away up the corridor.

When the DCI opened the door to his room, four expectant eyes bored in on him. "What did the commander want?" It was Twiggy, of course. The DCI remembered the notes in her file.

"Nothing much. He's given us a case."

"What! A real case?" The Captain sounded like an excited schoolboy.

"Yes, but not one we're expected to solve. It's just for a bit of protection if awkward questions are asked during the reorganisation committee meetings. Like I said, smoke and mirrors."

"But it's real so we can investigate it." Both the Captain and Twiggy were excited. "Anything's better than hanging around all day with nothing to do." "What's the case anyway?" Twiggy was living up to the notes in her file.

"I haven't looked but it came from the murder squad."

"Great!" Twiggy was smiling and walking around the room. Obviously unable to contain herself.

Steve felt he had to rein in his co-workers. "Listen, nothing's changed from yesterday. We're finished in six months, no matter what. We keep our heads down, don't rock the boat and collect our pot of gold at the end. This case is a bit of window dressing, that's all. None of us has ever worked a murder and to be honest, I don't think we would know where to start. This is politics, pure and simple."

"At least let's look at the file. You never know; we might find something."

The DCI admired Twiggy's enthusiasm, but it was getting a bit boring. He knew what the commander had told him and he had no intention of doing anything other than obey.

"Listen, Twiggy. There's the file." Steve opened it and put it on the table. "All one page of it. I haven't read it, nor led a murder inquiry before, but even I know a case file should be more than one A4 sheet." The DCI pushed the file into the middle of the tables that made the square.

"It's time I was in my other office. The Waterman's calling. You're welcome to join me." The DCI left his two colleagues to stare at the file in the middle of the table.

The DCI was sitting at the same corner table, just starting his second pint when his team arrived, looking excited. They refused a drink and Twiggy moved the DCI's beer away from him to the other side of the table. The DCI said nothing.

The Captain had the file. "Look Steve, Twiggy and I've read this file and have been talking." Steve noted the use of his Christian name and DC Rough's nickname. "Can we at least discuss it?" The Captain was almost pleading. "Let's not rule it out of hand as a political conjuring trick. Someone has actually been murdered."

Steve considered and thought back to their candid meeting yesterday and the conclusions he'd arrived at about his two colleagues. He supposed he could at least humour them and still work within Malcolm Clark's guidelines.

"OK, let's hear it, but don't expect too much."

The Captain opened the file, smiled and took out handwritten notes that he and Twiggy had worked on. "We made a few phone calls. The victim's name was Timothy Squires. He was 51, married and was a partner in an investment firm in the City. Initial inquiries reported he appeared to be well regarded. The file said so far investigations had not uncovered a likely motive. The file says he was hardworking, made friends easily and didn't seem to have any enemies or financial worries."

Steve was listening and looking at his beer that was out of reach, thanks to Twiggy.

Twiggy took over from the Captain. "The file makes interesting reading only because of what's not in it. The scene of crime report throws up more questions than answers. The initial autopsy report makes ordinary reading but confirms the area around the wound was wet. The final report should be ready any day."

"Hold on." Steve was staring at his large detective constable. "Just back up a minute. I didn't pay much attention to the file but even I know the CSI and autopsy reports weren't in that file."

"True. We just called them up online. With a police ID, it's easy."

"What!" The DCI was almost apoplectic. All thoughts of his unfinished beer gone. "You did what?" His rage carried to the volume of his voice such that other drinkers were now looking in his direction and expecting some form of altercation.

Undaunted, Twiggy rushed on, "Yes, well, you left the file presumably for us to read. It's obviously only a summary in the file so we asked why." The DCI had the same thought.

It was the Captain's turn to chip in. The DCI thought they had rehearsed this double act. "Like you said, none of us have worked a murder before, but we know basic police procedure and there should have been more details in the file."

The Captain looked at Steve. He was still showing a pleading face. "We know what you said about low profile, but we wanted to get as much information before we came here. The database search for the basic CSI and initial post-mortem findings was easy and we didn't speak to anyone about them. No one knows we have the information, so we're still invisible and below the radar." The Captain looked pleased with himself. "We're hoping to persuade you to change your mind and let us investigate this even if it's only low-key."

"Wouldn't it be great if we could solve this and give a two-finger salute on our way out?" Twiggy was back.

The DCI was impressed and annoyed at the same time. He felt a slippery slope approaching. He would have to be careful. If they only scratched the surface of the case, how would Malcolm Clark take it? He did say they could look as though they were investigating. On the other hand, if they found anything that might help the investigation without upsetting anyone then surely it would be a feather in the commander's cap.

Steve asked Twiggy for his beer back. He took a long swig of the dark liquid. He felt he needed it. "OK, let's hear what you have, but no promises."

The Captain and Twiggy smiled at each other and Twiggy began.

"The killing was six days ago, on Friday, 3 April. We know who the victim was, and we know he was shot in the head. First, the CSI guys combed the area and couldn't find any evidence of a spent bullet. A quick look at the body confirmed there was no exit wound so the bullet must still be in the brain. In the report, it says the victim's face and hair were wet on the side of the face where the bullet had entered. The strange thing is it wasn't raining and the way the body fell, the entry wound was showing and the other side of the head was on the pavement. If the victim had fallen into water, then the side of his face nearest the pavement would be wet. It wasn't. The CSIs looked for bottled water in case the victim was carrying any but again there was nothing."

"So, you're saying a guy is shot and the side of his head where the bullet entered was wet?"

"Yes. Don't you find it strange?"

The Captain took over. The double act again. "Forensics couldn't find anything at the scene but have done one of those 3D reconstructions back at their labs. The victim was six-foot one inch. The hole in his head was just above his left eye. They calculated the bullet struck him at an angle of approximately 20 degrees to the parallel and some eight degrees from his back."

"Hold on, how was the victim standing before he was shot?"

"According to witness statements, he was talking to his lunch partners. In their statements, this was a regular Thursday date and the victim always left by taxi. He was waiting for a taxi and had his back to the road facing in."

Steve smiled and asked, "I suppose you got the witness statements the same way you got the PM and CSI reports?"

"Well! They weren't in the original file, but they are now," said Twiggy.

The Captain carried on, "From their modelling, forensics were able to give the murder squad the angles. This should have given them a likely point that the shooter fired from. When a reconstruction was done, none of the angles made sense. There was no obvious point the bullet could have been fired from."

The Captain took a blank sheet of A4 and drew the scene so that the DCI would more easily understand. He showed the victim and drew a line that more or less represented the angles calculated by forensics. He then roughly drew the road and the buildings on the right-hand side of the road. To the left, there was a row of thick oak trees. The Captain sat back and moved the sheet in front of his DCI.

"You got this from the forensic and CSI reports?"

"Yes, and a copy of the murder squad's initial scene assessment."

Steve looked at Abul. "Don't tell me how you got this, but you know you're sailing close to the wind getting into murder squad files?"

"Trust me, Steve, we're still invisible. No one knows what we have. Forensics say the model's accurate and based on the fact that there's no line of sight through the trees on the left and the angles from the buildings on the right don't compute, no one has any idea where the shot could have come from."

"What you're saying is our only case is a mystery. An impossible killing? Well, that's a surprise." Steve's voice had a sarcastic tone to it. He finished his beer. His two washouts had given him a lot to think about.

Although his gut told him this was a complete waste of time, he eventually came to a decision. "Right, it sounds interesting but also a complete waste of time. We're no more qualified to solve this as I am to make chief constable of a minor force any time soon. But! I agree, it's a puzzle." Steve had to admit a growing sense of wanting to get on with this. At the back of his mind, a little voice kept asking, *Why give this to us?*

"What do you want to do? I suppose by looking into this, if nothing else, it'll keep us off the streets and stop us getting bored for the next few months."

Twiggy was first to speak. She was full of excitement and was almost radiant. "Well, let's treat it with an open mind. We should go to the crime scene and have a look and then follow up on the witness statements. The murder squad only took statements from the victim's lunch buddies. No one else."

The Captain looked at Twiggy. "There was no one else. Nothing. No witnesses. We have no motive, no weapon, no place the bullet could have been fired from and a damp patch around the entry wound. It's an impossible murder. We've nothing to go on but it's intriguing so let's give it a shot. If you'll excuse the pun?"

"We don't know there's nothing. Just because those lazy buggers in the murder squad haven't found anything doesn't mean we can't. There was no house to house. Somebody must have seen something. There's a body in the morgue after all."

The DCI sprang into action, although in his case 'sprang' wasn't a true statement. He decided more slowly and deliberately. "Captain, can you sign out a pool car tomorrow morning? We'll go look at the crime scene and see where we go. But remember, no promises. Captain, you have my address and the location of the crime scene?" The Captain confirmed he did. "Pick me up tomorrow at 10 o'clock. We'll pick Twiggy up here at 10.15."

"If you don't mind, Steve, I'd rather make my own way there. I have something to do first thing tomorrow, but I'll meet you there at say, 11 o'clock."

"Fair enough, Twiggy. So, Captain, 10 o'clock at mine and straight to the crime scene. Right, who wants a drink to celebrate our taking on our first case?" As usual, a pint of IPA for Steve, a half of lager for the Captain and a diet coke for Twiggy. The DCI paid again. He hoped he hadn't just opened a can of worms!

Chapter Twelve

The Captain picked the DCI up at exactly 10 o'clock and they arrived at the crime scene just after 10.50. There was no obvious parking, so the Captain bumped up the kerb and parked on the pavement. This was outside the restaurant used by the victim on the day of his killing. The pavement was wider than usual and crescent shaped. They found the spot where Timothy Squires had died. There was still a dark purple-coloured stain on the pavement. From this spot, the DCI surveyed what the scene of crime and forensic officers would have seen. Just another road full of cars driven by people going about their lawful business.

From yesterday's briefing, the DCI recalled the victim had been standing with his back to the road and as the DCI was standing facing the road, then the kill shot must have come from the left. He turned left and saw exactly what he had been shown on the Captain's sketch. A row of trees on the left and a row of buildings with shops underneath, all joined together, running up the right-hand side of the road. The only part of the row of mixed shops with flats above that had a view over the kill scene was the gable end of the first block. This gable end didn't have any windows, so the shooter didn't fire from there. The DCI surmised that if the shooter had fired from any of the apartments above these shops, he must have stretched at least six feet out of a window, turned 90 degrees, taken aim and fired with the skill of a marksman. A bit unlikely.

Just as the DCI was about to mention this to the Captain, Twiggy arrived, driving an apple-green Fiat 500 car, which boasted not only a sunroof but a 25-year-old air cooled engine that sounded every day of its age. Sticking out of the sunroof was a long piece of wood. One end was resting on the back seat and the other end was high in the air and protruded beyond the front of the car. Twiggy couldn't see a parking space so, like the Captain, elected to bump up the kerb onto the pavement. Unlike the pool car, the Fiat sat lower on the road and its suspension was considerably older. The poor old Fiat reluctantly climbed onto the pavement, but the DCI thought terminal damage may have been done.

Twiggy reversed her ample body from the car, grabbed the piece of wood together with a collapsible stool and a larger than normal knitting needle. She struggled to move her bulk plus carry her props but didn't ask either of her male colleagues for assistance. As best she could, she almost ran to greet her fellow officers. With a bright smile, she proudly held the four inch by two-inch-thick plank vertically. "Good morning. Sorry I'm a bit late but I had to collect Mr Squires here from a friend of mine" She pointed to the wood.

The DCI was amused and intrigued at the same time. "What have you there?"

Twiggy gave a captivating grin, knowing both men were lost for words. "Mr Squires our victim was exactly six-foot one inch tall. This wood is exactly six-foot one inch long. Mr Squires had a hole on the side of his head just above his left eye. This piece of wood has a hole on the four-inch side just above where the victim's left eye would have been. Forensics gave us the angle of the bullet so the hole in this wood has been drilled precisely 20 degrees from the parallel and eight degrees from behind. If we stand my Mr Squires over the remains of the blood pool and put the needle in the hole, then look up the length of the needle, we should get an idea of exactly what went down on the day of the shooting." Twiggy stood back with her arms spread. Both the DCI and the Captain stood in awe of what Twiggy had just described. Both were dumbstruck. Without waiting for comments, Twiggy saw the purple stain and walked to it. She dropped the stool in such a way that it popped open. She then placed what looked like a large knitting needle in the hole and stood the wood vertically directly on the centre of the bloodstain on the pavement. The two-inch edge of the wood was nearest to the kerb and the needle pointed up the road.

"There. We now have a realistic representation of the scene of crime and forensic findings." Twiggy looked pleased with herself. The DCI had to admit he was impressed. The knitting needle pointed in the direction the bullet must have come from. It was a clever yet simple idea.

"Bloody hell, Twiggy. How did you think this up? It's brilliant!" The Captain could not contain his admiration for his partner.

"Yes. Good job, Twiggy. I think! So, what are we looking at? I can see the logic of the wood as a model. I suppose if the hole has been drilled exactly then by looking up the line of the needle, we should get to our kill site."

"Exactly, sir." Twiggy's not inconsiderable chest was swollen further by her pride in what she had produced. "If you stand on the stool, sir, you can have the honour of telling us where the shot came from." The DCI noted the use of sir but stood on the stool without comment. He closed one eye and stared along the knitting needle.

"Are we sure the wood's in the correct place?" The Captain was holding the timber vertically. "Can you rotate it a few degrees left and right?" The Captain obliged. The DCI stepped down from the stool, looking puzzled.

"Right, Twiggy, you have a look. I'll hold the wood and then the Captain can have a go." Twiggy was a bit puzzled by Steve's apparent lack of enthusiasm.

Twiggy used all her muscle power to climb onto the stool. Steve hoped it was strong enough. A Twiggy falling from a collapsed stool into his arms wasn't something he relished. She looked up the rod for a long time. She eventually, and with great effort, stood down and said nothing. The Captain took his turn. He asked for the wood to be rotated even more than the DCI had. He seemed to be looking at a greater arc presumably to get a different view up the needle. Like his two colleagues before him, the Captain stood down but said nothing.

A silence descended over the three detectives. Twiggy could sense a level of disappointment, including her own.

Once each officer had surveyed the view up the knitting needle, Twiggy put everything back in her car. This time, Steve and the Captain assisted. Having placed police on duty signs on the dashboards of their cars, they entered the same restaurant where Timothy Squires had eaten his last meal. The DCI wasn't sure if any passing traffic warden would pay much attention to the police notice on the dashboard of the Fiat but said nothing.

They ordered coffee and sat in a booth. The booth was set along a wall on the right of the dining space and the two male officers took one side, allowing Twiggy full use of the space on the other. She needed it!

"Right!" The DCI opened the discussion. "What did we see or learn from Twiggy's clever contraption?"

"I'm glad I had the idea and a friend of mine did a good job getting the angle right but from what I saw, the shot couldn't have been made unless it was from a helicopter or a drone. The needle pointed straight up the middle of the road."

"I think someone would have seen a helicopter or a drone and maybe even reported it." The DCI was trying to make light of their situation. "It can't be that common a sight around here. What about you, Captain?"

"I'm with Twiggy. I couldn't see anything that was even remotely possible as a firing point. Looking up the road and even changing the angles, there's just nowhere the shooter could have fired from unless he somehow was able to hover over the middle of the road. It just doesn't seem possible. Unless CSI and forensics got the crime scene wrong or the angles aren't correct. If everything checks out, then we seem to have an impossible shooting."

The trio sat in silence and it was obvious the results of Twiggy's experiment weren't what she had hoped for. It just confirmed what the commander had said: "It was an impossible case."

Steve broke the silence. "I agree. I couldn't see anywhere a shooter could've taken his shot but…There's a body in the morgue with a bloody great hole in its head. We have to assume that the angles worked out by forensics are correct, as they don't make those kinds of mistakes. The victim didn't put a hole in his head by himself and his lunch buddies couldn't have done it. So how the hell did the killing happen?" Silence.

The DCI made a steeple with his fingers in front of him while his team drank their coffee. A feeling of frustration started to creep over them, and Steve's mind was trying to figure out what was wrong with this whole puzzle. They sat in silence for about five minutes.

"Let's see what we've got. We definitely have a shooting, therefore we must have a shooter. But the shooter couldn't have set up anywhere to make the kill shot unless he was suspended over the middle of a busy road. We know the victim didn't put a hole in his own head. We know the bullet's still in the skull and the area around the entry wound was wet. The file we were handed was only one A4 page. We've been told this case is only for show and effectively we're not expected to solve it. Agreed so far?" A nod of heads agreed.

"But the case is only days old. No one's had a chance to work it. So why would the murder squad give it to us?"

"Maybe they recognised that it's an impossible murder and they just wanted shot of it."

"Could be, Captain, but it's still a murder. There's still a body and probably a grieving family."

"Well, I think your summary's spot on," said a weary Captain. "But I don't see where it gets us."

The DCI looked around the table. "I agree. I don't get it either. This case is doomed to failure. Maybe that's why we have been given it."

The atmosphere around the table was depressing. All three detectives were at a low point. What two of the three had thought was an exciting opportunity to prove themselves was now a frustrating dead end that would probably confirm that their impending dismissal was justified. None of them spoke. When the DCI broke the silence, his voice had a hard edge that neither the Captain nor Twiggy had heard before.

"I can't really believe I'm saying this." Steve paused and was shaking his head as he sat forwards. "You two said you wanted the challenge of this case but that was before we learnt how impossible it is. Do you still want to chase this knowing what we now know?"

Both detectives gave slight nods of their heads but said nothing. It was clear they were feeling down but, the DCI hoped, maybe not out. Twiggy again took the lead. "We might as well. We've nothing else to do." The Captain agreed.

The discoveries of the past few minutes had piqued Steve's interest more than he would admit.

"I hope I don't live to regret this, but I think we agree we should at least investigate this and run it as a proper inquiry." A pause while the DCI surveyed his team. "Somebody killed Mr Squires. We don't know who, we don't know why and we certainly don't know how. But we should at least try and find some answers. But listen, only if you're sure you're still up for it?"

The mood immediately picked up. Smiles all around. "But Steve! What about the commander?" It was the Captain speaking up. "If we get into this, then he is bound to find out what we're doing and you could be in a heap of trouble. I can't see how we can keep a full-blown investigation quiet."

"Don't worry about Malcolm Clark, Captain, we'll still keep this below the radar as best we can but if he gets wind, then I'll have to explain. But let's hope that day's not today."

"Right." Suddenly, Steve was re-energised. "Let's get this inquiry underway. Captain, I want you to be in charge of our record-keeping. Maintain the file and make sure we're all properly documented. First, I want you to go see the pathologist who did the PM on our victim. Try and get an off the record explanation of what they think we have here. Then I want you to see ballistics but on the quiet. Nothing official. Try and get an impression of what kind of rifle they think could've been used and what kind of bullet." The Captain nodded.

"Twiggy, you and I'll go and see Mrs Squires. From what you've said, she hasn't been interviewed nor made a statement. I think it's time we knew more about Timothy Squires. Let's meet up back at the other office at six tonight and debrief."

Twiggy pulled a face. "The Waterman isn't our office."

"Don't look at me that way, Twiggy. Just for you, I'll go on the wagon for the duration. No more booze till we solve this thing. The way it's looking, I'll be dry for a long time. OK, satisfied?"

Twiggy gave a shrug of her shoulders but was secretly pleased the DCI was taking the case seriously.

"Let's get on with it. Someone shot our victim, and we need to find him. But remember. Discretion at all times. No bull in a china shop antics."

The Captain almost jumped from his seat at the open end of the booth and was off with a purpose in his stride. Twiggy and Steve were left sitting.

"Oh, by the way, Twiggy, do we have a key for the office door?"

"I think so. It's in the lock on the inside. Why?"

"I want you to get two copies cut tomorrow. I have a feeling we should keep the door locked for the duration."

Chapter Thirteen

Friday, 10 April

When the DCI and Twiggy exited the restaurant, the DCI immediately realised his mistake. He looked at the little green Fiat with the wood sticking out the open roof. Then at the bulk of his DC. He wondered if they would both get into the car, let alone get to Mrs Squires' house. Certainly, it wouldn't be a comfortable journey. Twiggy must have had the same thought. "Don't worry, boss." Looking at her car. "She may be old, small and slow but she'll get us to Surrey."

The DCI realised he didn't know where the victim's house was. "When you say Surrey, you mean the Surrey in the home counties? The Surrey that'll feel as though it is a million miles away travelling in this car?" The DCI pointed at the Fiat.

"Well, boss," said Twiggy in a sympathetic voice, "there's no other car and Godalming is really not a million miles from here so don't exaggerate. We'll get there. Hop in." The DCI wished he had kept the pool car.

After stopping at a burger bar drive-through—a burger for Steve and a salad for Twiggy—they arrived at the home of Mr and Mrs Timothy Squires an hour after leaving the restaurant. It had been an eventful hour. As much as he liked Twiggy, the DCI had to admit she was not a small lady, especially when crammed in the front passenger seat of a very small car. Twiggy was capable of filling both seats. The DCI was not looking forward to the return journey.

The property was set in its own grounds and the street was obviously very upmarket. Painted white with exposed structural beams painted black, the appearance of the house was designed to look older than it was. It seemed to have two wings attached to a central building. Each wing was bigger than Steve's entire apartment block.

Without giving it a second thought, Twiggy drove the Fiat straight up the sweeping semi-circular drive and parked just outside the front door. The DCI felt a degree of embarrassment even though Twiggy clearly didn't. After all, a 25-

year-old Fiat 500 wasn't the usual official police transport. Off to one side sat a top of the range BMW gleaming in the weak sunshine. The Fiat didn't compare too favourably to the Beemer.

The door was opened by an ordinary-looking middle-aged woman. "I'm Detective Chief Inspector Burt. This is Detective Constable Rough." Both Steve and Twiggy unfolded their leather wallets that contained their warrant cards. Holding out his warrant card for the woman to inspect, Steve added, "We'd like to speak with Mrs Timothy Squires?"

The woman said nothing but grunted approval and ushered the pair in. She led them into a large square hallway and then through a door off to the right. They found themselves in what was obviously a grand reception room. The woman was dressed in black in what the DCI's mother would have called a twin set. She turned to the officers. "Please have a seat." The accent was very upper crust and Steve wasn't sure if it was natural or acquired. "I suppose you're here about my husband's murder?" the cultured voice continued. Steve thought she appeared to have taken her husband's death very well.

"Yes, and can we say we're very sorry for your loss. Have you had any contact with any of my colleagues?"

"No. Not since two policemen came and told me there had been an incident, and my husband was dead. They said he had been shot and that everything possible was being done to catch the person responsible. They said a post-mortem would have to be carried out and I would be notified when the body would be released for burial. You're only the second police officers I've seen since it happened. My son Sebastian went to the hospital to identify Timothy." Steve noticed Mrs Squires had dark bags under her eyes and looked like she hadn't slept much recently. So maybe she hadn't taken the death of her husband so well! He thought she must have been an attractive woman once but now looked somehow frail and vulnerable. Her high-class diction was being delivered in a softly spoken voice.

"Mrs Squires, we're investigating your husband's death and it would be useful if you could tell us something about him. You know, his hobbies, work, likes, dislikes. It'll help us paint a picture of the sort of man he was." Twiggy reached into her bag for her notebook.

"Inspector, my husband was a workaholic. He knew the importance of people to his business. He wined and dined a lot. From the outside, people took him to be a party animal but in reality, it was always work. He didn't have any hobbies and didn't play sports. We took two overseas holidays a year and Timothy would go abroad on business a few times. We led a quiet life. We watched TV, had a glass or two of wine in the evening and rarely went out to restaurants." Steve thought the longer Mrs Squires spoke; the more cultured voice was beginning to break down. "He said the high-life impression was for the clients, not for us." The DCI noticed the odd 't' was being dropped as she spoke. With a loud sob, the widow had tears in her eyes. "Who could possibly want to hurt my husband?" she pleaded.

Without waiting for her to regain her composure, Steve pressed on, "That's what we intend to find out, Mrs Squires. Can you tell me about your husband's work?"

Mrs Squires produced a small handkerchief from somewhere unseen by Steve and dabbed her eyes and nose. "He was a partner with SPS. That's Sneddon, Price and Squires. He bought into the partnership in 2010, I believe, not long after the financial troubles of 2008 and 2009. The partnership looks after a high-net-worth individuals and invests on their behalf. They give investment advice. There are hundreds of such firms in the City doing the same thing. Tim always said SPS was the best." The widow produced a shy smile.

"Do you know if he's had any trouble with any of his clients? Anyone who maybe felt they weren't making enough money from your husband's advice?"

"Not that I know of, but Tim never spoke to me about business. All I know of his work is little bits I've picked up from people I met at the occasional drinks parties SPS gave. I'm sure Frederick Sneddon of SPS will be able to tell you more of Tim's working life. I only saw Tim as my husband. Frederick is the senior partner at the firm."

The DCI felt he needed to know more about the victim but felt his wife could add no more. "You said your husband joined SPS in 2010. What did he do before then?"

"He was in partnership with three friends he had known from university. They set up a property investment company not long after leaving university. They called it TPPP. It stood for Tim, Peter, Percy and Philip. Very simple. All Tim ever said was that it was a time when people could get rich from property. I believe the firm got investors to put money into their property projects. All I know is that they bought property below value and sold it at a profit. I think their investors shared the profit from each sale. Tim seemed very happy and energetic in those days. I don't know much about what they did in detail." Mrs Squires seemed to drift off, looking into the distance, probably thinking of her life with her husband.

"Tim was the salesman, the people person. He said he brought in the money and his friends bought and sold the properties. He always said it was a perfect partnership." The widow appeared to be on the verge of breaking down.

"When the financial crash came, they all lost everything. It was a shame, they seemed to be doing so well. The firm was closed; everything was handed over to the banks. All four of them were declared bankrupt. It was a very distressing time. I remember we'd only just moved into this house. Tim was very bitter but in true Tim fashion, he bounced back. After the bankruptcy, we had a few months of soul searching and then Tim joined SPS in 2010."

"Yes, it must have been a difficult time. Is there anything else you can tell us?"

"No, I don't think so. He was a kind, hardworking man. I can't even begin to think who might want to hurt him." Mrs Squires at last started to cry and wipe her eyes. Talking about her deceased husband had been an ordeal.

Steve waited a few seconds before continuing, "Did your husband have a home office or study we could see?"

"He had a room above the garage he used when he worked from home. I'll show you over." The three walked in silence out a rear door and over a cobbled rear terrace to a large three-car garage with a metal outside stair fixed to the gable end. The stair led to a door at the top.

The room was built into the eaves of the garage and ran the whole length. There was a standard laminated desk set at one end. A large padded executive chair was behind the desk, which was clear of papers. A series of filing cabinets lined the wall behind the desk. There was a sideboard with a lamp and a tray of whiskey and gin bottles on it plus four glasses that looked like cut glass crystal. At the far end of the space sat two large Chesterfield sofas, a glass-topped coffee table and two angled floor lamps. The floor throughout was carpeted and the room gave the impression of a slightly down-at-heel gentleman's club.

"Did your husband often work in here?"

"Occasionally at weekends but not often during the week."

"Do you mind if we have a look around? It'll help us build our picture and if we find anything, we think might assist us, we'd like to take it. We'll, of course, give you a receipt."

"No no! That's fine, do what you have to. Please, just let yourselves out. Pull the door behind you. It will lock automatically. No point saying goodbye unless you have more questions." With that, the widow was gone, leaving Twiggy and the DCI alone in Timothy Squires' very own copy of his gentleman's club.

The DCI took the comfortable chair behind the desk. Twiggy was about to say something when she noticed he seemed to be staring at the far wall but with unfocussed eyes. "Are you alright, Steve?"

"What?" He shook himself back to the present. "Oh, yes, it's just something Mrs Squires said that's had me thinking. Twiggy, check with the Land Registry. Find out who owns this house and for how long. Try and get an idea of its value. There's a puzzle here but I can't quite see it yet." Steve looked around the room.

"Will do. Now, do we look through the drawers and filing cabinets or what?"

"You look through the filing cabinets and I'll take the desk." Fortunately, Mr Squires didn't seem too security conscious. Nothing was locked. The DCI thought that either the victim had nothing to hide or he kept things hidden in plain sight.

There was nothing of interest in the desk drawers. The DCI even took them out to check for anything taped behind or underneath but found nothing. The paperwork was all internal office gossip and letters to and from clients of SPS. The few letters the DCI scanned seemed normal and friendly. He didn't find anything threatening Mr Squires.

Twiggy had been pulling filing drawers out with great gusto. Steve was about to tell her to pack up when she jumped up. "I think I may have found something! It's a letter from a bank in Monaco confirming receipt of funds into an account marked TPPP. The letter's dated October 2008." She handed it to the DCI.

"Interesting; does it say how much or why? Could be innocent enough."

"The bank's only confirming they've received the funds. But why an overseas bank?"

"I've no idea. Better use your phone and take a picture in case it means something. Put the letter back where it was. Is there anything else?"

"No, it's all just letters. I can't see a laptop."

"Right, let's pack up and get over to the other office. If we leave now, we should get through the traffic in time to meet the Captain." As soon as he said it, he remembered with dread their mode of transport. He was already massaging his thighs and arms in anticipation of the journey back.

The little green Fiat was still parked outside the front door at the head of the long sweeping drive. They approached the car by walking around the boundary of the house. As they attempted a graceful entry into the car, Mrs Squires appeared and stood just outside her front door. She didn't look very happy. Once the two detectives had manoeuvred and pushed parts of their anatomy into strange positions and gotten to know each other better than they should have, they were ready for the drive back to the other office. The victim's wife walked towards the car. She spoke through the open sunroof. "Inspector, please take note that I have a position within this community to maintain and having this thing parked on my drive is not acceptable. If this is the transport the police are spending my rates money on, then I will seriously think about cancelling my payments. If you have to come again in this box on wheels, then please, park in the street and well away from my house." With that, she turned and stomped back into the house.

"Let's go, Twiggy, I guess not everyone's a fan of your car."

In response, all Twiggy said was, "Stuck up cow. No appreciation of a fine car!" The thin smile on her face said it all.

After a most uncomfortable and a more eventful journey than was good for anyone's nerves, Twiggy and the DCI arrived at the pub. The Captain was already there and had bagged the corner table. With great relish, Twiggy went to the bar and ordered. She returned with a half pint of lager and two diet cokes. Steve look at his drink—diet coke. "Twiggy, if you want me to stay off the booze, don't get me this fizzy rubbish. It's more likely to make me go back on the booze. Just for future reference, non-alcoholic beer is now my drink of choice." He took a sip of the Coke, made a face and put it down.

The Captain wanted to get his report in and be off. His wife was going out tonight and he was looking after the kids. "I didn't exactly draw a blank with the pathologist, Dr Green; it's just that she told me something weird." The Captain opened his notebook. Steve could see his notes looked neat and tidy. "I got all the official jargon first. The victim was male, aged around fifty. He was in good health and had good muscle tone. It was definitely the entry into his brain that was the cause of death. No doubt. But there's something really odd. Get this…" The Captain was enjoying his moment of attention. He was keeping the team in suspense.

"There's no evidence the wound was caused by a bullet." The Captain paused and looked at his colleagues. It took several seconds for this news to sink in. No one said anything but mouths were left open.

"Dr Green said she hadn't found a bullet or bullet fragments inside our victim's skull. She said if she didn't know it had been a shooting, she might have thought a spike of some sort could have been the murder weapon." The Captain consulted his notes. "The diameter of the hole measured 15 millimetres and whatever made the hole buried itself eight centimetres into the skull. The hole in the skull is tapered from 15 millimetres on the surface to 3.8 millimetres at the deepest point. Dr Green confirmed the head was damp when the body was first delivered. She'd no opinion as to where the water might have come from other than it was unlikely to have come from the victim." The Captain was silent and looked at his colleagues.

"Are you really telling us our victim was shot, but not with a bullet?"

"No, I'm saying there was no evidence that a bullet was used to shoot our victim. The wound wasn't a through and through, so whatever was used should still have been in the brain, but there was nothing!"

"Then what the hell are we looking at? A bloody bow and arrow or some sort of javelin?" The DCI couldn't take in what he'd just been told.

"No, our Dr Green says it could be a bullet but not as we know it. It certainly wasn't made of brass."

"Well, as if this case couldn't get any weirder." Steve shook his head. "What about ballistics?"

The Captain again referred to his notes. "Pretty much the same. The civilian tech who was at the crime scene told me that when he got there, the victim was, as described, flat down on the pavement with the left side of his face exposed. The tech, who's called Sammy Jones, saw the wound clearly and confirmed there was water on the victim's face around the wound. He was told by pathology on scene it wasn't a through and through. He scanned the area for evidence of anything that might give a clue to where the shot came from. He knew it was a waste of time. He told me the wound he saw was definitely caused by a high-velocity round probably fired from some distance away. He also said whoever fired must be a top marksman. Based on the surrounding buildings and lack of obvious firing points, he said the shot must have been made at maximum range. He was as surprised as anybody when he didn't get any bullet or fragments from the post-mortem to analyse."

"Did you ask him what the maximum range might be?"

"Yes, he was a bit vague. He said it depended on the rifle but if it was military grade and the shooter used competition rounds, the shot could have been made from up to 1,200 yards. He also said not to quote him. He's a civilian and not an expert on ranges of weapons." The Captain folded his notebook away.

"Thanks Captain, good work. Write it up in the morning. Twiggy, do you want to bring the Captain up to speed on our day but leave out the number of near-death experiences we had on the way here." The DCI smiled at them both.

Twiggy didn't! She took her notebook out with a flourish. "We interviewed Mrs Timothy Squires at her home in Godalming. She confirmed what the first officers to visit put in their report. The victim was hardworking, had no enemies and they had no money worries, certainly, looking at the house and the car. He was a partner in a firm called SPS. He bought his partnership in 2010, having previously been a partner in a property company he set up with three friends from university. They called it TPPP and we were told they bought property cheaply and sold it on for a profit. They had investors who put money in so as to get a share of the profits they made from buying and selling. The property fund collapsed at the end of 2008 into 2009 during the financial crash and our victim was declared bankrupt. The firm he now works with—SPS—seem to do the same thing. Invest money on behalf of other people but Mrs Squires didn't think it was in property. Mrs Squires said most of her husband's investors were high-net-worth individuals, whatever that means."

"It means they're loaded," interrupted the DCI. He saw Twiggy's notes were not as neat as the Captain's.

"Fine, whatever! Mrs Squires claimed not to know anything about her husband's work. He apparently didn't discuss business with her. If he did work at home, he used an office above the garage. Everything looked in order and we found nothing incriminating or anything that might shed any light on why he was murdered. The only unusual thing we found was a letter dated 2008 addressed to Squires at TPPP from a bank in Monaco saying funds had been received but no amount. I've a copy on my phone, it's probably nothing. There was no computer. That's about it, except that cow of a wife told me not to go back unless I had a better car. Cheeky witch!"

"Apart from the *Top Gear* reference, Twiggy, that was a good summary. Write it up and give it to the Captain. Right, any thoughts or comments so far?"

"Only that this case gets more impossible the deeper we look." Twiggy was in full summary flow. "We know we have no weapon, no kill spot and a guy with a hole in his head but no bullet. How's that for thoughts?"

"Just about spot on."

The Captain noted Twiggy's comments. "I'm sorry, boss, but I have to get home."

"Oh yes, Captain, I forgot. Before you go, on Monday can you get hold of maps of the crime scene area? Not the A-to-Z street kind. Proper ordnance survey maps. You know, one-inch equals ten feet. That sort of scale. We need a largescale map with a lot of detail going east from the kill spot. Given the way the victim was standing, we know the shot came from the east. Don't get anything that shows areas more than 200 yards from the straight line Twiggy's experiment showed us this morning. Never mind anything west. We only want east and get coverage up to…say, three miles out. Your ballistics mate Sammy said 1,200 yards was possibly the maximum range for the shot. The CSIs would only look for possible sites inside that range, but they didn't find anything." Steve's brain was working overtime.

"This case gets weirder so maybe we have to start thinking outside the box. What if our shooter was firing from further away? It could be a possible explanation. Even if ballistics think it's not possible, we should look into it. That's why I want the maps. You'll get the maps from the Ordnance Survey office. If they can't help, then try the Borough Surveyors and Planning Office, they probably open at 9 o'clock. Can you do that?"

"Yes, but what about money to buy these things?"

The DCI produced his wallet and gave the Captain £60. "I want a receipt. Remember, anything you spend, put it on expenses. If we're going to be sacked, we sure as hell aren't paying for the privilege."

Steve turned to Twiggy. "Twiggy, if you do the Land Registry and the keys on Monday morning and the Captain gets the maps, it sounds like an 11 o'clock meeting on Monday. When you're pulling the Land Registry info on the Squires' house, also pull the victim's financials. You know, bank statements, credit cards. I think we need to learn more about Mr Timothy Squires. If we can pinpoint something in his background, it might take us nearer to understanding his killing. If you're clean, you don't get shot in the head. There's something not right about him. I just have a feeling. The fact we didn't find a computer in his home office

72

must mean he has one in his office. We need to find it. We need to find a motive for his murder, and soon."

Chapter Fourteen

Monday, 13 April

The DCI was beginning to feel the effects of no alcohol in his bloodstream. His body was rebelling. He sat in his small kitchen nursing a headache reminiscent of a good night at the Bush. He'd taken a couple of tablets but still his body was calling for alcohol. The call of the Bush Bar had been strong over the weekend, but he'd successfully resisted it. He drank his second cup of coffee and was determined not to give in. He knew this would pass and he'd promised Twiggy he would be dry for the duration. He could only try!

He sat at his table and tried to ignore his head. He pondered the case. They had no motive, no murder weapon, no idea how the shooter had made the shot and no idea how the hole had been made in the victim's skull. He felt they would get nowhere until they knew where the shooter had fired from and what he'd used to shoot with. At the moment, the case was dead in the water. The DCI had never felt so useless or so frustrated when sober and working a case.

As he was leaving his flat, he paused by the tall wall-mounted mirror. He had to confess he looked better than he had last time he had looked. He decided to revisit Primark as his tailor of choice and buy another suit and a couple of shirts, maybe even a new tie.

The DCI was the first to arrive in the office on this Monday morning. He sat behind his desk and absently pulled a sheet of blank A4 paper from his desk. He doodled whilst trying to make any sense of what they knew. The biggest problems were the lack of a bullet and knowing where the shooter was when he took the shot. Things went round and round in the DCI's now slightly clearer head, but nothing jumped out.

He picked up the file that was now thicker than it had been 72 hours ago. The Captain had done a good job loading information into the file and lifting information from other sources. Steve found the telephone number he wanted and dialled. It was answered on the fourth ring. "SPS Investments. Good morning. How may I direct your call?"

"I'd like to speak with Frederick Sneddon please."

"One moment please. I'll see if he's free." The DCI was pleased, his introduction to SPS seemed to be cordial but he knew that could change.

A different and much more polished female voice was next on the line. "Good morning. May I ask who's calling?"

"Yes, you may but to whom am I talking?"

"I am Mr Sneddon's personal assistant and secretary. How may I help you? Mr eh…" Steve thought the voice was deliberate home counties but probably started in rural Yorkshire.

"My name is Burt, Detective Chief Inspector Burt. I would like to meet with Mr Sneddon this morning and wondered what time would be best for him."

There was a noticeable sharp intake of breath at the other end of the line. Just at that point, Twiggy arrived. The DCI signalled her to sit down and be quiet. He was obviously on the phone.

"Well, Mr Burt, I'm afraid Mr Sneddon is tied up with clients all day. I see from his diary he has a slot next Wednesday at…say, 3pm."

The DCI's headache suddenly intensified and his temper became shorter. Twiggy caught his attention and signalled coffee. The DCI very gently nodded his head as a yes. "Listen, lady. I'm not Mr Burt but Detective Chief Inspector Burt of Scotland Yard and I'm leading the investigation into the murder of one of your partners, Timothy Squires. It's very important I speak with Mr Sneddon this morning. This is a murder investigation so I suggest you look again at your boss's diary and tell me what time I should be at your offices this morning."

"Inspector—"

"Chief Inspector!" Steve was up for a fight.

"Yes, quite." The personal assistant drew a breath. "Chief Inspector." The tone was sounding condescending. The DCI didn't like it. "Please understand, here at SPS, everyone was very sorry to hear of Tim's death, but it has nothing to do with this firm. I must ask you to appreciate how busy Mr Sneddon is as a result of Mr Squires' demise. He is carrying Tim's clients as well as his own so has double the workload. Next Wednesday really is the first available time for Mr Sneddon to see you."

"What is your name?"

"Mrs Sneddon."

"I see, Mrs Sneddon!" Steve deliberately sounded surprised. "I presume your husband is the very busy Frederick Sneddon. All very cosy, keep it in the family." Steve's tone was equally condescending but also sarcastic. "As I said, this is a murder investigation and unless you and your husband can free up time this morning, I will arrest you both for obstruction. I have the handcuffs right here. I even have a matching set. One pair of pink ones for you and one pair of blue for your husband. Please don't make me do it but be in no doubt, unless I interview Mr Sneddon this morning, I will be around and I will bring the his-and-her cuffs."

"I have never heard anything so outrageous in my life!" At this point in the conversation, Twiggy returned with two coffees. "I'm sure you are exceeding your authority. I will be contacting our solicitors and reporting you to your superiors." So much for a low profile but the DCI's zero alcohol hangover was making him short-tempered and more cavalier than he might have been.

"Mrs Sneddon. You have that right as I have the right to arrest you both for obstruction in a murder inquiry. I expect to interview Mr Sneddon today and the interview should last no more than 30 minutes. I will be in your office at 12.30 today. Please make sure Mr Sneddon is there and available. Thank you, I believe we have no more to say."

With his final remark and not waiting for confirmation, Steve put the receiver back in its cradle. He massaged his temples and tightly closed his eyes, hoping this might ease the pounding in his head. If this were withdrawal symptoms from alcohol, then he might never drink again.

He stepped away from his desk and joined Twiggy at the square table made up of the three tables.

"Wow! Who was that you were onto?"

"That was SPS and we can expect a hostile reception at 12.30 this afternoon. By the way, I may have blown our low profile. If that witch Mrs Sneddon does file a complaint, then the game will be up. We'd better soft-soap her when we get to their offices."

Steve sipped his coffee and took another two tablets. He thought maybe his frank discussion with SPS had released some tension and he felt he was slowly beginning to re-enter the pain-free world, but only just.

The Captain arrived with a bang. His arms were stretched in front of him and piled up on them were paper tubes each about four foot long. He was using his chin to stop them rolling out of his arms. He barged into the room sideways so that the paper rolls would pass through the door. He went to a corner and brought his arms down to his sides. The paper rolls fell to the floor with a crash. The Captain looked up and simply declared, "Maps as requested."

"Good man, Captain; before we start, do you want a coffee?"

"Yes please."

Steve produced a £5 note and asked Twiggy to get three coffees. He felt everyone needed caffeine today. Whilst she was away, the Captain explained, "I first went to the Ordnance Survey offices. They were helpful up to a point and said the best they had was a scale of six inches to a quarter of a mile. They had a book listing the areas each series of maps covered. Each map seemed to overlap the next by a few inches so you could lay one on top of the other and get a continuous map. All the maps have numbers. It all looked very clever and professional. Anyway, I just told them what I wanted and they got the maps out. I got four and they charged me £10 a map." Steve calculated he had change to get from the Captain.

"From the OS offices, I thought I'd double-check with the Borough Surveyors and Planning. Turns out they use exactly the same maps, but they enhance them to show more detail. They even show property numbers, drains and so on. I got the same set from them with the extra detail, but they didn't charge me."

"I don't suppose you could get my forty quid back from the Ordnance Survey people?"

"Probably not but I've got your change and a receipt." The Captain enjoyed this exchange.

Once Twiggy returned with the coffees, the DCI went into official police mode. His headache wasn't helping his concentration. "Right. Twiggy, what did you find out?"

Twiggy again produced her notebook. "First, the land registry shows that the Squires' house is registered as belonging to Mrs Squires. It was bought in April 2008. There's never been a mortgage on it. The purchase price in 2008 was £789,000. I asked an estate agent friend of mine what property was going for in the Squires' road. He figures maybe £6 to £7 million."

"OK, so our victim buys an expensive property for cash in April 2008 just before the financial crash and is bankrupted within months of the purchase. The property can't be touched because he doesn't own it. What does that tell us?"

"He was a slimeball who looked after himself," said a slightly annoyed Twiggy.

"Right." The DCI looked a bit animated. "We may have found a motive. Suppose you were an investor in this guy's firm in 2009 and you lost all your money in the crash. You might expect the manager of your money to feel your pain. But instead, he declares himself bankrupt and carries on living in a mortgage-free mansion that, on paper, he doesn't own. What if Squires saw the crash coming and had it away with his client's money? If you were a client, wouldn't you be a bit pissed off? Wouldn't that be a motive for murder?"

"Back up, boss. The victim was only murdered two weeks ago. If what you say is true, it means that the killer waited around twelve years to get even. It seems a stretch, but suppose you're right. Suppose he did rip his clients off in 2009. Most of them will either be dead or at least elderly. But what if he's still at it? Isn't it more likely he ripped the wrong client off from his current lot of investors? They'll be younger and more able to get to him. Maybe someone on his SPS client list is our killer?"

"Mm! Good point, Captain. You mean if he was doing it in 2008 and 2009, he might still be at it?"

"Why not, a leopard doesn't change its spots."

"Thanks, Captain. I suppose it does seem unlikely something from twelve years ago would suddenly now be the motivation to kill. But remember, Twiggy did say we should keep an open mind." The DCI looked at the other two with a grin.

"What if Squires was a serial rip-off merchant? It could give us a strong motive. We need to find his computer and see what SPS has to say. How about his financials, Twiggy?"

Twiggy produced pages from her oversized handbag. "It seems he was a classic bank customer. His salary, or what I presume was his salary, was paid in every month. It was £14,000 each month—not bad, I wish I got that each month. I might even buy a new car." The room appreciated the humour. "He had the usual domestic outgoings for utilities, car lease, insurances, local rates and memberships of various clubs. He and his wife seemed to use credit cards for daily expenses. There were regular monthly credit card payments of around £6,000 for him and £1,500 for her. From his credit card charges, most of it seems to have been spent in restaurants or entertaining at sporting events. It looks like everything was on expenses, so it matched what his wife said. There was no evidence of him receiving any other payments from SPS apart from what I take to be reimbursement of his expenses. His closing balance as of yesterday was £136,000 in credit. He opened his current account as a new customer of NatWest when he joined SPS in 2010."

The DCI was again thinking. The team had already learned not to speak during these periods of silence.

"Where did he bank before?"

"I couldn't find out, so I've asked someone I know in financial crimes to do a low-key search on the quiet. You know, below the radar! He said it may take a while, but he'll get back to me as soon as he can."

"Good work, Twiggy. Right, let's get things moving. Captain, can you set up the maps on the table? We'll review everything when we get back. Also, remember to bring the file up to date. Twiggy and I are off to see SPS and we'd better not be late."

"Can do, Steve. I may have to tape the maps together and cut off bits that aren't relevant to try and make them fit the table. Do you want me to use the Borough maps?"

"Yes, you say they're more detailed. Right, Twiggy! Will you please call up a pool car? I don't think I'm strong enough for the Fiat today." They all laughed at the DCI's attempt at humour.

"I think we should take the Fiat but you're the boss. You're just not a good judge of cars. Here's your key to the office door. You have the original and Abul and I have the copies."

"Let's meet up for lunch in our other office at say, 2 o'clock. Captain, when you leave, remember to lock the office door."

"Will do."

Chapter Fifteen

Monday, 13 April

Twiggy and the DCI arrived at the palatial offices of Sneddon, Price and Squires at exactly 12.22pm. The receptionist, a neat-looking girl of around 20, had them sign in and produced security passes for them. They used their passes to swipe a card reader that opened a football-style turnstile that allowed them access into a plush waiting area.

To the DCI's surprise, the man himself, Mr Frederick Sneddon, arrived and welcomed them as though they were his best friends. The DCI had expected a level of animosity. Maybe all was forgiven and the investigation could continue under the radar after all.

"Chief Inspector, Constable." Sneddon gave a nod to each. "Please follow me to my office." Sneddon stepped out in front of the pair. Over his shoulder, he asked if tea or coffee would be acceptable. The DCI refused on behalf of both of them; although given his ongoing condition, he thought a beer might be acceptable.

"So! How can SPS help you in catching whoever carried out this terrible thing?" Everyone was seated in comfortable chairs and the senior partner had given up his desk to sit with the detectives.

"We're trying to get a picture of Mr Squires. You know, work, friends, clients, remuneration and so on. Anything you can tell us would be very helpful. To start with, how did Mr Squires come to work here and what does SPS do? How did Timothy Squires fit in? That sort of thing. I know nothing of how high finance works and what firms like this actually do."

The senior partner considered before he spoke. "That's a lot of information at once. Let me see." Frederick Sneddon was stroking his chin. The DCI thought he was buying a minute or two's thinking time. The room was air-conditioned and the DCI was feeling better in the cool air.

"My partner Peter Price and I set up the firm from the ashes of the financial crash of 2008 and 2009. We registered the firm as F and P Financial. We knew many serious investors who had been badly burned in the crash. These big investors are always hungry for the next deal but don't like losing money. They also bear a grudge and have long memories." Mr Sneddon paused and smiled more to himself than the detectives. "We knew many of them probably wouldn't trust big investment houses for some time so we thought there might be a place in the market for a small boutique operation that wasn't tainted by the crash. Hence, F and P Financial was born." Frederick Sneddon was full of pride.

"By 2010, just after the crash, things returned fairly quickly to more normal investment conditions. We were doing OK but realised we needed more exposure to our target audience of high-net-worth individuals."

Twiggy interrupted the senior partner's flow. "You mean rich people who still had money even after the crash?"

Mr Sneddon smiled at Twiggy as though she were a child who had just asked a silly question. "My dear, in the world of finance, there are always survivors who come through storms with money. Sometimes less than they might have hoped but money nonetheless." Sneddon wiped an invisible crumb from his silk tie before continuing.

"Now, where was I? Oh yes, we learned that Tim might be available as TPPP had folded a year earlier. We knew of him from his time at TPPP. He had a solid reputation as a real go-getter. A man who could bring in large investment sums. We thought this could be a man we could use to help build our business more quickly. Peter Price and I met him in mid-2010. We both instantly liked him. We saw he was an easy person to get along with and obviously a salesman to his roots. We offered him a job, but he wanted a partnership. He said he would be prepared to invest as an equity partner. He said he had researched us and was comfortable with what he'd discovered. We hadn't discussed bringing in another partner but didn't dismiss the idea. After all, if Tim was the man we thought he was, then there was little risk to us, especially if he was buying in."

"Sorry, Mr Sneddon. Are you saying Timothy Squires had money to buy a partnership here in 2010?"

"Yes, we agreed to a figure of £1million. The contracts were drawn up by our lawyers and Squires was added to Sneddon and Price. SPS was born. Tim paid his money and he commenced as a partner sometime in the second half of 2010. We haven't looked back."

The DCI's mind was working overtime trying to digest what Sneddon had told them. How could a man bankrupted one year invest a million the next?

"Thank you for that, sir. So how did Mr Squires get paid as an equity partner?"

"We all share our remuneration equally. Although I'm designated senior partner, it's only a cosmetic title. Tim was allocated a salary, paid monthly and subject to PAYE just like any other salaried employee. Peter and myself are similarly rewarded, we all take the same salary."

"How much is the salary?"

"Well, of course, our remuneration has increased since 2010. Tim would have been earning £300,000 or so this financial year as indeed will Peter and myself. Of course, this is before tax, national insurance and so on. His net take home would have been around £170,000 this year."

"Did he receive any other income?"

"Well, Inspector, we all work very hard for our clients and of course, we look to share in any increase in their wealth due to our efforts."

"OK sir; one of my original questions, what does SPS do?"

"Sorry. I wasn't avoiding your question. It's just as my wife says. Sometimes I talk too much, especially about the business." The mention of Mrs Sneddon caused Steve to blush slightly. He remembered his attitude when speaking to the lady earlier on.

"SPS was set up as I said as a boutique investment firm. We encourage high-net-worth individuals to give us their money to look after for them. In a nutshell, we use their money to make them even more money. You'd be surprised how lazy or stupid some high-net-worth individuals can be. Usually, they're greedy enough to want their money to earn more money but don't have the competence to do it themselves." Frederick Sneddon looked at his watch, indicating to the two detectives that time was moving on. He sensibly didn't say anything.

"We have over the past ten years been able to return an average growth rate of around 9% to our investors. The best year we had was 2017 when we achieved 17%." With a sense of pride, Sneddon continued, "We were the best performing investment firm in the City that year."

"Really?" said Steve only to show he was interested. "That must have been quite an achievement?"

"Yes indeed." Sneddon gave a small cough and adopted a more formal air. "We invest our clients' money across a wide range of investments in order to achieve a balanced portfolio of shares, bonds and directly in companies that can offer high yields, such as oil and gas ventures. We keep a certain amount in cash and speculate 3% of the fund in start-up businesses that we feel could be successful."

The senior partner stopped and adjusted his tie. Steve felt he had just been quoted and lectured at using the sales pitch from the company's brochure.

The DCI's mind was overwhelmed by the speed and intensity of the delivery Sneddon had just made. To calm himself down and for reasons he didn't know, Steve allowed his mind to wander to the senior partner's dress. He noted his silk tie, which was a bright striped pattern and thought he might get one like it. He also noted that the rather ordinary five-foot eight inch man was wearing a smart, three-piece striped business suit. The DCI didn't think the senior partner shopped in Primark.

Mr Sneddon carried on after drawing breath, "From our small beginning, we now have offices in New York, Los Angles and Tokyo. We employ worldwide just under 500 people, more than half of whom are analysts."

Steve cleared his mind of all thoughts of ties and suits. "That sounds very impressive. So how much money do you look after for your clients?"

"It's no secret; we currently have funds under management totalling some £800 million."

"And you're delivering 9% on average on this money?" The DCI heard Twiggy chip in for the first time since being referred to as 'my dear'.

"Yes, but remember, that's an average. We aim to return higher yields. Before you reach for your calculator, if we have an average year this year then that equates to £72 million our investors will collectively earn this year."

Twiggy persisted. "You said earlier that you and your fellow partners benefitted along with your investors. Do I take it that you meant you share in this £72 million? If so, would Mr Squires benefit also?"

"Why, yes, of course. The maths is simple. We charge 5% of the profits we generate for our clients. So, if the year ended now, our bonus would be £3.6 million. Our clients share a pot of £68.4 million."

Twiggy looked shocked. "Wow! That's a lot of money. So, the £3.6 million is shared equally among the three partners?"

"Yes. We are all equal," the senior partner said with more than a touch of indignation. Twiggy could swear he lifted his nose in the air as he spoke.

"In addition, we charge a small administration fee of 0.75%. We have significant overheads. This charge funds the operation and allows us to give our clients the best possible service that only a boutique business like ours can give."

Twiggy had been taking notes but both she and the DCI couldn't take in everything this dapper little man was saying. The DCI decided to change tack.

"Getting back to Timothy Squires. You're saying he would have had a salary of £300,000 this year, plus a third share of a £3.6 million pot. If my maths is correct, that would be £1.5 million just for this year." Steve showed he wasn't the simpleton he'd claimed to be earlier. "Again, if my maths is correct, you're raking in an additional £6 million for overheads. Is that about correct?"

The senior partner was beginning to colour up. "I'm not sure the term 'raking in' is appropriate. We run a successful business on behalf of our clients, and we share our success with them. It's all perfectly normal but your analysis represents a fair assessment."

"Did Mr Squires have any financial problems you're aware of? Say gambling or drugs."

"No, no. Tim was as straight as an arrow. He'd no problems of any kind." Given what the DCI suspected about Timothy Squires' past life, he wasn't too sure the arrow reference was accurate.

"How is the bonus paid?" Steve was warming to his subject. The air-conditioned air was still helping.

"By bearer bond. It isn't considered salary so not liable for PAYE. It's paid gross."

"If I remember from previous cases, bearer bonds are untraceable once issued?"

"Yes, I believe that is so." The senior partner was looking a little uncomfortable. He had certainly lost his earlier composure.

"It's a little unusual but isn't as uncommon within financial firms as you might think. How the recipient deals with the income is generally between them, their god and HMRC. The bond allows for unfettered transfer anywhere in the world."

"Did Squires send his out of the country?"

"Alas. As I said, what my partners do with their bonuses is between them and their god." The senior partner gave a little smile at his attempt at light-heartedness.

The DCI wondered where Mr Sneddon's bonus payments ended up.

"So, to the best of your knowledge, Squires would have no need to fleece his clients? He wasn't cheating any of them? No one might want to get even with him by killing him?"

"Inspector. You don't understand how we work. As I said, Timothy was a salesman. It was his job to bring funds into the firm. Once he had done so, the client became mine or Peter Randall's. We would select one of our analysts to work with a new client and decide on a portfolio. Tim had no access to funds once they were lodged."

The DCI was again in thought mode. Twiggy spoke up, "So, if Mr Squires was here for ten years, would it be that his bonus each year would have been around £1 million a year?"

"No, not quite, Constable. In the early years, we didn't control the level of funds we do today. In the first year or so, we didn't pay ourselves a bonus but over the past say seven years, it's fair you could say Tim's dividend would have been around £1 million a year."

Twiggy was making more notes.

The DCI hadn't taken in Twiggy's last question. His mind was elsewhere. Something was preying on his mind, but he couldn't bring it to the fore. He felt he now had enough information from the senior partner. He was exhausted listening to money numbers he could only dream of plus trying to get to grips with what it all meant.

The DCI stood and Twiggy did likewise. "Mr Sneddon, many thanks for your time. I'm sorry we have taken up so much of it. I know your wife said you were busy. We greatly appreciate your cooperation. Also, can you please pass on to Mrs Sneddon my apologies for my rather brusque manner on the telephone this morning?" The DCI thought it best to keep pouring on the charm in the hope any thought of a formal complaint would vanish.

"I certainly will. I know she sympathises with the great pressure every police officer looking for Tim's killer must be under." The DCI didn't get an impression the sentiment was too sincere.

"Thank you. Just a few more requests. Can we see Mr Squires' office, and could we have a list of your clients?"

"Viewing Tim's office is one thing but I'm not sure about the list. Our clients value their privacy. I feel that unless you can demonstrate an urgent need then I must decline."

"We can get a warrant but that takes time. We rely on people such as your good self to cooperate during a murder inquiry, especially when the victim is one of your own. We only need the list to try and establish if anyone on it might have had reason to harm Mr Squires."

"I see that, Detective Chief Inspector, but just the same. If you return with a warrant and our lawyers clear it then, of course, we will comply. Now, if you would come with me, I'll take you to Tim's office."

Twiggy and the DCI followed. They noticed that the senior partner checked his watch again but like last time sensibly said nothing.

Mr Sneddon showed the two detectives into a large corner office with glass on two sides. It was richly furnished and had a functional feel. Straightaway, Twiggy spotted a laptop sitting on the desk.

"This was Tim's office. Please take your time but you'll have to excuse me. I have a lunch meeting and I'm running late." The senior partner held out his hand to be shaken by the officers. He seemed to realise he had spoken out of turn. "Oh! Please. I didn't mean late because you kept me longer than you said. It's not a criticism. I was happy to help but I really must go." He shook both sets of hands again. As he left, he turned. "If you need anything, please ask Jane on reception." With that, the senior partner was gone.

"Right, Twiggy, bag the laptop." Looking at his watch, Steve took out his mobile phone and called the Captain. "We're running late here so our lunch date has to be postponed. Sorry! We'll be back in the office by three or just after. How have you made out with the maps?"

"Great. I think you'll be amazed by my cut-and-paste skills." The Captain giggled like a schoolboy. "Seriously, there's something you'll want to see. It doesn't make sense to me."

"After the meeting we've just had, you're not alone; see you later."

They did a cursory search of the office but knew they would find nothing to help. After 15 minutes of opening drawers, filing cabinets and cupboards, the DCI called a halt.

They explained to Jane on reception they were taking Mr Squires' laptop and gave her a receipt. The DCI knew he probably should have had a warrant based on his previous conversation with the senior partner and hoped this breach wouldn't come back to bite him. He also secretly hoped the laptop had client details they could use.

The DCI and Twiggy got back to the office at 2.50pm. They were met by the Captain leaning over the same three tables that formed the square in the middle of the room. The table was covered by street maps and the Captain seemed to have stuck a pin over the kill site. He was busy attaching a piece of string to the pin as the pair walked in.

"This looks impressive. Where'd you get the board?"

"Ah well. You see, I thought that if we're going to use the maps, we would need them mounted on something so we could move them from the table when we didn't need them. Then I had an idea that if we mounted them on a soft board, we could stick pins and all sorts in the maps to maybe better show what we're thinking."

"OK, Captain. Good thinking but where did the board come from?"

"Well. I got hold of a guy called Keith in maintenance and asked if he had a suitable board. This is the result, and by the way…I said you would stand him a large drink or two next Monday evening."

"Did you? I see you're free with my cash. Oh! And you still have my twenty quid." A smile showed the DCI was not serious. "Right, what have we got?"

The Captain took a deep breath and began, "This is a detailed map of the area to the east of the kill site. It stretches for about three miles from the kill site. As you can see, I've put a pin in the place where the victim was found. I've cut off the surplus parts of the map more than 200 yards either side of the estimated path of the shot." The Captain stopped and looked at his colleagues to see if they were following his explanation. "Right. I've tied a string to the pin. If we pull it along forensics' exact trajectory for the bullet…" The Captain held the string and walked around the table pulling the string tight. "Then we should see where the shooter was when he took the shot. Unfortunately, there's nothing there up to 1,200 yards out."

The DCI studied the map and took the end of the string from the Captain. He pulled it further out than the Captain along the kill line, following a pencil line drawn on the map to show the direction of the kill shot. The string was at least three-quarter ways up the map before it crossed a building.

"How far is it from the scene to this building?"

"It is exactly 1 mile, 1,677 yards. In other words, just under two miles. No way could the shooter have fired from that range. I've checked the maths."

The DCI stood over the map. He moved the string each side but realised there were no other buildings anywhere near that could have been used. "Captain, you have double-checked all this, haven't you?"

"Yes. More than once. There's no other building in the line of sight and the first possible building is too far away."

Twiggy, who had been looking on, asked, "What if the shooter had a rifle that could fire from two miles? Maybe he has a new state of the art weapon…say, made in Russia that we don't know about. If part logic says the only place the shot could've come from is this building and the other part says it couldn't, then surely we have to consider a weapon does exist that can fire from that range."

The DCI and the DS looked at Twiggy with something close to admiration. "You know what! You could be right; smart thinking, Twiggy. Why not a rifle that can fire that far? What you say makes sense. Right now, it's the only explanation that does."

The DCI sat down. "Alright, let's accept a super rifle exists as a working hypothesis. Captain, do you have the address of this building?"

"Yes. It's called Sedgwick Close. I've googled it. Seems to be an apartment block, not very upmarket but not council."

"Right. Let's put the map board against the wall and clear the table. Twiggy, how about getting some coffee? It's your shout anyway."

Sitting around the now cleared square table, the DCI started. "Let's recap where we are, although it shouldn't take long. We've got bugger all. Our victim was shot from what we believe was an impossible distance if we believe ballistics about maximum ranges for such a shot. Captain, first thing tomorrow, get onto the Collator's Office. Find out if anything has happened around the area of that building." The DCI didn't wait for a response. "The victim was shot in the head. There's no evidence of a bullet and his head was wet around the entry site. The victim seems to be well off, had a good job and although there might be a question of how he dealt with the tax man on his bonuses, he seems to have had enough money so as not to need to rip off his existing clients. Besides, his partner said he didn't have access to money once clients had invested." The DCI sipped his coffee and stared into the near distance.

"I don't think we're looking for a motive involving his working life. He just seemed to have it all. I don't buy a disgruntled investor. These guys don't go around shooting people. So, if he wasn't ripping people off, what's our motive?" Steve carried on thinking out loud. "He seems to have had some dealings with a bank in Monaco but that was in 2008. He's also made around £7 million in bonuses over the past seven years. This money doesn't appear on his bank statements. So where is it? Is the money our motive?" The DCI emerged from his thinking out loud.

"Twiggy, can you ask your friend in financial crimes to find out about this bank in Monaco? Oh! By the way, has he come back to you with details of the victim's previous bank?"

"No. Not yet. I'll chase him up."

"Right. We took the victim's laptop from his office earlier. See what you can get from it. I'm no expert, so I have to rely on you two to tell me."

"I'll take it home and see what I can do."

The DCI was still looking perturbed, almost talking to himself. "You know, I can't help feeling this Squires has paid for something in his past. I don't see him upsetting anyone involved with SPS enough to get himself killed. He's worked there ten years with no suggestion of trouble. Money can always be a motive, but he seems to have had enough. We'd better try and track down the £7 million if we can. I don't think it's relevant, but you never know. We don't know enough about his life before SPS. We know he bought that big house just before the crash and paid cash. Less than a year later, he was bankrupt. How did that happen? Then he paid for a partnership with SPS a year later. Where did that money come from? He was supposedly bankrupt. My head's spinning with all the finance stuff we got from Sneddon. I need to think in a quiet room."

Steve seemed to realise he'd been talking to himself. "I want to dig deeper into our victim's earlier life. I have a feeling that despite the ten-year time lag, that's where we'll find our motive. It can wait till tomorrow. Let's pack up now. We all need a break and some thinking time. See you both bright-eyed and bushy-tailed 9 o'clock in the morning. I think we have a lot to do this week."

Twiggy looked concerned. "Boss, you're not going drinking, I hope?"

"No, Twiggy. I'm going clothes shopping when I leave here and then White Hart Lane for Monday night football. Don't worry, I told you, dry for the duration."

The Captain had disappeared with a wave. Twiggy was gone. The DCI closed and locked the door. His second week as a DCI had begun. He felt good but had no idea where this case was heading.

Chapter Sixteen

Tuesday, 14 April

The killer had arrived the previous evening at the Holiday Inn at exactly 7pm. He'd phoned Friday afternoon and made a reservation for Monday night and had specified room 228. This was to be his kill room. He'd had a bit of a problem explaining he would pay cash. He didn't want to use a credit card that could be traced. Eventually, the girl on the end of the phone had agreed. He could pay cash on arrival.

He'd learned there was a shift change at 7pm and guessed anyone checking in during this time wouldn't be remembered too well. The killer had visited a Chinese emporium Saturday morning and bought a thick-framed black pair of near clear-lensed reading glasses, a cheap red baseball cap with a large peak, a long college-style woollen scarf and a set of luggage wheels that people used before wheels were built into suitcases. The glasses, cap and scarf were his disguise. The luggage wheels were instead of the warehouse sack barrow. He didn't think using the barrow was the best way to stay invisible on arrival or when leaving the hotel.

There were two girls behind the reception desk. As predicted, this must be the shift change. He entered, approached the desk and said he had a reservation in the name of Brown and he was paying by cash. Neither of the girls gave him a second look. His disguise was going to be adequate.

"Please fill out the details on the card. Your room is ready, and it'll be £69 for the night." The receptionist turned to her co-worker and carried on talking about some edict that had been handed down from their head office.

The killer placed exactly £69 on the reception counter, pushed the completed but totally fictitious registration card towards the woman who stopped talking just long enough to hand over the electronic room key and smile sweetly. "Have a nice stay with us. Breakfast's between 6.30am and 9.30am. Your bill will be ready for you in the morning." He was sure neither of the bimbos behind the desk would remember him in half an hour.

He carried a small bag so as to look like a guest checking in. He used the lift to make sure it was working. The carpark was only about a third full, so he knew the hotel wasn't busy. Once in his room, he emptied the contents of his bag and plugged in the electric flask containing the projectile for tomorrow. He would only get one shot.

He had parked his van at the far end of the carpark outside CCTV range. He was confident his disguise would stand up to CCTV scrutiny. Cameras only covered parts of the carpark, entrance and reception. He had kept his head down and had never given the cameras a clear view of him. He felt confident, nervous and excited all at the same time now that the clock to the kill was ticking.

The killer waited an hour before going down to the van for the first suitcase. He attached the old-fashioned wheel system to the case and pulled it through reception to the lift and up to his room. He still wore his disguise but the whole area was dead. He didn't see another human being. He waited an hour and repeated the process, wheeling in the second suitcase and brought the third in another hour later. No one paid him any attention. His killing machine was in his kill room.

He made a cup of tea using the room kettle and tea bags. As he sat on the bed and drank the strong brown liquid, he reflected on his first kill. It was a shame about the old lady but at least this time there would be no collateral damage. Just one dead body tomorrow. Somehow, this thought soothed the killer. He placed his cup on the bedside table and fell into a light sleep.

He hadn't meant to sleep, but when he awoke, he felt cleansed and fit. Almost ready for anything. The clock on his phone said 3am. It was Tuesday. His victim's last day on earth. He slowly and methodically set about assembling his killing machine. He meticulously made sure every part was properly screwed together and that the computer was plugged into the wall socket tightly. There had been provision for battery power, but the killer had adapted his machine to run on mains power. He called it a computer but knew it was more electromechanical than electronic. Despite being primitive by today's standards, it did the job.

He called up the local meteorological forecast. With the data he received, he dialled in the information on wind direction, speed and atmospheric pressure. He knew the range from the optics. He would amend the readings just before he took the kill shot. At 7am, he opened the window and positioned the killing machine ready for its next victim.

Waiting was now the enemy. Doubts started to enter his previously positive state of mind. *What if the green man is green when the target arrives at the pedestrian crossing and he doesn't stop?* This was his main fear. The target had to be stationary for the killer to get his shot away. As he thought about his victim, he became angry at what this man had done. He convinced himself yet again that this act of revenge was necessary. The killer was ready. Time ticked by. The countdown to a killing began.

08.57. The killer checked the connections one last time on the killing machine.

08.59. Everything was ready. The latest meteorological readings had been entered, the range settings had been re-entered and the machine was positioned.

09.00. The pre-alignment check was carried out and now only needed the target to appear in the optics for the final target lock.

09.03. The target appeared, coming around the corner, heading for the crossing.

09.03. The killer put on the industrial glove, opened the flask and as before, placed the projectile in the breach.

09.04. The propellant was placed in the breach and the breach closed and locked.

09.05. Everything was ready. The high-quality optics showed the target clearly together with the exact range.

09.06. The target arrived at the crossing. The killer locked on. The target was in the crosshairs of the optics. The green man was at red.

09.06. A small final adjustment. The target was clear and locked. The killer pushed the white button on the side of the machine.

09.08. The victim lay sprawled out on the pavement by the pedestrian crossing.

09.09. The green man said pedestrians could cross. The victim would never see another green man.

As before, the killer had a moment's regret. He had just taken another human life. He didn't like to think of it but then the rage set in. The killer believed at that moment that he was an avenging angel sent to seek revenge. The anger built up inside him until he hit his fist against the wall. Luckily, the wall wasn't damaged but the shock and pain brought the killer back to reality. He wondered as he had before whether he needed medical help. He didn't know.

Again, he knew they would never find him so he could take his time. He disassembled the killing machine, placed all the parts in the suitcases, packed his small bag and was ready to leave. As before, he had surmised that someone leaving a hotel with a suitcase, no matter how big, would attract no attention.

He collected his bill from reception and handed back his key card. The killer's escape was textbook. Well-planned and flawless. He was pleased with his cheap but effective disguise. Just in case any of the CCTV cameras spotted him in the carpark, he kept everything on until he was seated behind the wheel of his van. He could see no CCTV cameras covering guests arriving through the entrance. He had however spotted CCTV covering the exit. Despite his van having false plates, the killer exited through the entrance rather than the exit so as not to be caught on CCTV. He presumed the hotel was not concerned by who came in but wanted to nab anyone leaving with an outstanding bill. He didn't care. He'd just beaten their system. Yet again, he thought he had gotten away with murder.

Chapter Seventeen

Tuesday, 14 April

The DCI arrived fairly refreshed at 8.30am. He was wearing his new Primark suit, a new Primark shirt and even a new Primark tie, all bought last night. He didn't even have withdrawal symptoms and was clear-headed. He felt full of energy for the first time in months.

He'd been thinking about the case during the Spurs' defeat last night. This morning, he wanted to get things moving. He needed a clearer picture. Yet again, he went over what they knew.

One: The victim had been shot with something unknown but not a bullet.

Two: Whoever had shot the victim was an exceptional marksman or was using a sophisticated weapon unknown to police firearms experts.

Three: The victim's head was wet around the wound.

Four: It was unlikely the victim was involved in any fraud at SPS. He had no access to clients' cash. This probably ruled out the murderer being a client or investor. However, just to be sure, they needed to find out where the bonus payments had gone.

Five: There was no obvious weapon.

Six: The victim's life before 2010 wasn't transparent. It needed investigating. What had he been up to before 2010?

Seven: The victim had been declared bankrupt in 2009 but had bought an expensive house in 2008 with cash.

Eight: The victim had bought a partnership, creating SPS in 2010 only one year after being declared bankrupt.

Nine: Apart from a few financial questions, they had nothing to go on.

Ten: They had no motive, no means and no opportunity.

Steve summarised his thoughts on the whiteboard. He added an eleventh item: *Something from 2009 is wrong and why give us the case?*

The DCI was deep in thought, convincing himself the solution was in Timothy Squires' past when Twiggy arrived. "Wow, look at you, sir, very flash. Your evening shopping spree must have gone well."

"Yes, Primark's best. They even asked if I wanted a loyalty card. It was a bit scary. I almost said yes." They both laughed.

"Well, boss, I think you look the part." Twiggy settled her bulk behind the square table. "I took the victim's laptop home." Twiggy held up her hand to stop the DCI interrupting her. "I know. It's against the rules but we didn't exactly abide by the rules to get it, did we? Anyway, I told you last night I was doing it!"

"Yes, you did and no, I don't suppose it matters. We couldn't use anything you've found in court anyway without admitting we nicked the bloody thing. Now tell me you've found something and cracked the case."

"Not exactly. The whole thing was password protected. I got a friend of mine to help and he cracked it. I was able to get into the victim's files." Again, Twiggy held up her hand to stop the DCI interrupting her flow. "I know! I know! A civilian involved with evidence, but it was all done over the phone. No physical contact with the computer. Anyway, all I could see were emails and letters all to do with work. Nothing that looked suspicious or that jumped out at me." Twiggy stopped and tried to appear mysterious.

"However," she paused for effect, "there was a file marked Prospect List. What do you suppose that is?"

"It'll be a list of people he would see as potential clients. You know, punters! He'd keep in regular touch and try to sell something to them. All sales guys have a list. It's part of how they keep making their money. In this case, I suppose it was Timothy Squires' list of people he wanted to persuade to invest in SPS."

"Yes, well, this is some list. Everyone on the list is loaded. If I were looking for a rich husband, then this list is all I'd need. I suppose I may have to lose a few pounds first though?" Twiggy curled up, laughing at her own joke as did Steve.

The Captain chose that moment to enter the room. "What's so funny?"

"Twiggy's found a list of potential investors in SPS but thinks it would make a better dating agency list. She's just planning how much weight to lose."

"Are you looking for a husband, Twiggy?"

"Always but I won't find one around here."

"Ah, well, maybe you should interview everyone on the list. You might get lucky."

Twiggy looked slightly embarrassed and decided not to continue the conversation. "Oh, never mind."

"Nice outfit, Steve. Very sharp. Been down Saville Row?"

"No. I'm almost a Primark regular. Now can we get to work?"

"Good idea." Twiggy was back in charge. "Before you came in, Cap, I was explaining to Steve the only thing of interest on the SPS laptop is this Prospect List. You should see how much these guys are worth. None of them seems to have less than £50 million. There are about 40 names on the list. It gives addresses, contact numbers and how much they're worth."

"Good work, Twiggy, if a little unconventional. But where does it take us?"

"Hold on, Steve. There's more. One of the files is listed as Monaco 2009. The strange thing is the date, 2009. That's when Squires went bust, but get this. It was only transferred onto the laptop six months ago. It has a strange code attached to it and my friend couldn't unlock it over the phone. He tried for ages but no luck."

The Captain chipped in, "Couldn't your friend come here? If we kept the laptop in view all the time, we would preserve the evidence trail."

"Cap, the stunt we pulled to get this laptop means it can never be used as evidence. This is all a bit black market. It's not a bad idea. Twiggy, would your friend come here to take a look?" The DCI noted the Captain's nickname had been shortened to Cap by Twiggy. He thought this was a good sign. His team was bonding. Even if only for a few months.

"I can ask but—"

The office door opened without a knock. A man of about five foot nine stood in the doorway. No one in the room recognised him. The DCI saw that this person was dressed even more shabbily than he had been a few weeks ago.

"Detective Chief Inspector Burt?" The stranger looked at the three faces in front of him, expecting an answer.

"Yes, that's me," volunteered Steve.

"File for you from Inspector Lovat in the murder squad. Seems you're handling the Squires case. Mr Lovat thought you might like this one as well. The Collator's flagged it up as having a similar MO to the case you're working on.

"Seems you're listed as the senior investigating officer, so this is for you."

The DCI was temporarily lost for words. "If it's from Inspector Lovat, it must be a murder case?"

"I can see why you are a DCI and I'm only a constable." The constable's tone verged on the insubordinate. He read Steve's face and quickly added, "Sir."

"When did this murder take place?"

"It's in the file but about an hour ago. The SOCO and forensics are still on the scene. Not sure if the body's been moved yet. It's in Wimbledon. Good luck."

"Who are you?"

"I'm the bearer of news good and bad. I just go where I'm told. Detective Constable Mike Goodall at your service. 30 years a copper and heading for retirement in seven weeks. Roll on." With that, the detective constable was gone.

The DCI opened the file and read out loud from the initial summary:

"Shooting this morning, Tuesday, 14 April.
Time approximately 09.00.
Victim declared dead at the scene.
Victim not yet identified.
Location: pedestrian crossing, Penrose Road, Wimbledon.
First CID officer on scene: DC Robert Hollingsworth. Local station.
Victim appears to have been shot in the head.
Full scene of crime call out.
Senior Investigating Officer Detective Chief Inspector Steven Burt."

The DCI continued to stare at the file. "That's all it says. How the hell have we been given another one and what happened to low profile?" The DCI wasn't sure how to proceed. He took command. "OK. Change of plan."

"Right, boss. What do you need us to do?"

There was a sudden and obvious change in attitudes all around. An air of excitement and purpose filled the room.

"Cap, call down for a pool car. Twiggy, I need you to carry on chasing down details from the first case. See if your friend can come here sometime today and look at the laptop. Then follow up as we discussed. Talk with financial crimes. See if they can find evidence of Squires' banking before 2010 and see if there's any way they can trace the bearer bonds Squires was given as his bonuses. Also, the Cap will be with me so can you check with the Collator. See if there were any unusual incidents reported around Sedgwick Close on the second of this month. That's where we think the kill shot could have come from. OK?"

"Wow, yes, no problem. Let's get to it." Twiggy was full of enthusiasm.

"When you've done that, come out to Wimbledon. We'll need you there."

Steve looked at his now highly motivated team. "OK, any questions?" Silence. "This is a live one and we're in at the beginning. If this is the same killer, it could be our best chance to get to the bottom of the first murder. Let's give it our best shot. If you'll excuse the pun."

Chapter Eighteen

Tuesday, 14 April

Getting to the scene was a nightmare. Even with blues and twos blaring away, it took just over an hour to get to Penrose Road, Wimbledon. The road had been closed and the diversions obviously weren't ideal. Add this to rush hour traffic and the DCI could see a lot of motorists being very unhappy with the police.

As they arrived, they noted that a white spring-loaded tent had been erected over what the DCI suspected was the actual crime scene. An extravagance of blue and white police tape was circling the scene, keeping unwanted visitors out. A bunch of uniformed officers were stationed around the perimeter marked by the tape looking like sentries. As you always got when such things occurred, a small group of spectators had gathered but the uniforms were keeping them well back. There were three police cars and a couple of scene of crime vans parked at odd angles around the scene. The DCI noted the plain black morgue van lurking just on the periphery of what looked like a circus. These vans all looked the same.

As he approached the blue and white tape, a uniformed PC approached. The DCI showed his warrant card as did the Cap. As Steve walked towards the white tent, he was racking his memory to recall what he'd been taught about crime scene protocols. Especially murder scene protocols. He quickly realised he'd forgotten most of it.

They put their heads inside the tent and saw a body splayed out as though it had been crucified. There were two figures in white all-in-one disposable suits fingertip searching around the edge of the tent. A figure in the same white paper suit was kneeling beside the corpse and appeared to be talking to itself. The DCI gave a cough to attract attention.

The kneeling figure looked up with a 'who are you' look on its face. Because of the hood on the suit, it wasn't possible to see if the figure was male or female.

"I'm DCI Steve Burt, SIO on this case. And you are?"

The kneeling figure stood and turned to face the DCI. "I'm Dr Barbara Green." The doctor made a show of switching off her handheld recorder. "It's my misfortune to be the pathologist on call, which is why I'm here and not enjoying a few days' rest."

The DCI couldn't tell if she was serious or if this was just her way of dealing with any crime scene. Dr Green removed the hood of her paper suit. She appeared to be in her mid-40s, petite with a short rather boyish hairstyle.

"What can you tell me about the deceased?"

"You mean other than he's dead?" The pathologist wasn't in a good mood. She seemed to notice the Cap standing just behind his DCI. "Good morning, sergeant. Sorry I'm not good at remembering names but never forget a face."

"DS Ishmal. I spoke with you last week about another case similar to this."

"Ah! Yes, you did." The pathologist carried on as though the conversation with the Cap had not happened. She addressed Steve, "Male, probably mid-50s, looks like he was on his way to work." Dr Green pointed to the briefcase lying on the ground. "Time of death was within the last two hours. Say around 9 to 10 o'clock this morning. One thing you should know. He's been shot in the head and the wound and his hair are wet. I've seen this before. There was a similar shooting that had come for post-mortem examination about two weeks ago. The one your sergeant there came asking about. I'm fairly certain this'll turn out to be by the same hand, but I can't confirm that until I've done the PM. I'll set it up for…say, 2.30pm this afternoon, if that suits you?"

"Yes. Thank you, doctor; do we have an ID?"

"Everything he had on his person has been bagged and given to a young detective constable. I believe he's still here. We can bag the briefcase now and you can have it if you wish. I'm about done here."

"Thanks. See you at 2.30 this afternoon." The DCI and the Cap left the tent to seek out Detective Constable Hollingsworth. They found him talking to a woman who appeared to be segregated from the rest of the onlookers. As the pair approached the detective constable, he broke away from the woman to greet the two detectives.

Before anyone could ask, DC Hollingsworth volunteered. "That's Mrs Flora McLeod. She was standing beside the victim when he was shot. I've got her statement, but she can't tell us much. She said she just heard a whistling noise and the guy standing next to her keeled over. She's a bit upset."

"OK. If you've got her details, you can let her go. Do you have the victim's effects?" The DC handed over several sealed, plain plastic bags. One contained a wallet. A thought struck the DCI.

"Are you the only CID officer on scene?"

"Yes, sir. I was told a senior officer from the Met would be handling the case and I was to do the basics and hold on until you arrived."

"Mm. Good to know."

The DCI put on a pair of crime scene blue gloves, opened the bag with the wallet in it and removed it. He handed it to the Cap who also now had blue hands. The Cap opened it and took out various items, including a driving licence. "Looks like the victim is one Percival Booker, 16 Blackhope Crescent, Wimbledon."

Detective Constable Robert Hollingsworth chipped in, "That's just around the corner."

"So the pathologist was correct. He was on his way to work. He must have just left the house."

The DC suggested, "Must've been on his way to the station. It's only over the road."

"Did your Mrs McLeod say what time the kill took place?"

The DC looked up his notes. "Not exactly but says it must have been around 09.05 because that fits in with her daily routine. She does the same thing every morning Monday to Friday. She says she wouldn't have been at the crossing much outside that time."

"Good. So, we have a pretty accurate time of death. Thank you, Robert. Good work, we'll take it from here. Remember to let us have your report and the witness statement."

"It's Bob, sir. I'll get everything to you." The young Bob Hollingsworth turned and left.

"Cap. You and I had better go and see the widow if she's only around the corner. I don't suppose anybody has been to tell her."

Just as Steve and the Cap were about to set out to find number 16 Blackhope Crescent, Twiggy arrived in her apple-green Fiat. This time, there was no wood sticking up through the sunroof. Despite this, the engine still sounded like a cement mixer.

"What have I missed? Is it the same MO as the first victim?" She was obviously excited.

"Looks like it could be. Did you get all the bits you were working on and what about your computer friend?"

"Right. I have some really good intel. You'll hardly believe what I have, but yes. My friend says he can come to the office at around 6 o'clock tonight when he finishes work."

The DCI rubbed his chin in thought. "Twiggy, I want you to stay here and oversee the removal of the body. Then I want you back in the office working on the first victim. The data you have you can analyse and fit into what we know or don't know about our first victim. I don't want to be distracted from this second case just now. I have a feeling everything we learn about the first shooting will apply to this one. We could be nearer solving this thing than we know." The DCI was being very formal. "Sorry to put you office-bound for a while, Twiggy. Oh! Can you also phone our first victim's wife, Mrs Squires? Ask if she has ever heard her husband mention a Percival Booker. That's our second victim. See if she knows anything about him. It's a long shot but you never know."

"No problem, Steve. When will you be back? I really need to bring you up to speed."

"It's now 11.45. The Cap and I are off to see the widow Booker then we have to attend the post-mortem at 2.30pm. We should be back around 4 o'clock. By the way, I want to get that laptop back to SPS tomorrow before Frederick Sneddon notices it's missing and stirs things up." With a flourish of his arm and a "See you later", the two detectives left the detective constable standing inside the blue and white tape. Under her breath, Twiggy said, "Thank you very much, sir." She wasn't happy being put back in the office.

It was only a short walk to 16 Blackhope Crescent. The pair were impressed by the size of the place and the cars sitting outside. They agreed that Mr Booker must have been a very rich man.

The woman who opened the door was far from what either detective might have expected. She was tall, blonde, about 30 years old and, they could both see, was not afraid to show off her figure or her legs. She was well made up and looked more like she was leaving for a night out rather than doing her duty as a suburban housewife. Her skirt was pelmet-length and only just covered her bottom. Both detectives thought this was one stunningly good-looking woman.

Reaching for his warrant card, Steve approached the woman. "Good morning."

He thought he sounded like a door-to-door salesman. "I'm Detective Chief Inspector Burt and this is Detective Sergeant Ishmal. We would like to speak with Mrs Booker."

The woman looked a bit shocked at having two policemen on her doorstep but recovered quickly. "That's me; will you come in?" The voice was accented. Steve thought probably Eastern European but educated. As they followed her into the house, both men noticed the poise and grace of her walk, not to mention her long and very revealing legs. Steve wondered what a suburban housewife was doing dressed to impress late morning and wearing four-inch narrow heels inside the house. He let it pass but remained curious. The Cap was having similar thoughts.

They sat around a coffee table in a very large and well-furnished room. "Can you please tell me what this is about? My husband is at work. He usually deals with all official matters."

The Cap handed the DCI the plastic bag containing the wallet. "Mrs Booker, have you ever seen this wallet before?"

"I'm not sure. My husband has one like it."

"Mrs Booker. Inside this wallet, we found your husband's driving licence together with other cards, all of which bear your husband's name. Do you have a recent photograph of your husband?"

"Yes, there is one on the piano behind you. What is this about? You are beginning to scare me." The newly widowed woman had stood up and was pacing around behind the officers to retrieve a framed photograph of her husband. She handed it to Steve.

Steve saw the face of the man he had last seen on the ground by a pedestrian crossing. Even with a hole in his head, there was no doubt. The picture was of the victim standing on the deck of a large cabin cruiser-style boat. The photograph had been taken from the quay and was angled up, showing Mr Booker in full nautical gear. The DCI handed the picture frame to the Cap.

"Mrs Booker, would you please come and sit down again? We may have some bad news for you."

"There was in incident this morning at the pedestrian crossing in Penrose Road. A man answering your husband's description was killed, and looking at this photograph, I regret to say that it would appear the victim is your husband, Percival Booker."

The widow Booker sat, crossed her lovely legs and allowed her very short skirt to ride further up her thighs. "I'm sorry for your loss."

Steve had never been good at delivering bad news to relatives. He gave Mrs Booker a few moments to reflect on the news. "When you feel up to it, a policewoman will call for you and take you to see your husband. I'm afraid we'll need you to formally identify Mr Booker, unless he has a close relative who might be able to do it?"

"No, Percy was an only child."

"The formal identification can wait till tomorrow. We're fairly certain it is your husband."

Mrs Booker looked at the DCI without emotion. "Yes, of course."

"I'm sorry but I need to ask you a few questions."

"Yes, please, just ask." The widow was looking a little pale despite her expensively made-up face.

"What time did your husband leave the house this morning?"

"I believe at 9.00. That is his usual time. I didn't see him go. I was still in bed. I'm not very good first thing in the morning."

"What did your husband work at?"

"He is or was an accountant. I think he did tax returns for people. His boss should be able to help you. Dale Pollock runs the company, Tax 4 U. Their office is in the city."

"How long has your husband worked there?"

"Forever. I only married my husband five years ago and he was working for Dale then."

"Did your husband have any enemies you're aware of?"

"No. Percy went to work and came home. All we ever did was watch TV in the evening. We'd have an occasional evening out, but we led a very quiet life."

Steve wondered why the widow was so dressed up if she led such a quiet life.

"Who owns this house, Mrs Booker?"

"Well, I suppose I do now. I am my husband's sole beneficiary." Both detectives noted her English was very precise. Almost formal.

"Mrs Booker, can I ask where you are from originally?"

"I am from Estonia. I came to England eight years ago."

The DCI needed to buy some time to think. "I see." Although he didn't see anything. Everything Mrs Booker had told them about her husband painted a picture of him being ordinary and normal. Yet he'd been gunned down just like the first victim. The widow's accent was becoming more accented. She was showing no signs of grieving. Steve wondered if she was a trophy wife rather than a domestic wife. "Where did you meet your husband?"

"I worked for an estate agent in Pall Mall, all very upmarket. One day Percy walked in and asked if we could value this house. He was thinking of selling. In the end, he decided not to sell but phoned me to ask me to dinner as a compensation for not proceeding with a sale. We got married three months after our first date. That was five years ago."

The DCI noted this explanation was given as a statement of fact rather than with any emotion at the loss of her husband. "Did your husband ever mention a man called Timothy Squires?"

The widow appeared to think hard. "No…I don't think so. Is it important?"

"Probably not." Steve sighed. "Did your husband have a study or office here in the house?"

"Yes. It is upstairs. First door on the right. Do you want to see it?"

"Yes, if you don't mind. It could prove very useful. We'll only be in there a few minutes and then we can leave you in peace."

"Thank you."

The widow waved a hand as though the officers were now dismissed while she remained seated. Obviously, she wasn't going to show them into her husband's home office. As they left her, they noticed Mrs Booker was powdering her nose. Steve's mind wandered as he thought of the difference between Mrs Booker's perfect, if accented, diction and Mandy, his latest barber's, assassination of the language! He smiled and slightly shook his head.

The office was a smaller room than they had expected. A desk sat against a wall, meaning anyone sitting at it had to look at the wall. There was only one three-drawer filing cabinet and a small two-door cupboard. The filing cabinet and cupboard had keys in the locks. The DCI noted there were no pictures on the walls and no photographs of friends or family.

"I'll take the desk. You take the furniture."

The Cap understood but asked, "What are we looking for?"

"Anything that catches your eye and could have a bearing on the first killing. The MO is identical so I'm thinking both killings have to be linked. We just need to find it. You know what to look for. Things like bank statements, credit card statements. Anything that gives us an insight as to who Percival Booker was. People who lead ordinary lives don't get gunned down in the street."

The pair set to searching. The DCI found the desk drawers unlocked. He opened the drawer that ran across the top of the kneehole. Straightaway, he saw a laptop. "Cap, can you bag this? We'll take it with us."

One of the bottom drawers doubled as a filing cabinet. Steve went through all the files and found nothing until he saw a file marked Monaco. Inside were several letters addressed to Mr Booker from the Director of San Sotto Bank in Monaco. One dated 2008 welcoming the victim as a customer. Another, also dated 2008, thanking the victim for visiting the bank and trusting the bank with his funds. The other letters were dated 2008 and early 2009 and dealt with what appeared to be administrative issues concerning the victim's money. None of the letters mentioned how much money Booker had in the bank. There were no bank statements.

"Bingo, Cap. I think we may have a link. Can you bag these letters? Have you found anything?"

"No. Just bank statements from Lloyds and credit card statements. I'll bag them and look at them later but they're all fairly recent. They seem to all be dated from 2018."

"Good. OK, let's go. We'll tell the merry widow what we've taken."

They arrived at the mortuary at 2.25pm having fought the traffic. They had stopped *en route* for a Big Mac each from a burger drive-through. Dr Green was there, dressed in green scrubs with the trousers pushed down white wellingtons. She had a net covering her hair and wore protective goggles and standard-issue blue rubber gloves. Both detectives were dressed in plastic green disposable aprons and had blue covers over their shoes. It was obvious the pathologist didn't hang around. The post-mortem looked to be almost over, given they could see the body had been opened using the normal Y-shaped incision.

"Ah! Gentlemen. Are you late or did I start early?" Without stopping for breath, Dr Barbara Green carried on, "No matter, almost done." She pointed to the other person in the room. The detectives assumed this figure dressed in the same gear as the doctor was a technician there to do Dr Green's bidding.

"Finish up please, Eric."

She turned to address the detectives. She was all business. "As per our discussion at the scene, there's no doubt this is an exact copy of the shooting of Timothy Squires." She paused to gauge the reaction of the two police officers. She was disappointed not to get one. "As I said, I'm good with faces but not names so I looked the name up so you would know which case I was referring to. This poor sod has a hole in his head exactly the same as the previous victim, give or take a few very minor differences." The pathologist was walking around the metal table on which victim number two rested. Eric was washing the cadaver.

"The angle of penetration and site of penetration are, of course, different. Like our previous victim, there's no evidence of a through and through and there is no bullet nor bullet fragments inside the skull. The head was wet as you saw at the crime scene. Apart from a hole in the head, your man here was fit, healthy and would probably have lived for another 40 years."

"So, you're saying this isn't a copycat but the exact same killer?" The DCI felt he needed this clarification.

"No doubt about it. It's exactly the same. Do you have an identification for me or is he to remain John Doe?"

"His name is Percival Booker." The doctor nodded to her assistant.

"Thank you, doctor. No doubt we'll get your report in due course. I'll arrange for the widow to formally ID tomorrow. Say, 11 o'clock if that suits?"

"As good as any, I suppose. How did the wife take it? I hate grieving and sobbing widows."

"I don't think you'll have anything to worry about. Mrs Booker took the news very well."

Chapter Nineteen

Tuesday, 14 April

The DCI arrived back in the office at 3.35pm. The Cap was returning the pool car and would collect three coffees. Steve was paying—again. Twiggy was writing away on an A4 pad and had obviously been using the whiteboard. Steve's previous jottings on the board were still there. He had to admit the board looked impressive.

"Here we are, three coffees as ordered. Twiggy, what have you done to the board? It all looks very professional." The Cap was impressed.

"Thanks, Cap. When do you want to review things, sir?" Twiggy was still feeling a bit miffed that she hadn't been part of the crime scene investigation. The DCI recognised her mood but said nothing. All three now had their coffee.

Steve thought it best to give Twiggy her moment in the spotlight. It might put her in a better mood. "Let's get started then. The floor's all yours, Detective Constable Rough."

Twiggy stood up and edged towards the whiteboard. She noted the use of her title but said nothing. "I've had most of the day to think and review what we know, and time to add the extra information I gathered while you two were out enjoying yourselves." The DCI could see she wasn't so annoyed as she had been when he first returned to the office. She was being sarcastic. "First and most importantly, I spoke with Mrs Squires about our second victim, Percival Booker." The DCI could tell from Twiggy's big grin that she had something. "Booker was Squires' partner in the firm they set up out of university. We already know it went bust in 2009." An air of triumph filled the room.

"Wow! I didn't expect that," said the Cap as he threw his empty coffee cup into the waste basket.

"Good work, Twiggy. So, let's be sure. You're saying Timothy Squires, our first victim, knew our second victim, Percival Booker. Both men were partners in a firm that went bust in 2009 and both men were killed in exactly the same way within two weeks of each other. That's no coincidence. This gives us a definite link." The DCI had a sly chuckle to himself. This was progress.

Twiggy was still beaming when she put her hand up to interrupt the DCI before he could carry on. "There's more. Mrs Squires told me there were four partners. You remember in her statement she said her husband and three friends from university had set up their property investment company together. The other two partners were a Peter Randall and a Philip Du Bois. Mrs Squires explained the company name was TPPP. This was for Timothy, Percival, Peter and Philip, their Christian names. Apparently, Philip Du Bois was killed in a boating accident in 2006. Guess where it happened?" Before anyone could speak, Twiggy triumphantly announced, "Monaco."

"There's that Monaco connection again."

"Yes, Cap, there it is again. We need to dig deeper into this Monaco bank. What else did you learn, Twiggy?" The DCI was pleased with progress but deep down couldn't shake a feeling of apprehension.

Twiggy stood nearer the board. "Well…" She was looking far too pleased with herself not to have more interesting data to pass on. "In no particular order, I chased financial crimes. Turns out Squires had two accounts at NatWest from 1996 till 2008. The first was just a standard one but the address on the second account was in Monaco. This was before the serious clamp-down on money laundering. Squires seems to have used his first NatWest account to route money to his second and then onto a numbered account at San Soto Bank in Monaco. My friend in financial crimes couldn't get copies of any bank statements from Monaco for obvious reasons but said the amounts transferred ran into millions. He checked international money routes and as far as he can tell, there's been no activity on the Monaco account since 2009. Mr Squires has been very quiet. At best, my friend could tell the cash is just sitting there." Twiggy stopped to let this information sink in with her two colleagues.

She was still smiling. Still enjoying playing her audience.

"There's obviously more?"

"Well. Yes. Just a little." Twiggy was playing her audience like a professional performer. "Being a clever detective constable, I asked my friend to run a similar search on our second victim. Percival Booker." Twiggy paused for effect.

"Well, tell us, don't keep us in suspense." The Cap was all ears.

"Our second victim, Percival Booker, had a similar account in Monaco at the same bank as Squires. He also had two NatWest accounts between 1996 and 2008. It seems he transferred money using his NatWest accounts to Monaco just like Timothy Squires." She had the two detectives' full attention.

"There's even more. You wanted to know about bearer bonds. Well, bearer bonds are not traceable under normal circumstances, unless you know someone in financial crimes. These bonds leave a trail if you know how to follow it. The money has to come from somewhere and finish up somewhere. Anyway, my friend found that the trail went from an SPS account to San Soto Bank in Monaco. There's obviously no public record of Timothy Squires having a bank account at this bank. He must have been using a numbered account. But that's not easy, certainly today. My friend thinks he must have been converting the bonds to cash and using a safety deposit box at the bank or this bank runs a special secret account service only for selected clients. Same way numbered accounts in Switzerland used to operate and probably still do. It looks like Squires became legitimate around 2010. So since then, he's had a load of money in a secret account in Monaco that we can almost see and another load in cash that we can't." Twiggy just stood by the whiteboard. She seemed somehow drained after passing on her revelations.

"That's all I got from my friend except he says to tell you he called in a lot of favours and we all owe him big time."

"Twiggy, if that's all, then you and your friend have earned your pay this week. Well done. I'm not sure where this takes us, but I think it shows our Mr Squires and possibly Mr Booker were at it up until 2009. Squires seems to have been involved in a bit of tax avoidance on his bonuses, but God knows what he was up to before 2009."

"I'm not finished." Twiggy had been busy. "I checked with the Land Registry. It seems our Mr Booker bought his house in Blackhope Crescent in 2008 and paid cash. £749,000. The original deed was in his wife's name. Remember Squires' house was in his wife's name as well and bought around the same time. Just before their firm went bust." Twiggy raised an eyebrow and looked at her colleagues. "It seems the first Mrs Booker died in 2004 and under their joint wills, the property was re-titled into Mr Booker's name, so he now owns it. Or at least his widow will now."

Before anyone could draw breath, Twiggy was off again. "I also spoke with the collator and the intelligence unit to see if there'd been any unusual events around Sedgwick Close on the second of April. That was the date of the first shooting. It turns out there was a murder in the actual building. It was discovered on the fifth of April, but the pathology puts the death around three to five days previously. Also, a neighbour told the house-to-house boys that he had seen a uniformed police sergeant in the building on the first of the month and that he had seen a man loading suitcases into a white van on the second. The witness said he was certain of the dates because the second was his birthday. He said what caught his attention was that the man loading the van was the same police sergeant he had seen the previous day."

"Woah! Hang on. This is all too much to take in at once. I don't know about you, Cap, but I'm into information overload. Let's regroup and draw breath. I presume all this is on—" The phone rang. The DCI grabbed the receiver, not being pleased to be interrupted.

"Inspector Burt. This is Keith from maintenance. Your Oppo said you would stand your hand in the pub, so I was wondering about tonight. I just wondered which pub and at what time. I did him a favour, those boards are expensive you know, and I could get into trouble—"

The DCI cut him off, trying to remain civil. He could tell Keith was about to launch into some form of rant to justify asking for his drinks. "Yes, Keith, DS Ishmal told me you had been a great help. Look. I'm a bit tied up just now. How about if I put fifty quid in an envelope with your name on it and leave it at the main reception desk right now? You could maybe treat some of your mates on me?"

"Well, I was looking forward to a good old chinwag but as you're busy, I'll pick up the envelope in about half an hour. Thank you, Mr Burt. You're a scholar and a gentleman." With that, the line went dead and Steve was about to be fifty pounds poorer.

The DCI pulled two twenty-pound notes and a single ten from his wallet. "Cap, that was your friendly maintenance man. The one you promised I would buy drinks for." Handing Abul the money, he said, "Put that in an envelope and put his name on it. Then hand it to reception downstairs to be collected tonight."

"Right, Twiggy. This is very, very good work. Your technical friend should be here soon. We collected another laptop from the second victim's house. The Cap must have it in that great man-bag he carries." Twiggy picked up the man-bag and took out the laptop. "If he has time, can you ask your friend to check out this one as well?"

"No problem. I'll have a look first. I might get something off it."

"Fine. What I suggest is that the Cap and I leave you with your friend in here working on both laptops. The Cap and I'll go up to the canteen and have a debrief over a coffee. You've given us a lot to stew over. You've had time to digest this new info. We haven't. We need to catch up. Is that OK with you?"

"Yes. I'll go down to reception now in case he's early. You know how long it takes to get visitors signed into this place. I'll see you in the canteen if we crack anything anytime soon."

The Cap appeared, having successfully completed his delivery, as Twiggy was leaving. "We'll leave Twiggy to it. Let's go to the canteen. Bring the files with you and your notes from Twiggy's debrief. We've a lot to try and make sense of." The DCI knew he wasn't kidding himself.

Over coffee at a quiet table in the plastic tabletop side of the canteen, both detectives sighed and drank their coffee. "Look, Abul. We need to simplify this. Twiggy got a lot of data today and it's all useful in building a picture but it's not getting us any closer to our killer. My head's going round and round. I think we need to review the basics."

"I agree, boss. My head's full of dates and facts that I can't connect. We need to find our way through all this finance stuff. I'm not even sure it's helping our case."

Steve pulled a paper napkin from a dispenser and took out a ballpoint pen. "Right, let's put things into boxes." He drew a rectangular box on the napkin and wrote box 1. "We know our two victims were shot but we don't know how or what with. We have to find out as a priority. Agreed?"

"Agreed. Any thoughts?"

"I have a good mate in tactical firearms. I'll speak with him tomorrow. See if he has any ideas."

The DCI drew another box and wrote box 2. "Both victims knew each other and were partners in a property investment company from 1996 till 2009. Both paid cash for large houses just before the crash. We need to check if Booker was bankrupted at the same time as Squires."

"On it first thing, but didn't Mrs Squires say all four partners were declared bankrupt?"

"I'm not sure. It would make sense but check it anyway."

Steve drew box 3. "Twiggy gave us a lot of info about money but none of it ties up. The first victim appears to have been clean since he joined SPS in 2010, although we need to find out where the £1 million came from that he used to buy into the partnership. He seems to have been stashing money away at that bank in Monaco until 2009 so presumably it came from there. That'll be another job for Twiggy's friend in financial crimes. Apart from that, it looks like if Squires is guilty of anything over the past few years, it's not paying tax on his bonuses. We don't know enough about our second victim, but it seems they were joined at the hip until 2009 and possibly involved in some kind of fraud." The DCI gave a faint smile. "I don't think HMRC are bumping people off yet. Let's see if we can follow the money. I'm not sure it'll take us anywhere but just now we have nothing else. The £1 million is a start. I can't help this feeling that we should be looking into Squires' and Booker's lives before they went bust."

The Cap stared at the napkin the DCI was using as writing paper. He said nothing because he was equally confused and had no idea how these murders might be solved.

"If we're to get anywhere, I think we have to go back to this TPPP firm. Squires seems clean now, but he didn't buy a partnership nor a large house from bankruptcy without having been bent. All we know so far about Booker is he bought a large house presumably for cash in 2008. We'll get more on him tomorrow. I'm sure the secret's in the past. That's where we'll find our motive and our killer. The second murder is obviously linked to the first. If we solve one, then we solve both."

"Are you sure about this? Most of the people who invested up to 2009 with this TPPP will be getting on a bit. Would anybody wait over ten years to start killing these guys? And why now? I'm sorry, Steve, I just don't see it. The money has to be the motive."

"You could be right but if Squires, and we have to assume Booker, have been clean for the past ten years then where's the money motive? I just wish we had a list of clients from 2009. See who these guys were dealing with.

"We have Twiggy's marriage prospect list but that's only people Squires wanted to invest in SPS. There's been no sign of anything or anybody from their TPPP days as far as we know. If there is a list from 2009, it's well hidden." The Cap gave his shoulders a shrug. He felt deflated. They were going round in circles.

"No but I bet if we had that list, we'd crack both cases." Steve gave the Cap a wicked 'I told you so' grin. "I know you don't believe me but I'm telling you the answer is in the past."

The DCI knew it was just wishful thinking to believe a list of TPPP clients from 2009 would hold the key to solving this thing. He could only hope and dream.

But sometimes hopes and dreams come true!

"Let's go down and see how Twiggy and her computer wizard friend are doing. Drink up."

When the two arrived, Twiggy and Tom her friend were just sitting, talking and laughing. "Tom. This is my boss and the guy who will be paying you, Detective Chief Inspector Steve Burt. The other sad-looking individual is my second boss, Detective Sergeant Abul Ishmal."

"Good to meet you both." Tom was a stereotype techno nerd. Long hair, shaggy beard, black T shirt and jeans. He actually wore sandals with no socks.

Keen to get on and realising it was now after 8pm, the DCI became a bit more formal than he had intended to be. After all, Tom was doing the DCI a favour.

"So, Tom, have you solved the problems?"

"Yes, it was relatively easy once I had the binary code and hacked the password. Easy. People are really lazy about their computer security. Mind you, both these machines are museum pieces. I'd say they are at least 20 years old."

"Detective Rough mentioned payment. How much do I owe you?"

"My usual rate is £500 an hour but as you're a friend of Flo's here, we'll call it a pro bono job with future credits in case I ever get into a jam. I'll know who to call."

The DCI didn't tell Tom that as a cop, his reign as being a useful contact was a bit time-limited, but he thanked him and Twiggy showed him out.

When they were all back together, Steve wanted to know if Tom had succeeded. "Oh, yes, we have a lot of good stuff."

"Right. I suggest we call a halt and sleep on everything tonight. Did Tom get everything off the SPS laptop?"

"Did he ever. It's gold dust for the case."

"OK. If you're sure there's nothing of interest left on the SPS machine, take it back first thing tomorrow morning. If you have to deny all knowledge, do so.

"Just say you were asked to hand it in to Mr Squires' office. We'll schedule the Twiggy laptop tell-all show for tomorrow afternoon. Say, 2 o'clock. It'll be all eyes on you again then, Twiggy." Twiggy gave a shy smile but was happy to have her chance to shine. "Cap, you take Companies House. Just check to see if

Mr Booker was ever declared bankrupt. Also go and check out this witness at Sedgwick Close. If he did see a police sergeant, it could be significant, but I doubt it. Get the locals to open up the apartment where the murder took place. It must still be a crime scene so they can let you in. Have a look around. See if anything supports our theory that this could be the kill site. We also need to follow the £1 million Squires used to buy his partnership at SPS. Twiggy, maybe you could follow that up with your friend in financial crimes?"

Both detectives nodded their agreement. "I'll arrange a meeting with this Dale Pollock. According to Mrs Booker, he was Booker's boss at this company called Tax 4 U. It doesn't quite have a top five accountancy firm ring to it, does it?" This brought a smile to everyone's face. "I'll make the appointment for around 12.00. Twiggy, you'll be back here before the Cap so you can come with me. I'll call my mate in tactical firearms first thing and try and get a steer on our likely weapon. Everybody OK with that? Good. Twiggy, give me the laptop from Booker's place. I'll lock it in the desk."

Twiggy handed the laptop to Steve. "We've copied everything onto two memory sticks. I've got them here. I'll keep them and bring them in tomorrow if that's OK?"

Nods all around. "This is the longest day I've done in a long time. Not sure about you two but I'm shattered. See you both tomorrow."

With the door firmly locked, the three detectives left for the night.

Chapter Twenty

Wednesday, 15 April

Steve arrived early, intent on doing some thinking. He sat at his desk with a cup of coffee bought from a Costa on his way in. He wanted to lay out for his own benefit what they knew and what had to be done. Twiggy had thrown up more questions yesterday than answers. He wished he had a bigger team and wasn't having to work below the radar to satisfy Commander Clark. He was coming to the conclusion that given the second victim, his days of operating quietly could soon be over. He feared he might even be taken off the case.

Almost working on autopilot, he unlocked the top drawer of his desk and took out his A4 pad. Immediately, his brain entered into mild shock. The laptop he had locked in this drawer last night was gone. He frantically searched the drawer in the hope it was at the back but knowing all the time it was gone. He started to question his own actions but concluded he really had put the computer in the drawer and locked it. He examined the lock. There was no evidence of it having been forced or tampered with. If someone had been in this drawer, they must have had a key both for the drawer and the office door.

But who?

He sat for a few minutes considering the implications of this discovery. There was only one explanation as to why something would go missing in a building that was ultra-secure. The DCI couldn't get his head around the thought that someone inside the building had gone to the trouble of getting into the office and stolen the laptop from a locked desk. Surely, whoever had taken it must know the theft would be discovered. But why nick the thing in the first place?

Why go to the trouble? Was the theft to do with the two murders or was it just a coincidence? After a while, he decided he'd keep quiet until he understood why the laptop had been removed.

He called his contact in the tactical firearms support unit and was given the name of someone to talk to at the Imperial War Museum. A Major Simms. His mate in tactical support couldn't help with any ideas about what kind of rifle could have been used, especially when Steve told him about the suspected distance the shot had been made from. "Put it this way, Steve, if your guy has anything that can fire from that range and is hitting his target, then I would know about him. There aren't many, if any, who could pull off that shot. We keep a record of marksmen and I'm on that list. I doubt if I could hit a skull from that distance or even half that distance. Sorry but are you sure you've got this right?"

Steve thanked his friend and said he was following the forensics and reminded his mate that he had two dead bodies both shot in the head from what appeared to be excessive distances. A dead end.

After finishing with the weapons expert, Steve next looked up the number for Tax 4 U and dialled the number. After half a dozen rings, a voice appeared at the other end of the phone. "Yes?"

"Is that Tax 4 U?"

"Yes." The DCI thought this was not a good start. The voice was young, East London accent and clearly needed some training in how to answer a business telephone.

"Can I speak to Dale Pollock, please? This is Detective Chief Inspector Burt of Scotland Yard." Steve had found that using his full title and linking it with Scotland Yard, although a bit pompous, could be effective in getting people's attention. This was a case in point.

"Dale! Oh! I mean, like Mr Pollock is not in the office."

"When will he be in? It's very important I speak with him today."

"I could like call him on his mobile if you like. I'm sure he'll come in to meet you." The young voice was trying to be helpful, but Steve got a sense she might be a bit frightened of the police and a bit in awe.

"Fine. Call him and tell him I'll be at his office to meet him at 12 noon today. Please tell him it's very important and concerns a murder case."

"Oh! Yes, well, like. I'll make sure he gets the message. Who's been…like murdered?"

"Thank you." The DCI hung up.

His next call was to the Imperial War Museum. He was sure he would get a different reception. "Can I speak to Major Simms, please?"

"Who shall I say is calling?" The voice was home counties and sounded very professional. Not like Tax 4 U.

Steve explained and was put through within five seconds.

"Good morning, Chief Inspector. Hector Simms here. What can I do for the police today?" The voice was clipped, educated and full of authority. It was the voice of a career soldier.

"Good morning, sir. I understand from our firearms people that you're an expert in small arms. I have a bit of a dilemma and think you may be able to help. I was hoping I could come and see you later today if you were free…"

"Of course, old boy. Anything to help the boys in blue. I could certainly make time to see you later today. Say 16.30? Sorry. Old military habits. That's 4.30pm if that suits?"

"Ideal. Thank you, Major. See you then."

The DCI was pondering the stolen laptop when Twiggy breezed into the office.

"Morning, boss. You look a bit troubled."

"No, nothing. Just mulling over what little we know." Putting on a bright and light-hearted air he certainly didn't feel, the DCI carried on, "How did it go at SPS?"

"Well. It was a bit surreal. At first, the receptionist wouldn't take the laptop because it had belonged to Squires. She said she'd have to talk to Mrs Sneddon. I did as you suggested and played the downtrodden PC only carrying out orders. She must have had second thoughts and asked me what I was supposed to do. I couldn't believe the opening. So, I put on my best pathetic face and said I had been instructed to put it back in Mr Squires' office. Unbelievably, she took me along to the office and I left it on the desk. It seemed neither Mr nor Mrs Sneddon were in. So, mission accomplished. What about you? Anything good happen overnight?"

The DCI thought about the missing laptop. Surely Twiggy or the Cap wouldn't have taken it. They knew the information on it had already been downloaded by Twiggy's friend Tom and Twiggy had the memory sticks. So, if not one of them, then who else? He had no answer.

"No, not much. We have a meeting at Tax 4 U at 12 o'clock and I have a meeting with a weapons expert at 4.30pm. Remember, you have your big tell on the laptop presentation at 2 o'clock."

"How could I forget?" Twiggy said with a big grin.

The DCI leaned back in his chair and put his hands behind his head. "Twiggy, you are sure your pal Tom got everything off both those laptops yesterday, aren't you?"

"Oh yes. Pure gold dust. I've got all the info on two flash drives, like I said. I've got them here. Everything that was on both computers."

"Good." The DCI was relieved that at least the data from both laptops was safe. It was just the one laptop that had gone walkabout. He felt a little better.

Still leaning back casually in his chair. "I've been thinking about our two murders." Twiggy was taking things from her bag but she stopped and sat down if only on the edge of her chair to listen to Steve. "Both men knew each other as partners going way back. They were two out of four. According to Mrs Squires, one of the four—Philip Du Bois—was killed in 2006 in a boating accident in Monaco. According to the statement given by Mrs Squires, the fourth partner is a Peter Randall. What if our killer was going after all the partners in this TPPP firm? With two murdered and one already dead, our Mr Randall could be the next target. What do you think?"

"Well." Twiggy fiddled with her pen. "We have no evidence linking this Randall to anything but neither did we have anything linking our first two victims. I suppose it's possible he could be next. Shouldn't we go and see him anyway? If this is all connected to TPPP, it could even be he's our killer rather than our next victim. It's possible there's a pile of money locked away in this bank in Monaco and this guy wants the lot. Just a suggestion."

"Possible. It could be a motive. Money usually is but why now? These guys worked together over ten years ago." The DCI liked Twiggy's thinking. "It's not a bad idea though. Let's find out where he lives, and we'll go see him tomorrow morning. I think we have enough on our plate today. Tell you what! Get hold of the company accounts for this TPPP. Go back as far as you can. There could be something in them that we need to know. Your friend in financial crimes should be able to help."

Twiggy made a note.

At 11.51, the DCI and Twiggy entered the office building of Tax 4 U. Whilst the building was modern with a grand glass-fronted exterior and in Central London, the offices occupied by Dale Pollock and Tax 4 U were less grand. They were on the first floor. This floor seemed to be made up of a lot of little cubicle-sized rooms each with a different name on the door. It struck the DCI that perhaps these were serviced offices rented by the month. But then he recalled Percival Booker had worked here for ten years so probably not on a month-by-month rent. Compared to Timothy Squires' office, this place was a dump. Percival Booker didn't seem to be doing as well as his ex and equal partner.

119

Tax 4 U's office was at the end of a long corridor that ran from the front of the building to the back. When they got there, it was clear that the tax firm run by Dale Pollock was bigger than they thought. It seemed to occupy two of these cubicle-style rooms. Still not very imposing.

"Good morning. We're here to see Dale Pollock. We're from the police."

The girl behind the desk looked somehow frightened. She was young, probably no more than early twenties, a bit weedy looking with hair that had been dyed so many times the roots must have been dizzy. "Mr Pollock is expecting you." She was using what she thought was a very upper-crust accent. Unfortunately, it wasn't. "Second door on the left." Steve noted they were not being announced.

The DCI looked around the walls as they made their way to the second door on the left. There was no evidence of diplomas, testimonials, degrees or anything that you might find in a professional office. The DCI ushered Twiggy in front of him, so it was she who knocked on the door and entered, followed by the DCI.

A rather rotund man with grey hair, and not much of it, probably in his late 50s sat behind a desk. Steve had seen the same desk in IKEA. If this was Dale Pollock, then he didn't seem to be running a successful company. He and his operation were not very impressive so far. He was either running a temperature or sweated a lot.

"Ah! You must be the police. Detective Chief Inspector Burt, I presume." He smiled at his own David Livingstone joke. Neither detective responded to this attempt at humour. The DCI had to shuffle past Twiggy. There wasn't a lot of space in this office and Twiggy took up a lot of real estate.

"Yes, and this is Detective Constable Rough. We're looking into the death of one of your employees, a Mr Percival Booker."

"Yes. Sad thing. Mrs Booker phoned yesterday with the news. I understand he was shot?"

"Yes. What can you tell me about Mr Booker? What did he do here?"

"Inspector, you should be aware that Mr Booker didn't work for me, I worked for him."

There was a stunned silence and a sharp intake of breath. The DCI and Twiggy exchanged astonished glances before Twiggy blurted out, "What! So, who owns this firm?"

"Percy. He did almost all of the work. I just look after the office and route clients' questions to Percy. But to be honest, that didn't happen very often."

The DCI gave Twiggy a sour look that said don't do that again. "What does this firm actually do?"

"To be honest, I don't rightly know." Mr Pollock was sweating even more and was playing with the end of his tie. "Percy would arrive Monday to Friday always between ten minutes to ten and five past ten. He would talk to me and Paula, that's our receptionist, for about ten minutes and then go into his office. We might see him if he went to the bathroom but apart from that, we never saw him."

"What about client visits, phone calls, mail? That sort of thing. Surely you had to see him during the day?"

"I've worked for Percy for seven years. I've never known of any client visit here. Paula collected the mail from downstairs every day although there wasn't a lot of it. When the phone rang, it was usually to Percy's direct line in his office. If anyone called on the office number, Paula took the call, but like I say. We're a very quiet office. Paula and I don't have a lot to do."

"Are you actually telling us you have no idea what this company does? A company you've worked for, for seven years?" Steve was lost for words.

"I think Percy did a bit of tax work. The name's a bit of a giveaway." Dale Pollock's attempt at humour fell flat. "When Percy hired me, he made it quite clear that I wasn't to get too involved. My job was to fetch and carry."

"Mm! Unbelievable. I suppose you get a salary?"

"Oh! Yes. Each month. Never misses."

"Is there anything you can tell us about Mr Booker or his work?"

"Like I said. All I did was fetch and carry and not too much of that."

"Can we see Mr Bookers' office?"

"Sorry. It's locked. Percy keeps it locked and he has the only key."

"We'll need to get a locksmith to open the door with your permission."

"Yes. No problem. After all, he's dead. I don't know what Paula and I will do now." He got no sympathy from the detectives.

Twiggy got on her mobile and after a few frustrating calls got what she wanted.

In the meantime, Paula produced some very ordinary instant coffee.

"A local guy will be here in ten minutes, sir, he said he needs to be paid cash." Twiggy smiled. She knew Steve had been handing out money all through the investigation. She hoped he'd get it back on expenses.

It took the locksmith five minutes to open the door, ten minutes to fit a new lock to Percival Booker's office and a few seconds to relieve the DCI of £175. Steve reflected being SIO was an expensive business and he'd just handed over the bulk of his self-imposed weekly living allowance. Good thing he was off the booze.

Steve and Twiggy stood in the office with the newly unlocked office door firmly closed. "Well, this is strange. I don't have the foggiest where to begin or even think what's going on here. His wife said he was an accountant doing people's tax returns. Now this. This thing's getting weirder by the hour. Why would a guy tell his wife he worked for someone else, but he owned the firm? Better get hold of the accounts for Tax 4 U."

"Right."

"Well, at least the office is tidy. It shouldn't take too long to have a look around."

As was becoming the norm, Steve took the desk and Twiggy went to work looking through the filing cabinets. Apart from the desk and two filing cabinets, there was no other furniture in the office except two small upholstered chairs.

They searched their respective areas. The desk yielded nothing. Twiggy was working through the cabinets. She had started at 'A'. Steve, having gotten nothing from the desk, went to help and started at the other end with 'Z'.

All the files were orderly and contained little correspondence. What there was consisted of single-sheet letters to clients about tax rebates and reminders about tax returns. Both Twiggy and Steve saw there were not many letters and even fewer clients. Twiggy noticed each file with a letter of the alphabet attached to the outside only contained one client. Some files were empty. Mr Booker had not been a busy man. It was boring work looking through this paper until Twiggy coughed. She was looking at the DCI and was holding up a file. "It says 'M' and inside it says Monaco."

Twiggy took the file to the desk so that they could both look at the contents. There were several letters from San Soto Bank dating from 2008 until a week ago. It all looked fairly routine stuff. Interest rates, deposit rates and so on but interestingly, one of the letters mentioned Timothy Squires, the first victim.

There seemed to be lot of nonsense talk within the letters. Not what either the DCI or his DC would have expected in business correspondence. Things like the weather in London, football scores and reference to cars various people were driving. There was too much to take in. These letters needed going over when they had more time. At least they had another connection between the two men.

"Anything else catch your attention?"

"Well, there are odd files with no names. Just references and what's in them looks like receipts or something but there's not a lot of detail. Some of the receipts, if that's what they are, run into tens of thousands. Not sure what I'm looking at."

"Right. Let's get going. Bring all the files you want. I've got the Monaco one. I don't see a computer so maybe the one we took yesterday from the house will tell us more."

"Steve, when Tom and I were going through Booker's laptop yesterday, Tom said he felt some of the letters may have been in code. I'll explain later but some of these letters are just as odd. I wonder if Tom was right?"

"Good on you, Twiggy. Don't spoil the show. Keep it till 2 o'clock. Let's get out of here and grab a bite to eat on the way."

Not only had the locksmith opened the office door and changed the lock he had also given Steve two keys for the new lock. Now the DCI was the only one who could get into Percival Booker's office. As Steve locked the office door, he decided not to give Dale Pollock the second key.

Chapter Twenty-One

Wednesday, 15 April

When Twiggy had returned the pool car, she gathered up three coffees and returned to the office. Both Steve and the Cap were sitting around the square table. It was time for another Twiggy tell-all show.

Twiggy opened her oversized handbag and produced her own laptop. It was obviously not police issue. The Force didn't give out pink-coloured computers with flowers pasted on the lid. Twiggy got down to business. She was once again front and centre.

"I want to start with victim one. You remember I was able to get into some of the files, especially the prospect list, but nothing I could read was of much use." There was no humour today. Twiggy was taking this very seriously. "Tom was able to open the file marked Monaco. He said it was an old file and had only recently been loaded onto the laptop." She stopped for effect. "The file was a list of investors in TPPP going back to 1996. It has names, ages, addresses, amounts invested, how much each investor got back each time their investments were sold and if any investor was a multiple investor." Twiggy looked pleased with herself. "In other words, people who reinvested their cash, including their profit." She stopped to await Steve's reaction to this information.

The DCI couldn't believe what he was hearing. This was the list he had been hoping, even praying, would turn up. If he was right, this list could be the key to solving the case—although he knew the Cap disagreed. He was ecstatic but knew Twiggy had more. He kept quiet.

Twiggy continued, "The file totalled up the amounts they received from investors each year and gave a summary for each year. There's a lot of pages. They seemed to have started small with only £127,000 in investments in the first year. That's 1996. They took in the same more or less each year until 2000. In that year, they took in over £900,000." Twiggy looked at her notes. "The investments grew each year. They were pulling in millions from people and in

2008, just before they went bust, they collected over £40 million in cash. They also took cash in 2009 but not so much. It's all on this memory stick if you want me to load it onto my laptop."

Twiggy perched on the front of her chair and sat back as best she could, obviously pleased with herself.

"This is great stuff, Twiggy." The DCI was buoyant. "How many names on the investor list?" The DCI's mind was racing.

"We didn't count them; I can find out quickly but at a rough estimate—300. That would be 300 individuals from 1996 till they went bust in 2009."

"You said the list showed what each person put in and how much they had received back. What does it show for investors from…say, 2007?"

"I don't know but I can check. Hold on, just give me a minute." Twiggy set about booting up her computer and inserting the memory stick.

While Twiggy was busy, Steve looked at the Cap. "What do you think?"

"I think you could be right. So far, we've drawn a blank everywhere we've looked. All we have is a load of financial stuff that may or may not help but doesn't seem to take us to a motive. If you're right, then the motive for the killings could be in that file, especially if they were ripping off their clients. There's something dodgy about this TPPP. You don't have £40 million to play with one year and go bankrupt the next, especially if you buy a great bloody mansion before you're bankrupted. I don't know how it hangs together but I bet someone was ripped off big time by this Squires guy and probably his mates. There's the motive."

"You think our killer could be on this TPPP list?"

"Possible. We don't have anything else and it's a plausible theory. I still don't get the ten-year wait though. Something must have happened to bring the killer out if he's on this list. These high rollers tend to be a bit long in the tooth if they have made their fortunes themselves, so, if he stopped investing when the firm went bust, how old is he now?"

Before the DCI could answer, Twiggy took control again. "Right, it seems in 2007, the amount of money investors got back was a lot lower than in previous years. Seems they all got their original stake back and some even got a small profit. But looking at the money coming in, it was still getting bigger each year until it stopped in 2009. In 2007, they took in £47 million."

"So, in 2007, most investors who expected their money back got it back but not with much profit. Is that correct?"

"Seems so."

"And in 2007, they took in around £47million?"

"Right again."

Steve was struggling to curb his growing excitement. "Does it say how long people left their money with TPPP?"

"No but there's a pattern of people putting their money in and being repaid a couple of years later. Most seem to have re-invested when they got their pay-out. Looks likely a lot of them were in for two years each time they invested."

"Right. Twiggy, this is important. Does the list show how many people put money in and didn't get anything back?"

"Just a minute." Twiggy was hitting keys at breakneck speed even with only two fingers. "There are 23 people who put in money in 2006, 2007 and 2008 that don't seem to have had their money back. There's another 12 from 2009. The list doesn't show anything being paid back to any of them. So, 35 people in total put money in and got zilch back."

"How much did these 35 people invest?" Steve was getting more interested.

Twiggy went to work with speed on the keyboard. "Looks like £52 million, give or take."

"OK. Let's look at this." The DCI was back at the whiteboard.

"Stay with me on this, Twiggy. Of the people who invested up to 2007, most got either all or some of their money back but no or little profit. Is that correct?"

"Seems so. There's a couple who put their money in during 2006 but don't seem to have had it back either."

"OK. Some people who put money in during 2007, 2008 and 2009 got nothing back. Is that correct?"

"Yes. Looks like it."

"And you say there are 35 of them who got nothing back at all. They lost all their money?"

"That's it; also, according to my friend in financial crimes, by early 2008 most people in the City knew a crash was coming. So, if this TPPP took money in either 2008 or 2009, they must have had no intention of investing it."

"Are we saying this TPPP outfit deliberately took investors' money knowing the property boom was about up and we think they've stashed the cash away somewhere where they hope it can't be found? Say, a dodgy bank in Monaco?"

"It's a theory and it fits what we know." The Cap was drinking the last of his cold coffee. He screwed his face up at the taste.

The DCI stood up and clapped his hands. "I think we may have just found not only our motive but potentially our killer. Someone on that list who lost all their cash clearly has motive. Being ripped off and losing your money could drive anyone to murder. But why now?"

All three detectives sat looking at each other and each was silently digesting this latest information.

Steve broke their concentration. "Twiggy reckons the remaining partner in TPPP, the one who is still breathing, could be our killer. He could have motive if he's decided he wants to pocket all their ill-gotten gains for himself. Hopefully, we'll see tomorrow if Randall is victim or killer." He looked at Twiggy and smiled.

"We now have two lines of inquiry where an hour ago, we had none."

"Twiggy, I could kiss you, but all your friends might object." Smiles all around.

The Cap stood up. "I'll go and get celebration coffees." He stopped to look at Twiggy. "You clever girl, well done, partner."

While the pair waited for their coffee, the DCI asked Twiggy to print out the list. "But not here. Can you print it at home? Sorry to have to ask you but I'm a bit concerned about security just now. Don't leave anything important in the office overnight even if it's in a locked drawer."

"Understood and yes, I can print off the list. Should I make two copies if you're worried about security?"

"Good idea but leave the second copy in your flat."

The Cap arrived back, and Steve took his coffee gratefully. "Twiggy have a bit of a rest. Take a breather and enjoy your coffee. Cap, how did you get on this morning?"

The Cap sipped his coffee and placed it on the table before beginning.

"Mr Booker was declared bankrupt in 2009 just like Timothy Squires. While I was at Companies House, I asked if they had accounts filled for TPPP going back to 1996." The Cap raised his voice an octave. "A nice young man," the Cap made a gesture with his hand and wrist, "told me such things were public record and I could look them up. I think financial crimes might be our best bet if Twiggy's friend doesn't mind."

The Cap drank some more of his coffee. "I went to Sedgwick Close and interviewed the witness. He was firm on his recollection and stood by everything he had said in his statement. Although he did add one interesting thing. He said the uniformed sergeant looked like a copper. He said he could spot one of us a mile off. He also confirmed that he saw this sergeant load some heavy boxes or cases into a white van. That was the afternoon of the second of April. He thought it was about half-past three. He remembered because it was his birthday so he knew the date. The second of April was the date of the first shooting. If the witness is right and we know the shooting happened at 2.30, then the times match." The Cap waited for this detail to sink in. He carried on.

"A local bobby opened the flat. All pretty ordinary. Old lady living alone. Old-style furniture, old TV. Everything dated. I checked the view from the main window. If the shooter had fired from there, he must be some superhuman marksman. True, you could just about see the restaurant, but it was a bloody long way away. The old lady must have had some renovations done and a new wooden floor put down. It looked new. There were scratches on the floor in front of the window and I found a puddle of clear liquid beside the skirting board. I don't know if SOCO spotted it, but I took a sample." The Cap held up a small clear plastic bottle. "I think it's oil, but I'll get it to the lab later today, that's about it."

"So, you wouldn't rule out that address as the kill spot?"

"If the killer can shoot like we all think he can, then no. It could be the spot. But what kind of weapon did he use? It's a bloody long way."

"If it is the spot, then not only is our shooter a killer with a rifle but he's also a coldblooded murderer. We have to assume it was him who strangled the old lady who lived there."

Everyone took in Steve's words and began to realise the importance of catching this killer. He had killed three people already.

They finished their coffee in silence. The DCI had been in deep thought. Before he could speak, Twiggy chipped in, "Steve, you asked where the million came from that Squires used to buy into SPS?" Twiggy was reading from an A4 sheet. "It came from his NatWest account. Money was transferred in from an unknown source. Financial crimes are looking into it but it was 2010. May take a while."

"Thanks, Twiggy, I've been thinking over what we think we know. Suppose you were an old woman living alone; you might be reluctant to open your door to a stranger. Agreed?" Nods all around. "But if someone came to your door in a police uniform, you're more likely to open your door and even let them in."

"Agreed?" Again, nods all around.

"Say the copper at your door spoke about needing to check your security or was from the neighbourhood watch. The witness at Sedgwick Close said he walked and looked like a copper." Steve stroked his chin. "Is it possible we're looking for a killer who's a real cop?"

There was stunned silence at Steve's comments.

"Slow down, boss. We're nowhere near that deduction yet!"

"Yeah, you're right. But let's factor it in when we do the next review. It's not impossible." Steve was thinking.

All three were silent, lost in their own thoughts.

"Cap, did you check any CCTV for the van and any joy on the make or model?"

"There were no CCTV cameras in the building or outside. The nearest seemed to be along the main road but a good half mile from Sedgwick Close. There must be thousands of white vans around and spotting our one would be impossible. Our witness didn't get even a partial number from the registration. And no, the witness didn't know the make. All he knew was it was a small van. Smaller than a Transit; apparently, he knows what a Transit looks like." The Cap raised his eyebrows.

"Let's get all this in the file and on the board. OK, Twiggy. What did you and Tom get from the second computer?"

Twiggy removed the memory stick from her computer containing the data from the first victim's computer and inserted the second memory stick. She read from her notes.

"Tom said it was easy getting into Booker's machine. It was hardly password protected. The files were mainly letters to clients, invoices and a few copy tax returns but not a lot of anything. There was nothing to say Booker was running a successful business. There was a file marked Monaco, but it was only copies of letters like the ones we took this morning. You know, to and from that San Soto Bank. The second laptop wasn't as well protected as Squires' machine. Like I said this morning, Tom thought some of the language in the correspondence was odd. He even thought there could be some underlying code but maybe that's too James Bond. There wasn't a lot to help us on the second laptop. Anyone could have opened it. It got us to thinking that either Booker had nothing to hide or the documents themselves were somehow coded for protection. Maybe Tom was right. Sorry, Steve, but we didn't get much except that some of the correspondence was recent. Within the last few weeks."

"Mm! Don't worry too much, Twiggy. You got enough from the first machine." The DCI sat back and drew a deep breath. "Let's see where we are. You know, I can't help thinking all this financial stuff's a distraction. Agreed there's something going on but I'm not sure it concerns us or even helps us. If we stand back from the numbers, what do we have?" The DCI stood and went to the whiteboard once again, picking up a black marker pen from his desk.

He wrote as he spoke, "Victim one. Shot from long range, probably from Sedgwick Close. A police sergeant who may or may not be a copper was seen acting suspiciously in and around Sedgwick Close at the time of the first murders. That's Mrs Boyd and our first victim, Timothy Squires. We have evidence that the victim seems to have been involved in some sort of financial scam around 2008 and 2009. We know the £1 million he used to buy into SPS seems to have just appeared in Squires' bank account. But from where?

"There are people who gave this TPPP firm money to invest and didn't get anything back. If we're right about the list, then that's 35 potential suspects. Looks like the partners took the money with no intention of investing it due to the crash. This could be our motive but why wait so long? Our killer is a first-class marksman, but we don't know what kind of weapon or bullet he's using." The DCI stopped suddenly. A flash of inspiration.

"If our killer is such a marksman, we should check for serving or ex-military. Why didn't I think of it before? Twiggy. Check and see how many people from the TPPP investors list were in the military. Only look at the 35 who lost the lot."

"Will do."

"We may have motive and a list of potential suspects if our killer is on the list but we still don't know how he's doing it. Anything to add on our first victim?"

"No."

"OK. Our second victim almost fits exactly into the profile of our first. They were partners, same MO. Shot in the head but not with a conventional bullet. The two victims were partners so must have been in the scam together. That's the only link between the two. The second victim could have still been scamming. Looking at the office setup, I wouldn't be surprised. He was running a company he apparently didn't admit to owning. Even his wife thought he was employed by Tax 4 U. She had no idea he owned it." Steve looked at the two faces staring at him.

"We'll have to get Twiggy's friend in financial crimes to look over the stuff we brought back from Booker's office. Even if our second victim was still at it, our first victim, apart from his bearer bonds, seems to have been clean since 2010."

"Where does that leave us, Steve?" This was the Cap who was looking a little deflated following the highs of Twiggy's previous news.

"I'm not sure but we don't give up. There's a way through this. We keep using good police procedure but let's not get too involved in finance and accounts. We need to catch a murderer. But check this thought out. If Squires has been clean since 2010 but Booker has carried on with his dodgy deals, is it not more likely that the motive goes back to pre-2010?"

"You mean both men were working after their firm collapsed but not together, so their contacts going forward would be different after 2010, so the common link is pre-2010?"

"Exactly, Cap."

"Well, it would support your theory."

The DCI changed tack. "We have the list and we have Peter Randall as either potential next victim or killer. We've more than we've had so far. We keep working and digging."

Neither the Cap nor Twiggy had seen Steve so animated during the short time they'd known him. Silence fell and covered all three detectives. The DCI took control.

"Right, Twiggy. You check for military connections from the list. You'll have to get onto the MOD personnel department. Give them the names of all 35 people on the list who lost all their money. We have their ages so that should help cut down the search. I think we can discount anybody who's over 75 now. Also, but as a secondary task, check with your friend in financial crimes. Get details of TPPP accounts and while you're at it, ask him to check into Tax 4 U. But remember, concentrate on the list. I'm sure our killer is on it. Cap, check with forensics. The 3D modelling of our second victim will be done by now. Follow what we did with the first killing. We should be able to work this one from the maps without Twiggy's piece of wood and knitting needles."

Everyone recognised Steve's attempt to lighten the mood. "Go over to the Borough Council for planning maps. We know the victim was facing the crossing and that the wound was to the area above his left eye. We saw it for ourselves. It means the shot came from the north along Penrose Road so again, only get maps going north and only…say, 200 yards either side of Pembroke Road. Maybe you can work your magic again and mount the maps on the other side of my expensive board from maintenance. The post-mortem report's in the file. It came in this morning. Right. All good?"

"Yes, but my friend in financial crimes may not be too happy with all the info we're asking him to check."

"Just smile sweetly, Twiggy. You can do it. I'm off to meet a military man who hopefully can give us a steer on the weapon and maybe even the marksman. See you both in the morning and remember to lock the door and leave nothing in the office." The DCI was still thinking about who could have stolen the laptop. "Twiggy. You and I will go see this Peter Randall tomorrow so look up his address." With that, the DCI set off for the Imperial War Museum.

Chapter Twenty-Two

Wednesday, 15 April

The DCI arrived at the Imperial War Museum about five minutes late. When he entered, he saw a man dressed smartly in blazer, grey trousers and an obvious regimental tie. Steve recognised it as Royal Engineers. The man approached the DCI and thrust out his hand.

"You must be Detective Chief Inspector Burt? Nice to meet you, I'm Hector Simms."

"Thank you for agreeing to see me at such short notice, Major."

"Not at all, and please, it's Hector. To be honest, meeting a policeman is a welcome distraction from the routine of this place. If you come with me, we'll adjourn to my office. Get a bit of peace and quiet." Major Simms had an air of efficiency about him.

The Major led the way and the DCI followed. There was something about the Major that Steve instantly liked. Maybe it was meeting a fellow officer and that the service mentality was more deeply ingrained than he thought. Being in this museum with all its military connections, Steve began to feel a sense of nostalgia for service life and for a fraction of a second drifted back to what might have been.

The Major entered his office, which was huge. In some ways, it resembled a church with rectangular stained-glass windows positioned high up on three walls and a ceiling height of at least 15 feet. The walls were covered in dark wood.

Hector showed Steve to one of two comfortable leather armchairs positioned either side of an open fire. The fire wasn't lit.

"Can I get you something to drink? Coffee, tea or something stronger?"

"Coffee would be fine, just black, no sugar."

"Excellent. You won't mind if I have a small libation? I usually have a medicinal whisky around this time. After all, the sun's over the yard arm somewhere in the world. What!" The Major seemed a very jolly character.

Hector gave a belly laugh as he wandered over to his desk and phoned someone to bring coffee. He opened a cupboard that stood in a corner to reveal an almost fully stocked bar. When he saw the DCI looking with interest, he said, "Oh! It's not all mine. This office doubles as the Officers Mess when we have a function. Lucky for me, eh!" Hector had a twinkle in his eyes. "I just sign on a chitty and square up my bill at the end of the month. Usual thing but sometimes the bill's a shocker."

"Yes." He liked this obviously retired major with the clipped military voice and the ramrod straight back. The DCI's coffee was almost instantly produced and delivered by a waiter in a white jacket. Despite the speed of production, the coffee was hot and very good. Once both men were settled, the Major asked the obvious question. "Now. What's this all about. How can I help you?"

"Well, Major. Sorry, Hector. It's a bit of a long story so please bear with me."

"Absolutely, old boy. The bar is fully stocked, and we have all the time in the world." Hector smiled at Steve.

"We had a shooting a few weeks back. Victim was shot in the head at what we believe could have been around a two-mile range. When we got the victim to the morgue and the pathologist opened him up, there were no bullet fragments nor a spent round inside the skull. There was no exit wound, so we expected to find something. The victim's head was wet around the entry wound. On Tuesday of this week, we had another shooting with exactly the same MO. We haven't calculated the range yet, but it looks to be very long. Maybe even longer than the first shooting. Again, the site of the entry wound was wet and it wasn't a through and through. When the pathologist opened up the skull on our second victim, again there was no evidence of any bullet or bullet fragments inside the wound."

"Hm! Interesting. Do go on." Hector sipped his whisky.

"Well, that's about it. An impossibly good shot from an impossible range with no obvious bullet. But we still have two dead bodies. I was hoping to pick your brains and hoped you might have some thoughts on any weapon that's capable of firing accurately from that range and if you know of any ammunition that vanishes within the wound."

"That's a tall story, Detective Chief Inspector. It may require a few shots of brain fluid to even begin to think on this." Hector held up his whisky glass.

"Sir, if you want me to call you Hector, then please call me Steve."

"Right you are. Well, Steve. Offhand, I can't think of anything that might help. Perhaps another snifter might get the old grey cells working." Holding up his now-empty glass in Steve's direction, Hector rose from his chair. "Are you sure you won't join me?"

"No thanks. I'm on duty." Steve was thinking of his promise to Twiggy and thought maybe he shouldn't have made it.

"Ah! The policeman's burden. No booze when working. Just as well it didn't apply to the army in my day. I daresay soldiers in the modern setup are like policemen. Only get a glow from alcohol when off duty and no one's looking." Hector refilled his glass and re-joined Steve.

The Major settled down and sipped his whisky. He was trying to decide how much information he could pass on to this policeman.

"You know, we keep ourselves pretty much up to snuff on new weapons here. It's not all relics from past conflicts. In fact, we have a full team of intelligence chaps based here who spend their lives ferreting away at secret works around the world. If any research is going on that looks likely to produce something significant in weaponry, then they would know about it sooner rather than later. We share intelligence with other services, of course, and even some spooks from MI5 and MI6. No one wants to be out-gunned these days." Hector took a sip of his whisky.

It was obvious that retired Major Hector Simms was no fool and despite being retired was somehow still dialled into the nerve centre of UK military weaponry. Steve had come to the right man.

The Major carried on, "We have monthly briefings on what is going on in the world of weapon development. We know pretty well every new or planned weapon being worked on anywhere in the world. Just to give you an example: at our last briefing, we learned that groups in the Baltic States are spending large sums trying to perfect a light machine gun that will fire tank shells." Hector laughed out loud then giggled to himself. "You couldn't make it up, old boy, could you? They're still working on it and our side is unofficially helping them spend their money. The thing will never work but we keep feeding them bogus technical data that convinces them they're almost there. What fools."

Hector took a handkerchief from his pocket and cleared his eyes of tears of laughter.

"This is the same team that claimed to have perfected a rifle that could shoot round corners." Hector was in his element. "Sheer lunacy but we know about it. That's the thing you see. Keep your enemies close.

"This is the type of intelligence we get up to here. Not high level but if any individual or organisation is playing at inventing something new, we tend to help them. That way, we know what's up. You'd be surprised how many times apparently useless and silly weapon research has led us to discovering terrorist activities." Hector savoured another sip of his drink.

"But that's a whole different thing. Regrettably, I'm pretty sure we haven't had any briefings about a super rifle capable of doing what you say. If there was such a weapon, we'd know about it. I could suggest several international marksmen who could possibly make the shot you say happened but without a weapon, it's just not possible. As to the lack of bullet, it sounds impossible. If you want to shoot someone then you have to fire something into them. I'm afraid, old boy, you have a real conundrum on your hands. I'm just sorry I can't be of more help."

"Well, thank you for trying. I thought it was worth asking. You never know. You might have solved this for us."

Both men just sat and stared at nothing in particular. Major Simms seemed as disappointed as Steve. Steve gave it one last chance.

"Can you think of any weapon that might come close to being able to deliver such a shot?"

"Frankly, no." Hector was still staring into infinity when he suddenly seemed to come alive. "Actually, old boy, let's go to the small arms library. There may be something but I'm not sure it'll help. Over the years, we Brits have experimented with all sorts of silly ideas. You never know. There may be something in the archives. I have a vague recollection of something delightfully eccentric that was being worked on during WW2. I can't remember the exact details. I came across the reference during a bit of research I was doing for a book I'm writing. Let's go have a peek."

The library was a small room, about 12-foot square. Every wall was jammed with books of all sizes. Against each wall was a ladder that seemed to be on rollers suspended from the top bookshelf. In the middle of the room was a small square table and two chairs. There was a reading lamp on the table. The room had no windows and smelt of old leather and wood polish. Hector drew a large book from one of the lowest shelves. "This is our reference to the location of each book in here," he explained. "I can't remember which book I was referencing when I came across what might just be of interest to you. I'm not saying it's the answer, mind you."

Steve stayed quiet so as not to interrupt Hector's thought processes. After a few minutes of page turning, Hector exclaimed, "Ah! This is it." He put the reference volume back and moved one of the ladders until it covered the section of books he wanted.

Steve was surprised how nimble Hector was at climbing the ladder and even more impressed when he descended holding a large leather-bound book cradled in his arms. With the book on the table, Steve saw it was not a bound book after all but a series of typed sheets and folded drawings all fitted between the two outer covers that made this collection look like a book.

Hector rummaged through the contents slowly and deliberately, putting to one side the items he was not interested in. Then he pulled out what looked like a complete file. It seemed full of individually typed sheets and larger sheets that were folded. From the file, he produced one of these folded documents. The edges were brown, indicating the paper had some age to it. The Major opened the folded document and carefully laid it on the table. "There it is!" he exclaimed. "The Mk 1 LRSR. Circa 1942." Hector was reading from a written section in the lower left-hand corner of the sheet. "It was designed by the Browning Small Arms Company to meet War Office Department Specification 42/bfs/1. This called for a weapon capable of hitting a target at up to four miles range with 99% accuracy." Hector opened his arms wide, showing the document to Steve.

Hector then spent some time reading the sheets of paper in the file. Finally, he said, "Remember, during WW2, all sort of schemes were hatched and companies across the country were asked to design things that would never be used. The specification for this weapon, apart from the extreme range, was that it be sniper-suitable, portable and robust enough to withstand battlefield conditions. It also called for a form of automatic gunsight lock to allow less proficient marksmen to use it. Have a look." Hector pointed to the table.

What Steve saw made no sense to him. He was not an engineer and this sheet looked like a typical engineering drawing. Steve could see it looked like a weapon but beyond that had no idea what he was looking at. All he could say was, "So did it work?"

"Ha! Well. You must remember this was war time. Even government departments were capable of coming up with silly ideas." Hector rummaged through more papers. "Here we are. Each request for experimental kit had to be justified and a form JJ01 filled in. Luckily, the form has survived so we know the thinking behind it. Don't we Brits know how to look after our history? Marvellous!" The Major was full of pride.

He read on, "This contraption was to be used to assassinate Adolf Hitler if you please." Hector cocked an eyebrow and looked quizzically at Steve. "It says the only way to achieve the goal of removing Hitler was to use a long-range sniper from over three miles. Hitler was too well guarded at closer ranges." Again, Hector looked directly at Steve.

"Fascinating. It's real history but could it be my weapon?" Steve was getting frustrated by the Major's history lesson. He wasn't interested in World War 2.

"Well, I'd be surprised. These documents in the file show that three of these prototype weapons were manufactured and sent for testing at the Small Arms School at Hythe in Kent. The file only refers to initial tests being promising but then there's a note saying the project was cancelled in 1943. It doesn't say why."

Steve was visibly crestfallen. He had begun to allow himself to believe he might have found the weapon used to gun down his two victims.

Hector picked up on Steve's disappointment. "If you've seen enough then let's go back to the office. Just leave these things here. I'll get it tidied and put back tomorrow."

Hector offered Steve a snifter, which was again refused. Steve had a soda water instead. He was considering the implications of his history lesson with Hector. He quickly concluded it was a dead end.

Sitting back in his armchair and working on his third whisky, Hector carried on with his narrative, "From documents we have downstairs and putting two and two together, I believe it's likely that a committee of government in 1942 came up with the idea to assassinate Adolf Hitler as a way of shortening the war. I came across this concept often when I was doing research for my book. I believe the plan was for a sniper to take a long-range shot but, of course, no weapon existed that could deliver the shot. It was impossible to get close to Hitler at any time, never mind close enough to kill him. From the papers downstairs, it's obvious it was this plan that led to the government issuing the specification for the Mk1 LRSR or long-range sniper rifle. Browning must have been asked to develop something to meet the specification."

Hector took a long sip of his whisky. "I'm sorry, Steve, but I think the LRSR is the only thing I can think of that could possibly do the job. I don't know of anything more modern that has either been designed or is being designed to fire from those distances. What we're looking at was a long time ago and apparently didn't work. If it had worked, then why cancel it?"

Steve sat back and finished his soda. He hadn't expected much from his visit but had hoped the Major could give him some guidance. Instead, all he had was a defunct weapon from 1943 that had been designed to kill the leader of Germany in 1943. Apart from getting a history lesson, he was no further forward. But at least, he'd met Hector Simms. It hadn't been a complete waste.

"Well, thank you, Hector. It was worth a try and who knows? Maybe your 1943 weapon could have been the answer to my problem." Both men stood. "If only it had worked." Steve gave a shrug of his shoulders and said, "Ah well. Never mind. We tried." Both men started to walk to the door.

"It was a real pleasure to have met you, Major. I hope we can keep in touch?"

"What will you do now?"

"I don't know. If you as an expert can't think of a weapon capable of firing a non-bullet over a range of almost two miles, then I have nowhere else to go. We still have two dead bodies and no idea how they died."

Hector finished the last of his whisky as they walked. "Steve, just a thought, old boy. If, as I suspect, there are no modern weapon systems that can do what you're asking, something clearly did, and you have dead bodies to prove it. The only weapon we can find that might possibly have made those shots is the LRSR. It could be they did test it and it worked back in 1943? The file only says it was cancelled. It doesn't say why. What if this is the weapon killing your victims? In the absence of any other explanation, is it not worth considering the possibility that one of these weapons might have survived?"

"Well, you are right, of course, but how could I find out after all this time? Everyone from that time must be dead. It's a real long shot, if you'll excuse the pun." Both men smiled.

"Good point. Let me do a bit of digging in the morning. See if I can find anything that might help."

"Major, you've been very helpful and understanding. I think I would have enjoyed serving under you."

"Very kind of you to say so, Captain. I looked you up, you know, before you arrived. Not too difficult in a place like this. I took a punt you might have served. The record isn't too full of detail, but can I say you were a bloody fool?"

"Yes, sir, you can, and I was. I've been lucky enough to find another career. Anything you can come up with will be gratefully received. Thank you for your time and your insight."

The two men shook hands. Steve handed over his business card and set off to catch the tube to home. He didn't tell his new friend the Major that his second career was all but over.

Chapter Twenty-Three

Thursday, 16 April

The DCI arrived late at the office the next morning. He had overslept so had not shaved. He also realised his washing machine hadn't been in action for a few days, meaning his supply of clean shirts stood at zero. He'd recycled one that was in the wash. He hadn't had any breakfast and was feeling a bit rough around the edges. On his way out, he had once again stood in front of his wall mirror. What he saw didn't fill him with confidence. He looked like a busy door to door salesman or what he thought such a person would look like. He noted his Primark suit was beginning to look very second-hand and thought for fifty quid, it should have retained its shape longer than it obviously had.

When he entered the office, Twiggy was hard at it on her laptop and seemed to be making notes. He recalled the Cap would be out getting maps. "Morning. You look busy."

"Yeah, I am." Twiggy put down her pen and addressed the DCI. "I remember you said not to get tied down with the financial stuff, but I couldn't help think there has to be a connection. You said yourself that the motive had to be about money."

"Yes, I did." Steve wondered what was coming next.

"Don't worry. I haven't disobeyed your command, my leader." Twiggy looked at Steve with a wicked grin. "In my own time, last night, I looked again at what we had from both laptops. You remember I said yesterday the second machine from Percy Booker didn't have much on it?"

"Err, yes." The DCI had no idea where Twiggy was going.

"Oh, how wrong I was. I looked at the correspondence files Tom and I had just skirted over as being boring and full of nonsense comments."

Steve was beginning to get more curious. "Come on then. You're dying to tell. What have you found?"

"Not so fast. Please, sir, let a lady have her moment." Twiggy preened herself. "You remember I told you there was a letter to Squires in Booker's file in his office, the one we took? Well, I found more letters from Booker on Tax 4 U-headed paper addressed to Squires at the SPS address. All very formal and on the surface just correspondence between businesses. In each letter, Booker is saying to Squires that he was happy to recommend clients of Tax 4 U to SPS. The computer file shows that 'ALL' of Booker's clients invested in SPS. The amounts mentioned range from £100,000 to over £1 million."

"So, Booker was feeding clients to Squires. There's no law against that. I presume Booker was making the recommendations to his clients as part of a tax saving scheme?"

"No boss. You're not getting it. Every Tax 4 U client I can find has invested in SPS. How odd is that? Every single client in these files." Twiggy was getting animated.

"There's more. On the surface, you could be right. Maybe Tax 4 U directed all their clients to SPS so that they could save a few pounds in tax, but before you can save tax, you have to pay it." Twiggy sat back as best she could in triumph. "I took two names and addresses at random of clients referred to SPS by Booker.

"One was investing £600,000. The other £450,000. I went upstairs first thing this morning to see my friend in financial crimes. I asked him to access the two investors' tax records on the 'QT'. By the way, he wasn't keen and told me no more. He said this plus the other stuff he's doing for me is just too much. So, I guess we're on our own now." Steve wasn't surprised and a little relieved. He'd never really believed all the financial information they had gathered was really helping solve the murders. Twiggy continued, "My friend, Derek by the way, could find no record of either investor ever paying tax or even having existed. He said it was possible both investors were legit, and their records were filed somewhere else. But…"

Twiggy again looked at Steve and shrugged her shoulders. "Derek wants to take this to his boss and asked for everything we have. He wants to go official. He thinks some sort of money laundering and serious tax avoidance is going on. I've asked him to hold off until you decide what to do. Involving financial could officially blow our low-profile cover."

"Yes, you're not wrong. Commander Clark would be all over us if financial made anything official." Steve was thinking how the information Twiggy had just given him fitted into the case.

"If I read you correctly, you're saying Tax 4 U is a front for money being channelled through SPS and that Tax 4 U doesn't have any real clients?"

"I don't know but it looks that way. We need to dig deeper, but I think the evidence is there. Also, I wonder if the pompous Mr Frederick Sneddon and the equally delightful Mrs Sneddon knew where Timothy Squires was getting his investors?"

Steve looked at his watch. 10.45. Time to be off. "OK Twiggy, good job. Let's sit on this for now at least. But remember, I don't think this financial thing is getting us any nearer our killer. Let's go see Peter Randall and try to figure out where he fits into this. Did you get his address?"

"Sure did, he lives in Esher. Will I take the Fiat?"

"I don't want to hurt your feelings and I appreciate the offer, but I think a pool car. Can you call one up?" Twiggy made a light-hearted show of being miffed but lifted the phone.

With Twiggy at the wheel of a very ordinary-looking Honda Accord, Steve learned that the army had not been too helpful with her request for service record information. The officer she had spoken with claimed he didn't have the resources to search 35 random names without more information. He said service numbers would help. Without at least a Regiment or Branch, it was impossible. Steve knew it would be difficult but felt Twiggy had been short-changed. The army kept immaculate records and any search was possible. "Well. We tried. We'll go back once we get more information," was all he said once Twiggy had explained. Twiggy asked about his museum visit. "Nothing much to tell. The nearest we could get to any kind of weapon was an old gun from WW2 that was junked before it was used. Another dead end. Let's hope Mr Randall has something to say." The drive took just over an hour and passed mainly in silence.

Peter Randall lived in a gated community in a very upmarket neighbourhood on the outskirts of Esher. Twiggy stopped the Honda just short of the closed gate. There was a guard on the gates who appeared to need to know your inside leg measurement before letting you in.

"We're here to see Mr Randall," said Twiggy in her poshest accent.

The guard, dressed in an American-style mustard-coloured uniform, was seated inside the guard station beside an open window. He rose slowly from his seat and equally slowly exited his station. He rounded the front of the Honda towards the driver's side. Despite an attempt to look like an American cop, Steve was relieved to note he didn't have a gun strapped to his thigh.

"Is Mr Booker expecting you, ma'am?"

Almost an American accent. Steve noted he carried a clipboard with a pad of forms attached. Not a good sign.

"No, but I think he'll see us. Just let us in, please."

"Oh! I can't just do that, miss. I'm security and have to vet everybody who comes in." The guard was obviously enjoying his position of power. Twiggy noticed although he wasn't carrying a gun, he was carrying a large beer belly so that his shirt buttons were under great strain. This was not a fit man. The guard was preparing to fill in a form on his clipboard. He produced a pen from his top pocket. Had it been a pencil, Twiggy was sure he would have licked the end before starting to write.

"Name?"

"Police." The guard stopped writing. Twiggy produced her warrant card. He looked a little shocked. He quickly regained his composure and was about to ask his next question when Steve leaned towards Twiggy's driver's side. Even in the bigger Honda, this wasn't easy.

"We're here on matters relating to a double murder so stop playing at cops and let us in."

The guard's jaw dropped. "I'm sorry, sir, but like you I have my job to do. The security of our residents is at stake. We can't circumvent protocols." Steve was amazed how pompous certain individuals could be. He was slightly amused. He thought he might as well enjoy himself.

"If you don't open the gate in the next five seconds, I'll protocol you into a cell!" The guard was stunned and shuffled back to his guard station without another word. Twiggy was impressed by her boss. Through the window, Steve could see the pompous guard was phoning someone. Presumably Mr Peter Randall.

The gate in front of the pool car opened just as the guard reappeared on Steve's side of the car. "Mr Randall lives in 'The Pines'. Just follow the road round to the left and 'The Pines' is the house straight ahead at the end of the road." Twiggy didn't give Steve a chance to acknowledge the guard's directions. As soon as the gate opened just wide enough for the Honda to get through, Twiggy was off.

As they drove towards Peter Randall's mansion, they were both impressed by the real estate they were passing through. Each house looked like the White House in Washington DC, only a bit smaller. The gardens were large, back and front, and all seemed well tended. Three-car garages were the norm and in the first few minutes of their drive, they must have passed £6 million in fancy cars just sitting outside the main entrances.

"Wow! Who can afford to live here?"

"I suppose footballers and rock stars, plus the odd merchant banker and London underworld boss." Twiggy looked sideways at Steve, not sure if he was being serious, especially about the underworld bosses.

As Twiggy drove on, she noted, "They don't have house numbers. Must be too posh for that. Look at that one there. It's just called Home." Twiggy gave out a true belly laugh. "What kind of a poser lives there?"

They arrived at 'The Pines', parked in the sprawling driveway and got out. The house was not out of place with its neighbours. In fact, it looked to be one of the bigger properties on the estate. As they walked towards the front door, it opened and two dogs dashed out towards the detectives. As they barked and jumped up, a voice called them to heel.

The voice belonged to a man of about five foot eight inches tall, dressed casually but even to the casual observer, his dress was expensive. He was a handsome devil, probably early 50s with lush blonde hair, no beer pot and even from a distance, he had a warm friendly personality. As the dogs returned to their owner, he walked towards the two detectives with his hand held out.

"Hello, sorry about the dogs. They just like to play and meet people. My wife usually has them during the day so that I can work. I'm having a lazy day today.

"Usually, I lock myself away in my study and get a good solid ten hours work in. We all need some time to relax." He gave a wide smile that showed his perfect teeth. "By the way, I'm Peter Randall. Please come in." Walking in front of the detectives, Randall half-turned and over his shoulder said, "I understand you're from the police. George, our security man, was all of a flutter when he phoned to say you were on your way. A double murder, he said?" Neither officer commented but continued to follow Peter Randall towards his front door. "I'm sure he'll get a few free beers down the pub tonight on that information." The handsome devil cracked a smile that seemed to light up his face. Twiggy was close to swooning!

As they reached the front door, both Steve and Twiggy produced their warrant cards for Peter Randall to inspect. "I'm DCI Steve Burt. This is DC Florance Rough."

Randall gave the warrant cards only a cursory glance and waved the detectives through the front door. The front door opened onto a massive circular hallway that Steve estimated was the same square footage as his flat. There was an enormous glass dome in the roof above the hallway that allowed light to flood in.

"Please." Peter Randall ushered his guests through a door off the hallway. This door took the group into a comfortable living room with patio doors out to the large and beautifully kept garden. A large swimming pool was obvious through the glass. "Can I get you anything? Tea, coffee. Just name it." As Steve hadn't had anything, he asked for a black coffee. Twiggy did the same. Peter Randall opened his arms, inviting the detectives to sit whilst lifting a phone and asking for coffee for three.

"Now, how can I help you?" Steve noticed that Twiggy was a bit starstruck. She'd taken out her notebook but was smiling to herself and appeared to be miles away.

Steve took the lead. "I understand you know a Timothy Squires and a Percival Booker?"

"Yes. We were partners up until about ten years ago. Why do you ask?"

"Both Mr Squires and Mr Booker have been murdered during the past two weeks." Steve studied Randall's face for any hint that he already knew. He saw none.

The handsome devil drew a long breath. "Well. What can I say? How did they die?"

"They were shot," Steve added this fact with a force in his voice to gauge a reaction. "From very long range." He saw nothing in Randall's face. "Where were you on Monday of this week between 8.30 and 9.30 in the morning?"

"I was here."

"Can anyone confirm that?"

"Well, if they had to, I suppose so. My wife was here until 8.30. She takes the girls to school at that time every day. She also usually takes the dogs. But as you saw, not today." Randall was attempting to lighten the mood.

"What time did she get back?"

"Oh, not till the afternoon. After she drops the girls off, she goes on to see her mother. Her father died a few months back and her mother isn't coping very well. That's why she takes the dogs. They're company for her mother."

"Did anyone see you here after 8.30?"

"Yes." This was drawn out as Randall gathered his thoughts. "Our gardeners arrived just after 8.00 and were here until around noon. Why are you asking all this?"

"Just a process of elimination, sir. I presume your gardeners work outside. Did anyone actually see you if you were indoors?"

"Actually yes, our gardeners. Monday was a beautiful day and after Susan, my wife, left, I took my coffee onto the terrace and read my *Times*. I usually start my day at 8.00 but decided to have a break. The gardeners would have seen me right up until probably around 10.30. Our maid would also confirm I was here. She brought me an extra cup of coffee."

Steve was about to ask another question when the door opened and a maid dressed in traditional black and white entered with a tray. Coffee had arrived. Steve noticed there were biscuits. Peter Randall served and offered the biscuits around. Steve took two. He noticed Twiggy declined. "How long have you lived in this house, sir?"

"We bought it in 2007 so I suppose that makes it about 14 years, give or take."

"Can I ask what you do for a living?"

"I'm what we call a day trader in the jargon." Randall saw the confused look on Twiggy's face as she tried to understand for her notes. He looked at the detective constable. She almost fainted. "Simply, I buy and sell shares from home. I start with an amount of money each morning and usually an empty basket. I pick shares I think will go up in value during the day and I buy them. Before the market closes, I sell all my shares and hopefully, the shares have risen and I make a profit. I do the same thing each day."

Twiggy didn't really follow but made her notes. She could feel her face reddening.

"Judging by this place," —The DCI waved an arm around— "you must be a successful trader?"

"Yes, I don't do badly." Something close to a grin appeared on Randall's handsome face. Steve was beginning to think Peter Randall could be a pompous ass. He suspected not a view Twiggy would agree with.

Steve went into official police mode, speaking directly to Peter Randall. "Mr Randall. We have reason to believe that the killing of your two ex-partners may have something to do with your company TPPP. I know it was a long time ago, but can you think of anyone from that time who might have a reason to kill your partners?"

Peter Randall stood and walked slowly around the room. He was obviously shocked and thinking hard. No one spoke and both detectives were waiting for their host to speak. Eventually, Peter Randall spoke, "Inspector, there are a few truths you should know, but can we keep what I'm going to tell you off the record? It was a long time ago and no one was hurt." The handsome face looked like it was pleading.

"I can't make promises or deals, Mr Randall. If you tell me what you know, and I think it's relevant, then I will be duty-bound to use the information."

"Understood. It's just we all have things in our past we're not proud of. My time at TPPP is one of those things." The DCI had concluded this handsome man was not their killer but was he the next victim?

"Why don't you start at the beginning and tell us everything? If we don't need to use certain pieces of information, then we won't."

Peter Randall returned to his chair, crossed his legs and stared into the distance, not focussing on either of the detectives.

"We all met at university. That's Tim, Percy, Philip and me. When we graduated, we didn't have a clue what to do with our lives. I can't remember exactly how it started but we somehow formed TPPP in around 1996. The TPPP name comes from our Christian names. T for Tim, P for Percy and so on. It was Percy who had come up with the idea of investing in property. He said we couldn't go wrong. Fortunes were there to be made in bricks and mortar." Peter Randall stood again and went to the telephone. "Would you like another coffee?" Both Twiggy and Steve could feel the story Randall was about to tell would be a long one so they both said yes.

He returned to his chair and resumed the same faraway look. "We worked from a small rented office by Tower Bridge. After a few false dawns, we settled into our roles in the partnership. Tim was the salesman, Percy was the finance guy, Philip and I were the deal makers. Tim would persuade people with spare cash to invest with us. We then went out and found properties we could buy cheaply and sell on for a profit. Remember, the London property bubble was a few years away, but you could still make money. For the first two to three years, we did OK. We weren't getting rich, but we were learning." As Peter Randall was about to continue, the second round of coffee arrived. This time they each helped themselves.

"Then one day, in 2000 I believe, Tim arrived in the office with a cheque made out to TPPP for half a million pounds. It was the biggest cheque any of us had ever seen. Tim explained he had found an investor who wanted to invest big with us but only if we bought certain new-build properties. I suppose we were a bit innocent and overwhelmed. We just took everything Tim said at face value. Tim was told the property we had to buy, and we did. Two months later, we got a cheque for £50,000 in the post made out to TPPP. There was a note saying it was for us to spend and not for investment. It was our commission on the £500,000 we had invested on behalf of Tim's client."

Peter Randall stopped to finish his coffee. The detectives sat and said nothing.

"As I remember it, Tim brought another £500,000 cheque in a few months later. We invested it again for his client in stipulated property projects and got our commission as before. We questioned Tim on who he was getting the money from. Eventually, he told us it was a large bank based in Monaco who were investing in London property on behalf of their international clients. It all seemed above board. We were getting rich, so we carried on. We'd stopped looking for our own clients. Apart from a few of our original small investors, the Monaco bank was our only client." Peter Randall sighed before he continued, "With hindsight, I suppose we should have been more suspicious.

"Then Percy had the idea that if we went back to having our own independent clients again then we could invest alongside the bank deals and make more money for ourselves and other clients. Remember, it was 2000 and between commissions from the bank and our own clients, we were raking in around £100,000 a month split between the four of us. Our office expenses and general overheads were low so most of the money came to us. We thought Percy's idea was a good one because we didn't know how long the deal Tim had would last. Percy was ambitious and thought we should raise our sights. You know, not trawl in a small pond but go looking for high-net-worth guys with serious cash to invest."

In an effort to speed up Randall's narrative, Steve said, "So you started bringing in individual investors?" Peter Randall was looking a bit sorry for himself. He held his hands on his lap.

"Yes. Tim was good at it and soon we were pulling in around £500,000 a month of our own plus a million or so from the bank. Percy then had another idea. If we borrowed from the banks the same amounts we were raising, we could invest the Monaco bank's money plus our UK bank's money and keep the client's funds in reserve."

Steve held up a hand. "You mean you kept your own clients' money for yourselves?"

"You could put it that way. We stored it in a separate account and just watched it grow. We didn't touch any of it until the crash."

The DCI was amazed this guy could sit here and admit to what amounted to fraud. Randall carried on with his narrative, "We were still getting deals from the bank in Monaco, so we had enough money to service the bank interest and return a profit to our investors even though we weren't using their cash. This was around 2005. The London market was red hot. Anything to do with property was a licence to print money. We knew it probably wasn't strictly legal, but it worked. The investors were happy, and we were making money hand over fist."

"Is this what is now called a Ponzi Scheme?"

"Yes, I suppose it was, but we didn't think of it as that. You see, everyone was happy and making money. In that environment, no one asks too many questions."

Peter Randall stopped for breath and to gather his thoughts. It was clear to Steve that the way he was explaining things, he was seeking to justify his actions.

"It all started to unravel around the end of 2006. The Monaco bank stopped asking us to invest. We weren't sure why so Philip flew to Monaco to meet with the bank's managing director. We didn't see him again. He was killed in a speedboat accident in Monaco. We had a letter from the bank saying how sorry they were but that was it. We never found out what happened. We tried contacting the local police but drew a blank. Philip wasn't a sailor. What he was doing by himself in a speedboat we never found out."

There was a pause while Randall pulled himself together.

"The door to the Monaco bank was closed but we still had our other clients. We figured that now that there were only three of us to share the profits, we could carry on without the bank's deals. Money was coming in from investors at a rate of knots. One month, we took in over £6 million. Most of our investors were in for two years so we had time to make things work. We were still rolling."

Steve again interrupted in an effort to get to the end of the story, "And then the financial crash came?"

"Yes, but not straight away. Tim had found a way of plugging the hole left when Monaco pulled out. He learned that pensioners with large pension pots made ideal investors. They would willingly invest in what they could understand. Property. They typically invested for two years in what they saw as the safe haven of property, got an annual profit of around 10% and their capital back after two years. We invested in some good deals, so we were still able to repay the UK bank interest and accrue our own windfall money. That's how we saw it. Then, as you say—the crash."

Peter Randall was telling a good story.

"We had gotten used to a lavish lifestyle and our expenses were increasing all the time—new offices, chauffeur-driven cars, you name it, we could afford it. We didn't want to give anything up. We saw the writing on the wall towards the end of 2007. Percy decided it would be prudent to preserve our cash by not investing but keeping clients' funds in the bank. We stopped matching clients' funds with more UK bank loans but we owed the banks millions. Percy thought it was only a matter of time before they asked for their money back. We hatched a survival plan. We each bought expensive but not flashy houses and registered them in our wives' names. We thought that given the turmoil in the market, what might normally be seen as a fraudulent transaction would be missed, and it was." Randall gave a slight smile. Steve could have punched him. He let him carry on.

"Tim kept selling and bringing in cash right up till early 2009 as though everything was normal, so we still had money coming in. Of course, the bottom had fallen out of property by mid-2008." For the first time, Randall was looking uncomfortable.

Steve was getting the picture. "The money you brought in during late 2008 and early 2009, was this totally from pensioners?"

"Well, yes, exclusively."

"Was it ever your intention to invest this money?"

"No. You see, we found that pensioners generally weren't sophisticated investors. All they saw was the money we were making them. They were happy to keep investing. They didn't really know about the market beginning to tank. They were content to let their nest egg roll into our next deal."

Twiggy was listening and making notes. She was no longer in awe of this crook.

"As part of our contingency plan, we moved our own money offshore and opened numbered accounts in San Soto Bank in Monaco. After all, we knew the people there. By early 2009, it was clear we couldn't carry on and that closing the business and us each declaring bankruptcy was the only thing to do. We had a pot of investor money in our bona fide business account here in London. Instead of leaving it for the Receiver, Percy closed the account and moved the money to our personal numbered accounts in Monaco. From that point on, the business had no money, we individually had no money or assets and the company owed the banks and investors millions. On paper, we had no choice but to close down the business and declare bankruptcy in 2009."

Twiggy looked at Peter Randall with daggers and anger. "But you had all this money in Monaco, so you weren't bankrupt. You stole money from your investors who were pensioners. How much money was in Monaco by 2009?"

For the first time, Randall's handsome face didn't look quite so healthy. "I suppose we each had around £30 million."

"What!" Twiggy exploded.

Steve could see a problem so he stepped in. "Are you saying some people lost everything?"

"I'm afraid so. I've had sleepless nights over what we did but I can't go back and start again. I wish I could. I've tried to be honest and frank with you, Inspector." The DCI didn't think this man had ever had a sleepless night in his life worrying about his investors. He was still living the grand life looking at his house.

"Just to be clear. The people who invested towards the end. They were mainly pensioners. Not your high-net-worth investors?"

"As I said before. Sophisticated investors like the high-net guys would've seen what was coming and stopped investing. The unsophisticated investor like pensioners just carried on, expecting everything to be normal."

"Am I correct in saying you don't have a mortgage on this house?"

"Er, yes."

Peter Randall looked defeated, but Steve suspected this was an act. This man loved money and didn't care what he had to do to get it or keep it. Steve almost smiled when he thought of his next statement.

"Mr Randall, thank you for sharing with us. However, we believe someone from your 2009 scam may be responsible for the deaths of your two colleagues.

We also suspect that you could be the next target." Steve sat back, satisfied, and let this information sink in.

"What! Surely not, it's been over ten years."

"Nonetheless, that's our working theory. Can you think of any of your investors from then who might have been angrier than most or who made threats against you?"

"No. We just closed up shop and didn't hear from any investors again. We had a few crank letters but nothing serious. The only squeaky moments we had were with the financial regulator but that was all."

Steve stood and Twiggy followed. "Well, sir, please be careful. I would advise you not to leave this house until we catch this killer. If you do go out, then go by car and do not stand still at any time in public. Remember, we believe this murderer shoots from long range."

As the three walked into the grand round hallway and towards the front door, Peter Randall asked, "Do you seriously think that after all this time I'm a target?"

"Yes, I do, sir, and based on what you've told us, I'm not surprised. It's only our working hypothesis that one killer is after all the partners involved in TPPP. If we're correct, then you're the last of the four still alive. If we're right then yes, you are a target."

"What about police protection? If you're right, then I'm in danger." The handsome devil was getting panicked. "You can't just leave me."

"As I said, sir, stay in this house. Don't go out. You're behind a wall of security here. I doubt there's little more we could do to protect you. Remember, this killer shoots from long range, so if you don't go out, you should be safe enough. If I had been an investor in your company, sir, I might be the one pulling the trigger. Good day." Steve was hot under the collar. Twiggy was incandescent with rage. Peter Randall stood in a state of shock.

"I've told you everything. What's going to happen to me?"

Steve couldn't resist it. "Well, sir, if the killer doesn't get you, then it's likely our fraud department might be paying you a visit."

Steve and Twiggy walked off. Peter Randall closed the door and applied all the locks.

A Twiggy behind the wheel of the pool car, still angry after the interview with Peter Randall, was even more of a danger on the road than when she was in the Fiat. The DCI had his eyes closed most of the way back to the office. He tried not to listen to the foul language Twiggy was reciting under her breath. "How could that crook steal money from pensioners just so he could maintain his lifestyle? He's worse than the bloody killer. I'm beginning to bat for our murderer. How did that bunch of scum get away with it?" There was more. A lot more but Steve didn't respond, although he agreed with her sentiment.

The journey back took 20 minutes less than getting to Esher. And the traffic was heavier! Steve vowed never to let Twiggy drive anything when she was angry. His nerves couldn't stand it.

Neither of them discussed the interview with Peter Randall beyond Twiggy's under-her-breath narrative. Twiggy was too angry. Steve was too frightened.

Thank goodness they weren't in the Fiat!

Chapter Twenty-Four

Thursday, 16 April

Steve went to the office while a now calmer Twiggy returned the pool car. The Cap was in the office, working on his new maps. He'd cut and pasted as before and had taped the maps together and to the board, so they were a good fit for the board. He'd also cut everything off that was more than 200 yards from the supposed shot line. He was placing the pin in the spot where the victim was shot and knotting his string when the DCI walked in.

"Hi boss. There was a call for you from some posh guy called Hector. Can you call him back? Also, the commander was looking for you. Said to go see him the minute you got back."

"What did you tell him?"

"Not a lot. He just looked at the whiteboard. Didn't ask what I was doing but asked where you were. I just said out and I didn't know where you were."

"Good man. I suppose I had better see what God wants."

Steve made his way to the twelfth floor and the office of Commander Malcolm Clark. He wasn't sure why his saviour wanted to see him, but he knew it couldn't be good. He knocked and was shouted in. The commander was sitting behind a large desk. His office wasn't as luxurious as Steve had thought it might be. The walls were covered in graphs, bar charts and all sorts of organisational flow charts. The commander was obviously a busy man.

"DCI Burt. What part of low profile and don't rock the boat don't you understand?" The commander was all business. He put down his pen and looked up at the DCI.

"I'm sorry, sir, I don't know what you mean." Steve was confused but also worried.

"Let me enlighten you. I've had Superintendent Jackson from financial crimes in to see me. He was complaining that a certain overweight DC working for Special Resources has been up asking one of his DCs to do her favours on

155

the quiet. Then she asks for information that is beyond the DC's pay grade. He was smart enough to see what she was asking and reported it to his governor, who reported it to *his* governor, who came to see me this morning. What have you been up to, for Christ's sake?"

Steve was relieved this was all the commander wanted to talk about.

"Well, sir. You know we now have two cases that have similar MOs."

"What! Just a minute. What do you mean two cases? Last time I looked, you had one case and a clear instruction to pay lip service to solving it and keeping your head down. Where did the second case come from?"

"The murder squad handed it over on Tuesday morning. It's identical to the first case you gave us. I thought you'd approved it," the DCI lied.

"You got the first shooting case just so it would look like your department actually did something. I wasn't expecting Sherlock bloody Holmes to get involved with other cases. Let's leave that for now. Tell me why financial have their knickers in a twist?"

The DCI decided it was better to give Malcolm as little information as possible. He thought this was his best chance of staying on the case. If he could make it look like progress was slow then the commander might accept that his low-profile instruction was still being obeyed.

"Well, sir. We took a quick look at the first case. It's a bit of a bummer. No forensics and nothing to go on. By the way, the second shooting is the same— nothing to get a handle on. So, as we were trying to make sense of things, we found that the two victims were no boy scouts. We think we may have found some sort of money laundering operation. DC Rough has a friend in financial and has been using him to try and unpick what we've found, which isn't much. We thought maybe if we understood what was going on with the money, we might find a motive at least for the killings. That's it, sir. Nothing more. I'd no idea DC Rough was taking up so much time with financial."

"Mm. I see." The commander may be a pen-pushing political cop, but he was still a cop and not easily fooled. "And that's all? Just looking into accounts that none of you are qualified to do?"

"Yes, sir. That's why we've had to involve financial."

"Mm!" Again, the commander was considering his DCI's reply. "Any of this link to the murders?"

"None that we can find, sir," Steve lied beautifully.

"OK. Get your large lady to hand over everything you have about this money laundering thing and then forget it. Just do as I said before. Keep your nose clean and in six months, you'll be free of all of this. Oh! By the way. What was your DS doing with a board full of maps?"

"Oh! That's just an exercise to keep him busy. Just looking at the crime scene in more detail. It's a real dead end. It also looks like we're working."

The commander gave another Mm and said, "Alright but remember. Low profile. I'll tell Superintendent Jackson to expect a visit from your walking roadblock. Now let me get on with my work. Oh! And you look a mess."

"Thank you, sir. I missed a shave this morning, that's all."

"I thought you were sorting yourself out, man? Try and at least look like a police officer." The commander reflected that the DCI was still the same mess as when he had ended his three-month suspension. No real change. Any hopes that he might learn a lesson appeared dashed. The only change was he didn't smell, and his suit was newer. The commander gave a satisfied smile.

Steve was dismissed. He didn't know why but he felt uneasy about not coming clean with the commander. He could have shared a lot more with his saviour but had chosen not to. He wondered why.

When he got back to the office, Twiggy was there and drinking coffee with the Cap. An insulated cup was on Steve's desk.

"What did God want?" This was the Cap.

"Only to give me a mild shafting. He's not happy about involving financial. It seems Twiggy's friend Derek jumped the gun and told his boss we were using him." Twiggy was about to speak. "Don't worry; no one's in trouble. So, Twiggy, I need you to pull together all the financial and background stuff we have on our victims plus Peter Randall.

"You'd better write up your report from today's interview with Randall as well. When you have everything, and I mean everything, go and see a Superintendent Jackson in financial crimes. But don't include the TPPP investor list nor mention your pal Tom. I think we can keep that to ourselves. Talk Jackson through what you have but don't, for Christ's sake, mention anything about our two shootings. You can give him Tax 4 U as well, including this bank in Monaco, but be careful. I've a feeling anything you say will be relayed straight to the top floor."

"Will do, but it'll take a while. I'll try and get it done tonight and see this Superintendent in the morning. After all, I've nothing else to do except track down 32 suspects from 2009." Twiggy had still not fully calmed down from their interview in the morning.

The DCI decided not to comment except to say, "Thanks, Twiggy. And don't give Jackson our suspect list either."

The room was quiet until the Cap said, "Steve. Remember, you have to call that guy Hector. He seemed a bit insistent."

"Right." The DCI lifted the receiver and dialled the Major's number.

Hector answered on the second ring. "Major Simms here." Steve heard the same clipped military voice of authority.

"Hello, Major. It's Steve Burt returning your call. Sorry it's taken a while, but I've been out."

"No problem, old boy. I assumed you would be a might busy. What!" A chuckle came down the line. "I won't ask how you're getting on. It's not my place.

"However. I was thinking about your little problem. I've looked into the Small Arms School records for 1940 onwards. It seems there were very few permanent military staff posted there and I suppose, only a few instructors. It was after all a school so most postings would be for training courses. So, no joy among the military, I'm afraid. All permanent staff except for instructors were from the REME. Royal Electrical and Mechanical Engineers, you know."

"Hector, I hope you've found more than that or you wouldn't have called."

"Just so, old boy. Just so. I found there were a few civilians on strength throughout the war and after. Most of them were armourers or clerks. Of course, they'll mostly all be dead by now. However, I may have something for you." Steve couldn't see it, but the Major had a distinct glint in his eye.

"It seems a young apprentice was taken on in 1941 as a gunsmith. Name of Albert Spinks. Must be a good age by now but my spies tell me he's still alive and in a care home in Rye, West Sussex. He was employed right through the time our Mk 1 LRSR was being tested. He only retired in 1991 when we closed the place. It may be a wild goose chase, but I thought it might help."

"Hector, sir, thank you. I'm not sure if this'll lead anywhere but I'm grateful for your help. I'll chase down anything at the moment. I don't suppose you know the care home this old chap's in?"

"Ah! Well. Military training, don't you know! Never give intelligence that's not complete. He's in the View Care Home. Don't know it myself and hope I never have to. Anyway. I trust this may be of some help. I'm sorry but it's the best I could do."

"Thank you, Major. I'll follow it up and I promise to keep you posted."

"Very kind of you, Captain. Goodbye for now." With that, the line went dead.

Steve noted the use of his old rank. He wasn't sure if a 60-year-old gun was the answer, but he had nothing else to go on. "Cap. Can we leave your map till tomorrow? It's getting late and I'm knackered."

"No problem but based on the modelling, I can't get the angles to work just on paper. Any chance Twiggy could get her other friend to knock up another plank and a knitting needle?"

"Oh yeah, along with all the other little jobs I have." Twiggy was not a good actress and both Steve and the Cap knew she was joking. Or they hoped she was. "Leave the PM and 3D report and I'll talk to my friend tonight, but I can't promise when we'll get it."

"No rush; let's plan to go to the crime scene later tomorrow. We'll go over your maps first thing. OK?"

The Cap stood up and stretched his arms. "Fine. By the way, I got the analysis back on that liquid I found in Sedgwick Close. I was right. It's light oil normally used with guns."

"So, we could have our firing point for the first shooting."

"Could be."

"Right. See you all tomorrow. Don't work too late, Twiggy. We need you alert tomorrow if you're going to the crime scene in the Fiat." Steve let out a bit of a giggle. "Remember to lock the door when you leave."

Twiggy said nothing but carried on pressing keys on her laptop.

Chapter Twenty-Five

Friday, 17 April

Everyone was in the office before 9am. All three detectives were seated around the square table that was made up of three other tables, drinking coffee. Twiggy was in front of a pile of papers. All neatly stacked and with two memory sticks placed on top. "I'm ready. When do you think I should go up?"

"I'd leave it for a while. Give them time to read their *Financial Times* and check their stocks and shares. How can you be a real copper if all you do all day is only look at numbers?" the Cap spoke with feeling.

"You're sure you have everything, Twiggy?"

"Yes, boss. I've been through it twice. TPPP, SPS and Tax 4 U plus bank details, accounts, details of San Soto Bank and a full report of Peter Randall's statement from yesterday. I've even put in the reports from the Land Registry that gives the dates of the three house purchases in 2008. But don't worry, like you said, I've deleted the list of investors in TPPP."

"Well done. Good work, Twiggy."

Twiggy looked pleased at the praise from her boss but knew the work that had gone into getting everything ready. She thought about asking for overtime but thought better of it.

The DCI wanted to share his current thoughts with his two colleagues but was worried if he shared too much, then they would all be aware just how little they had. Steve decided to plough on. "Let's have a recap. See where we are now that all the financial stuff is off our hands."

The Cap pulled an A4 pad to him, ready to take notes.

"We have two identical murders, both shot with something that isn't a conventional bullet, from long range." Steve interrupted himself, "Cap, we should confirm the second shooting was from long range later today but at the moment that's what we're thinking. Correct?"

"Yes."

"Right. We believe the killer is linked to a scam pulled by the four partners in TPPP, possibly going back to 2009. One partner died in a boating accident in 2006. Two have been murdered and the last one standing, Peter Randall, has admitted they ran a scam before they went bust in 2009. This cost a lot of people a lot of money. From what we know, 35 investors were well and truly shafted. So, we're pretty confident in our working theory that one of these 35 is our shooter. Agreed?"

"I wasn't convinced in the beginning, Steve, but I have to agree it looks more likely. They're the ones that were ripped off big time. So yes, agreed."

"Right. So, going forward. Do we think Randall could be the next target?"

"If we're running with our theory, then yes. After seeing him yesterday, I think he's a scumbag but not a murderer."

"I think you're right, Twiggy, but check out his alibi with the gardening company anyway. I'm sure he's telling the truth, but best to be sure."

"Just another little task then for me then?" Twiggy wasn't too amused at being given more research work.

"So just to be certain. We're agreed our killer is on our list of 35 names?" Yesses all around. "We also agreed any one of them could be our killer. The downside is, it was over ten years ago and a lot of the names will be either dead or too old to have carried out the shootings." The DCI paused to think before carrying on. His team were silent.

"Twiggy is looking at a possible military connection although army records weren't too helpful. People don't shoot like our killer without expert training.

"We don't know if there is a military connection but it's a strong possibility. Twiggy, keep on at the MOD. We'll need access if we can narrow down the list to a couple of suspects." Twiggy just nodded. "While Twiggy is looking at this angle, I want you, Cap, to take the same 35 names and run them down as civilians. Let's see where these people are today." The Cap made a note and nodded.

"The thing we're missing is a weapon and a bullet. No one seems to think anything exists that could possibly have made these shots plus whoever heard of a rifle that didn't fire bullets?" No one answered the DCI.

"All we have is a possible WW2 gun that was built for some daft assassination plot during the war. It was apparently built to fire from the long ranges we're looking at, but it didn't work and was scrapped. Not sure the murder squad would be impressed if we told them we think the weapon is a 60-year-old museum piece that didn't work." Steve sat back and chuckled. "Have I missed anything?"

"Yes. We still don't have a bullet."

"The last part of our puzzle."

"Where do we go if the killer isn't on the list and these shootings have nothing to do with the scam?"

"Good question, Twiggy. I don't know. We've exhausted every avenue we can think of. I suppose we shut up shop. Do as the commander wants, keep our heads down and wait for our redundancy notices. Unless the second crime scene throws up something new, we're stuffed. I think we are all out of ideas."

The three sat in silence for a few minutes. "There's just one other thing. Did either of you take the computer we collected from Booker's place? The Tax 4 U guy."

Both detectives shook their heads. "It was in your top drawer."

"Yes, it was. A couple of days ago, I went to get it and it was gone. Someone's been in here when we've been out. The office door wasn't forced nor was the lock on my desk drawer. Whoever it was, had keys."

Again, silence descended as the three detectives digested the information. No one had anything to suggest. Twiggy, feeling responsible for the laptops, spoke up, "Why take a laptop knowing it'll be missed? We got everything off it, but it was Tom who opened the encrypted files. He said the security was weak but still, unless our thief knows computers, it's not going to be much use to him."

"Unless he has his own Tom." The Cap was smiling.

"OK. It's another strange event. Let's not think too much about it. There could be a straightforward explanation." The DCI didn't believe it.

"Twiggy, you'd better get up to financial. The Cap and I'll get over to Wimbledon and hope we learn something from the second killing. Did your friend finish the plank?"

"Yes. He did it last night. It's in the Fiat."

"Great. OK, Cap, let's go see what the crime scene can tell us"

All three left. Twiggy to the 9th floor and Steve and the Cap to the garage to pick up a pool car.

Steve and the Cap arrived before Twiggy. The Cap had the file. Both men stood silently looking at the buildings that ran along Penrose Road. There was no obvious site that a gunman could have fired from. Just like the first case. They

162

stood facing the crossing as Percival Booker must have done on Tuesday. The Cap stood over the crimson stain.

"What was the angle of the shot?"

"According to the file," The Cap opened the buff-coloured cover. "it was 41 degrees from the front. They show it as being measured from the centre of the nose and coming from the left. So, if the victim was standing here," The Cap put the flat of his hand at 90 degrees to his nose and moved it left to simulate something near 41 degrees. "then the shot must have come from there." He pointed straight up Penrose Road.

Steve joined him and stood behind. "What was the other angle of penetration?"

The Cap again looked in the file. "It was 21 degrees from the horizontal."

"Stand there, Cap, where our victim would have been." Steve stood behind the Cap and draped his right arm around the Cap's neck and angled it to the left. He used his right-hand index finger and tried to incorporate both angles to try and simulate the trajectory of the bullet. "It's only rough but it looks like another impossible shot." It dawned on Steve that if a uniform went past, there was a good chance they might be arrested for something improper. Two men standing one behind the other with one of them having his arm around the other's head. Steve quickly stood back. Just in case!

"We'll have to wait for Twiggy's wood to be sure but where the hell could our killer have shot from?"

Both men were at a loss. They continued to walk around the crime scene and survey their surroundings, but nothing helped. "It's another dead end. Exactly the same as the first. I'd hoped because we got this one early, we might get a head start." The DCI was depressed. "But look at what we have. Nothing."

"Not quite true, is it? We think we know where the kill shot came from for the first murder. Who's to say we're not looking at the same again? The kill site is out there. It's just further away."

As both men tried to remain positive, Twiggy arrived in the green Fiat. It didn't sound any better than before and the Cap was sure he could see steam and smoke coming from the exhaust. A plank was again sticking through the sunroof. Twiggy, as before, parked on the pavement. Fortunately, the kerb was low and the Fiat seemed to manage climbing over it with a bit more ease.

Twiggy was rushing to get the plank, stool and knitting needles out of the car. The Cap went to help. Twiggy was obviously in a foul mood so neither male officer spoke. As Twiggy handed the plank to Steve, she let off a torrent, "That bloody pen pusher. He kept me waiting 20 minutes then tore me off a strip for using his staff without permission. When I gave him the file, he just put it on a table in his room and said he would talk to my DCI in due course. No bloody thank you. No good job. No thank you for working half the night to get everything in order. Great bloody plonker."

Steve could sympathise but just said, "Yes, he sounds like a great bloody plonker."

Twiggy smiled. "Yes, well. He got right up my nose."

They set up the wood as at the first scene. The height matched exactly the victim's and the hole in the four-inch side of the plank matched the position of the hole in the body. Twiggy set up the stool and positioned the wood over the crimson stain. The knitting needle was stuck in the hole and they were ready. Steve didn't think they would learn anything new but lived in hope. The Cap had the first go. He looked along the needle and asked Steve who was holding the wood to rotate it left and right. They reversed roles and Steve took his turn. Again, he asked for the timber to be rotated.

They moved away from the crossing and stood against low railings that bordered some terraced houses beside the crossing. Twiggy held the timber.

"You first, Cap."

"Nothing, just like last time. I've just remembered something the pathologist Dr Green said. The angle that any bullet enters a body is not the angle the shot was taken at. If you're firing over a distance, the bullet has been fired high so that it's on its way down when it hits the target. We didn't allow for this but I'm sure the 3D model did. It's probably not relevant. We know it was a long-range shot."

"You're right, I remember from rifle training in the army. You adjusted your sights for the distance of the shot." Steve was momentarily back at the rifle ranges at Aldershot. His memory bank kicked in. "Hold on, Cap, you may have something. If our shooter's firing from a long way away, then his rifle must almost be pointing at the sky when he pulled the trigger. That means he must be using some very sophisticated sighting equipment. Maybe we need to check with suppliers and manufacturers to see how many high-end sights have been sold recently. I don't think it matters just now but it might give us another lead."

Without being asked, Twiggy volunteered. She felt she should continue to play the downtrodden female, although she was enjoying the chase.

"We need to concentrate on the angle of delivery. It's all we have. From Twiggy's model, the shot must have come down Penrose Road. Let's walk up it and see if anything looks possible. It may make more sense when we look at your map later, Cap."

"What about my car?"

"I think it's safe. Twiggy, put the wood in the car and get back to the office.

"You have more than enough to get on with. Chase down those names with the military. Remind them it's a double murder inquiry. Don't take any excuses and feel free to threaten them with anyone you like, including me."

"Oh yeah, carry a lot of influence then, sir?"

"Detective Constable, just get the information." Both Steve and Twiggy giggled at each other. "Oh and remember to check on sales of upmarket gun sights."

Twiggy would rather have joined in the search for a kill site but did as Steve suggested.

The DCI and the DS set off on foot up Penrose Road.

Penrose Road was a typical London suburban road. Shops lining the pavements with flats or offices above. The detectives walked slowly, trying to look for any vantage point a gunman might use. They continually turned to look back at the crossing and tried to keep the crossing in view. They walked on.

After about 19 minutes of walking, the Cap said what Steve was thinking. "Boss, this is getting us nowhere. We can hardly see the crossing now and the road's beginning to curve."

"Yeah, I see, but where the hell did he shoot from?" The DCI was equally stumped. "Suppose you were higher up. You'd still be able to see the crossing, wouldn't you?"

"Yes, good point, except you'd need wings. Where could anyone hang to get a shot in?"

"Let's keep walking. We need the exercise. Let's give it another five minutes." The two detectives carried on.

They stopped again after a few minutes, totally dejected. "There's nothing here." Steve was getting more and more depressed. He felt they were getting nowhere fast. "Cap," he said with a heartfelt sigh, "we need your map. I don't know how far we've walked but it seems a long way and I need a coffee.

"There's a Holiday Inn there, they're bound to have a coffee shop."

The Cap stood still. Just staring. "Steve, it may have a coffee shop, but it also has high windows facing straight down the road. What if our shooter was here?"

The detectives entered the hotel and asked for the manager. The manager was helpful and agreed to show Steve and the Cap the top floor rooms to the front that looked straight down Penrose Road. The first was room 228. It had an uninterrupted view straight down the road and from the window, Steve could just about see the crossing. The manager showed the adjoining rooms but both Steve and the Cap felt room 228 was the best positioned.

"Was this room occupied on Monday night?" Steve was less depressed now. Something positive was happening and you never knew. This could be a breakthrough.

"I'm not sure. I would have to check."

"Please do; we also need to know if anyone has stayed in this room after Monday."

The manager, who was in her early 30s and a little on the thin side, was beginning to look a bit flustered. "I'll get what you want and will be at reception once you've finished with the room."

"Well, Steve. What do you think?"

"If the shooter is in fact such a great shot and if he has a rifle, we know nothing about and if he has bullets that aren't bullets, then we could have something." Steve raised his eyebrows at the Cap.

"This seems to be the only logical place that has a line of sight that might match the angle of the shot." Steve paced the room. "But we still don't know how he does it. Let's go see what she has downstairs."

The manager who, according to her name badge, was called Petra had copied out details of the guest who had stayed in room 228 on Monday night. She handed a sheet of paper to Steve. "So, it was a John Brown. Address in Canterbury. He didn't register a car. How did he get here?"

"Some of our guests walk from the station. Or he could have had a car but didn't register it on his booking form. Some guests don't."

"Were you on duty on Monday?"

"Yes. From noon till around 9 o'clock."

"So, you checked this Mr Brown in?"

"I must have. I'm usually at the front desk or in the office just behind."

"Can you remember what he looked like?"

"Not really. I think he was quite large, maybe a bit overweight. He was wearing glasses but now you ask…" A startled expression appeared on Petra's face. "There was a funny thing I remember. He was wearing a red baseball cap. I remember thinking at the time he was a bit old for the hat."

"How old would you say he was?"

"Not sure; probably around late 50s but I didn't pay much attention."

The Cap looked at the CCTV cameras in the ceiling around reception. "We'll need the CCTV tapes or dvds if you're digital from Monday and Tuesday. Do you have cameras covering the carpark?"

"Yes, but only the exit."

"We'll need the carpark tapes as well."

Steve asked, "Has anyone stayed in room 228 since Monday night?"

"Yes, it's been booked every night by different guests. All our rooms are cleaned daily, regardless of whether they've been let."

"So, boss, no point us getting forensics over."

"Get them in anyway. There could be something."

"Let's get the CCTV pictures and head back to the office."

On the way back, both men discussed what they had learned. Steve had picked up on the shooter's age. "Cap, if this bloke in the red cap is our shooter, then according to Petra, he's late fifty, maybe even early sixties. Check the list of the 35 names. See if any of them match that age. If any of them do…"

"Then flag them up as our prime suspects?" The Cap was on the ball and both detectives were feeling a lot more positive about the case. "Also, I'll contact Canterbury. See if anyone answering to Mr Brown's description, such as it is, is known to them. You never know. Mr Brown might even be his real name."

Steve admired the Cap's optimism but maybe they were getting closer. One step at a time.

Chapter Twenty-Six

Friday, 17 April

Back in the headquarters building, all three detectives met in the offices of Technical Support. The dvds from the Holiday Inn were already loaded into a very sophisticated-looking machine that had as many lights and dials as a spaceship. The technician ran the Monday tape first. The detectives knew from the manager that Mr Brown had checked in around 7 o'clock in the evening.

As the time clock on the screen arrived at this time, the technician slowed the speed of the image. At 7.03pm, a figure appeared at the reception desk.

Steve was standing behind the chair Twiggy had grabbed. Pointing at the screen— "That's our man, red baseball cap and glasses."

They watched the screen until Mr Brown walked out of camera shot. "He was disguised, and did you see the way he never looked at the cameras?"

The film was played again but the result was the same. It was no help in identifying the man they thought could be the killer. The technician offered to try and enhance the image but said he didn't think it would change much.

"Can you run it on? Let's see if he reappears."

The technician did and the red cap was seen three more times before midnight. Each time he was recorded wheeling a large suitcase into the hotel and presumably taking it to his room.

There was nothing else of interest on the Monday recording, so the technician loaded in the disc from Tuesday starting at 01.00. The red-capped Mr Brown was seen passing through reception Tuesday morning from 10.01 on three separate occasions, again wheeling a large suitcase each time. The team took it this was him leaving. From the size of the cases, they also assumed he must have a car or a van. The last image was timed at 10.34. He was seen at reception again but only briefly. He didn't look at the CCTV cameras.

The tape from the carpark revealed nothing, just cars leaving. Steve thought back to the witness statement from the first shooting about a white van being seen. He had hoped to see a white van but there was nothing. Not even an estate car on the disc.

They returned to the office. "Twiggy, get on your laptop. I don't suppose Brown is his real name, but you never know. Check out the Canterbury address. See if it exists. The Cap's checking with Kent Constabulary but it's a long shot."

Twiggy got on to it. "Oh, by the way, Steve. I checked out high-end rifle sights. The main importer for a German-made sight told me no sight in the world could adjust for a long-range shot over about 1,500 yards. I was told the German sight is the best in the world. If it can't do it, nothing can. Sorry but it's a dead end."

"It was a long shot anyway, Twiggy." Steve was still disappointed to find another dead end.

"You know, Cap, if we're right and that room in the hotel was the kill spot then it's likely we've seen our killer. I wonder what was in the suitcases?"

"Maybe our killer is a woman and she was travelling light." The Cap attempted to lighten the mood. Steve looked at him and gave a sarcastic "Ha ha".

Twiggy spoke up, "There are a lot of Browns on the Canterbury census but the street name he gave doesn't exist." She rested one of her chins on her right folded arm.

No one spoke. Steve stepped in to try and lift spirits. "We think we've identified our two kill spots. We've seen what we think is our killer, so we know he exists. Despite the Cap's humour,"—Steve looked directly at the Cap— "we're sure it's a man of stocky build in his late 50s or maybe early 60s and he travels with three large suitcases. This is a lot more than we had 24 hours ago."

"Boss, if our killer is, say, sixty, is he on the investor list?"

"Really, Twiggy, why didn't I think of that?" This was said with a certain amount of sarcastic humour. Still smiling, the DCI apologised. "Sorry, Twiggy, but the Cap is supposed to be working on it."

The Cap was quietly scrutinising his list. They waited for him to finish making notes and crossing names from his list. "Well, of the 35 on the list, there are nine who in 2009 were between forty-two and fifty. No one was younger than 42. This could be our new suspect pool."

The re-energised DCI looked at his team. There was a twinkle in his eyes. "If our assumption is correct and someone on that list is our murderer, and we now have a witness that places him today at between late 50s and early 60s, then one of the nine names the Cap has come up with should be our man."

The DCI pumped the air with a loud "Yes!"

The Cap and Twiggy smiled at each other but didn't yet have their DCI's enthusiasm. They knew they would be the ones doing the follow ups. "You two have been looking into the names. You, Twiggy, for military connections. You, Cap, at civilians. From now on, we concentrate only on these nine names.

"Twiggy, can you print it out and we'll all have a copy?" Twiggy did.

"I think it's best if you work the nine names on the list together. You know, take one name at a time. Twiggy, you check military and Cap, you check out civilian. With luck, we'll find that our man served in the infantry and now works locally. As each name comes up as a dead end, move on to the next one. One of these names is our killer."

Both detectives nodded.

"It's the weekend. Let's review things again on Monday. Try and relax and recharge. I've a good feeling that when you run down those names, we'll have our man. I think I'll go to the seaside tomorrow and follow up on a lead." The DCI was in a playful mood. He'd decided to go and see the old boy Hector had put him on to and stay overnight at the seaside. He told himself he needed a treat.

"Boss, I've been thinking…"

"Oh! Always a bad sign, Cap." Steve was in a happy place. After all, they seemed to be getting closer to catching a very clever killer. Or so they hoped!

"What about the last man standing? This guy Randall. Shouldn't we give him some police protection? If one of the nine people on the list is our killer and, as looks likely, is targeting the owners of this TPPP, it means Randall as the last of the original four has to be the next victim."

"Yes. You're right, Cap. If our killer sticks to long-range shots, I think Randall is safe enough if he stays in that great mansion of his. I don't like the scumbag but I suppose that's no reason to get him killed. Let's set it up on Monday."

Chapter Twenty-Seven

Friday, 17 April

The killer had a problem. His third and last victim was proving difficult to target. He knew the target's address. He knew how many family members he had. He had detailed maps of the area. The problem was that there was no obvious location or time when the target seemed likely to present a clean shot.

The killer had been staking out the estate Peter Randall lived in since just after he had taken down his second victim. He had spent days walking and driving past the guarded entrance. Unless the target came out, it would be difficult to get to him.

The killer was not downhearted. He knew that good planning was the key. He told himself he would succeed. He just couldn't see how for the moment. He had to rationalise. He had to think. He had to be patient.

It was obvious that his third victim worked from home. He lived behind a security fence with a 24-hour guard. From the maps, it was clear that the estate was surrounded on three sides by light forests. It was impossible to guarantee a clean shot through trees. As with his first two victims, the killer knew he could get the kill shot away but he needed victim three to leave his house.

He had the DVLA data for the target's cars, but this didn't help. The target never came out. So how would he get to him? He had no idea, but he knew apart from planning, good surveillance was essential. So he kept watch at various times around the clock.

The killer was patient, but he knew he had to get this kill over with. He kept repeating his mantra that good planning would win through, but he was beginning to feel frustrated. With frustration came anger and the need for retribution grew. He admitted to himself that he liked the thrill of the challenge and it helped keep him alert and less likely to make a mistake. But still! How to get to victim number three?

Over several days, he had seen the target's wife leave around 08.30 with two girls in the car. He also saw two largish dogs in the back of the estate car. She was obviously on a school run. Other cars came and went through the security gate during the day but none with the correct registration numbers that said they belonged to his target. The killer was again angry and frustrated. He knew deep down that more direct action was going to be needed. He didn't like direct action. It meant he could be identified and there was always the possibility of witnesses. Also, he would be face to face with his victim. The killer didn't think of himself as a murderer. He didn't want to murder anyone, but he had to have revenge. He preferred the more sterile method of a long-range shot rather than having to look into his victim's eyes as he pulled the trigger. But if his target wouldn't come out then he would have to go in. He had no choice. He couldn't wait any longer.

At 3.44pm on Friday afternoon, the 17th of April, a uniformed police sergeant drove up to the security barrier at a very posh and upmarket estate. He stopped as required at the barrier and left the car. He walked slowly towards the security guard who was seated inside a brick-built hut. The hut had a large glass sliding window facing the barrier. The police sergeant didn't know it, but it was the same guard Steve and Twiggy had met during their earlier visit to Peter Randall.

"Good afternoon, you guys working in security have an easy number," said the sergeant, making conversation.

"It's not all just sitting down, you know." The guard was full of his own importance.

"Oh well, when I retire, I think I'll look for a job like yours. Good pay and regular hours, not like the police. I've only got a year left and I'm finished." The guard didn't comment but wondered why the police were here again.

"They've already put me out to pasture. Got me doing security checks on all the large estates. Seems there've been a few perimeter breaches around the place recently."

"So, is that why you're here?"

"Yes. Your office should've had a letter but the way the paper shufflers work, I wouldn't be surprised if it was still on some civilian clerk's desk, waiting to be signed in triplicate." The sergeant gave a laugh and the guard joined in. This was good. The killer felt he was putting the guard at his ease.

He looked at the guard. He was flabby and clearly not fit. "If you can open the gate, I just need to drive around and inspect the boundary fences that don't belong to the residents. Only the ones that surround the common areas." He knew this was a safe ploy. The maps showed a lot of open green spaces and he knew such upmarket estates always had play and walking areas. "Well, I'm not supposed to let anyone in without permission."

"Look, I'll be in and out before you know it. The letter to your bosses will be in the post so you've nothing to fear. I'm sure your residents will appreciate your initiative, especially if I find a gap in the fence."

This did the trick. "OK, but don't be too long just in case I get an inspection. They do that sometimes, you know. Just turn up to make sure you're not asleep on the job."

The gate opened and with a wave, the sergeant was in.

He drove around until he found 'The Pines'. Looking at the mansion, his anger returned. This was evidence that it was one rule for the rich and sod the rest. This was why Peter Randall had to die.

He parked his car, which had false plates fixed over the real registration, and holding an official-looking file started to walk towards 'The Pines'. He was only looking to get the lie of the land, but his sixth sense told him to go as far as he could. He wasn't ready to kill Randall yet, but he needed a look inside the house. All part of good planning. He told himself again that unless his target went out, he would have to do the deed up close and personal. He didn't relish the prospect. He didn't like killing people close up but if that was the only way then he knew he could do it. Revenge would be sweet.

He rang the bell of 'The Pines'. It was answered by a small, neat woman dressed as though she was out of an Agatha Christie novel. He had last seen a black and white maid's outfit like hers on television in a 1930s drama.

"I'm Sergeant Brown with the police. I need to inspect the perimeter of this property. There have been a few burglaries recently," he lied. He knew a uniform always gave an air of authority and when someone with a menial job was asked by authority to do something, they usually just went with the line of least resistance.

"I'm sure it'll be OK. Do you need to come inside?" Her voice was East London.

"Only for a quick look. I won't disturb anything. Is anyone else in the house?"

"Only the owner, Mr Randall. But he's in his study at the back of the house."

"Does he spend a lot of time in his study?"

"Oh! Yes, he never seems to leave it. It's full of computers and phones. Apart from something to eat or an odd coffee, he's in there working from first thing until Mrs Randall gets back about five in the afternoon."

The killer stored this information. He was beginning to form a picture.

The maid showed the sergeant around the ground floor of this vast structure. He tried not to show it, but the killer was again getting angry seeing all this opulence. His thirst for revenge was taking over. He could have killed right there and then. All this wealth and grand living from scamming people of their hard-earned savings. He would have his revenge.

He had to stop, and with a high degree of self-control, drew deep breaths. The maid showed him all the downstairs rooms but only pointed out the study door. The killer was close to his next victim, but revenge would be all the sweeter when it came. "Thank you for the tour. I'll leave now and check out the outside. You've been very helpful."

The maid showed the sergeant out. He immediately went to his car and sat for a few minutes, considering what he'd seen. He now had a plan and an even stronger resolve to kill Peter Randall. He would have to get up close to kill this rogue. He would do it on Monday. Give the victim his last weekend of enjoyment.

He drove back through the security barrier and waved to the guard, noting that he would be collateral damage, just like poor Mrs Jemima Boyd. The guard had seen him so he would have to die as would the maid.

The killer now had a plan.

Chapter Twenty-Eight

Saturday, 18 April

Saturday morning arrived with a clear blue sky and a large orange ball in the sky. The DCI had arrived midmorning and signed out a pool car for two days.

He was heading for Rye in a fairly new Volkswagen Golf. He'd phoned the View Nursing home earlier and so was expected. He was told Albert Spinks was well and alert as always. The nurse he spoke to had said she would tell Mr Spinks that he was having a visitor in the afternoon. The kindly sounding nurse told Steve that Albert didn't get many visitors so this visit would cheer him up.

Steve had decided to make a weekend of it. After all, they were close to solving a double murder. Dressed in a new polo shirt and chinos bought during his last visit to Primark, he was feeling relaxed and fit. He had shaved and even his hair looked neat and tidy. As he drove, he thought how well his two rejects were performing. The Cap and Twiggy. It was a pity all three of them would be looking for jobs in a few months' time. He knew he couldn't help them find jobs but somehow, he wished he could.

The roads in these parts of Kent and West Sussex that the DCI was travelling weren't motorways. They were traditional narrow country lanes that didn't allow for high-speed driving. The DCI was in no rush and was enjoying the drive. He had made a reservation at the Bull Hotel in Rye. It looked full of old-world charm on its website. Steve was looking forward to getting there and checking in.

He arrived just around lunchtime. Checked in and went down to a magnificent dining room for some lunch. After three courses of the most delicious food served with bottled water and washed down with a strong black coffee, the DCI was ready to face the world.

His Golf had a satnav, so he found the View Care Home with ease. As he entered, he smelt a mixture of bleach, human sweat, furniture polish and another smell he'd always associated with old people. The building was a modern single storey with large glass windows. The front hallway was carpeted in a design that

Steve remembered his parents having in their lounge. The walls were papered in a neutral pattern and there were various prints of country scenes on the walls.

As Steve started to walk up the corridor that led from the main hallway, a voice called from behind him, "Can I help you?"

The DCI turned to face a lady in her late fifties, not small and wearing a dark blue nurse's uniform. "Yes, you probably can. I'm here to see an Albert Spinks."

"You must be Mr Burt. We spoke this morning. If you come with me, I'll take you to Bert. He's in his room. It'll be quieter and you can have a nice chat. I'll send in some tea and biscuits in about half an hour."

"Thank you. Sorry, I didn't get your name on the phone?"

"It's Mabel. Mabel Forsyth. I'm in charge here." With a smile that seemed to light up the corridor, Mabel admitted, "I don't know what I did wrong in an earlier life to finish up here." She chuckled away to herself.

Mabel stopped outside a door with the number 11 painted on it. She knocked lightly and opened the door without being invited in. "Bert. This is the visitor I was telling you about. Mr Burt. He's come down from London." She had raised her voice a few decibels. Steve wondered if Mr Spinks was deaf. Without further comment, Mabel eased Steve into the room and closed the door.

Albert Spinks was sitting in a traditional high-backed winged chair favoured by older people. It was positioned by the window facing south overlooking the gardens. Albert Spinks looked frail but still had a full head of hair and was sitting upright in his chair. Steve noticed his hands shook a bit and were like bird claws. There was a dining room-style chair opposite Bert Spinks. Steve took it and sat down before speaking.

"Mr Spinks. My name is Steve Burt. I'm a policeman from London. Thanks for agreeing to see me."

Bert looked through his small watering eyes. "I was curious what a copper from London wanted with me. I haven't robbed anywhere in a few years." Bert gave a thunderous laugh as though he had just said the funniest thing in the world. Steve thought the sound couldn't possibly have come from this frail-looking old man.

The DCI smiled to humour Bert.

"So, what's this about?" The old man's voice was surprisingly strong with what sounded like a Kent accent.

"Mr Spinks—"

"Please call me Bert. My father was Mr Spinks."

Steve started again, "Bert. I understand you worked at the Army Small Arms School during World War 2? I was hoping you might remember a rifle that was tested there around 1942 or 43. I think it was called an Mk1 LRSR."

Bert closed his eyes as though asleep. "Made by Browning, yes, I remember. A wonderfully engineered piece of kit but it wasn't a rifle. Oh! No. It was a gun." The DCI took this information on board but didn't know what it meant. "I was only 16 and a year into my apprenticeship. My dad was in the Home Guard and was based at the School. He got me in. I was a gunsmith. Reserved occupation, you see. It was a proper job. Proper apprenticeship. Not like these apprentices today, three years and they think they know it all. They are only half-trained and semi-skilled, most of them."

Steve thought it was going to be a long interview. He decided to let Bert talk. After all, it was a nice day and he'd been promised tea and biscuits.

Bert carried on, "Well, you know, me being the youngest in the camp I suppose I was also the nosiest. What do you want to know, it was a long time ago?"

"Anything you can remember about it. How it worked. That kind of thing."

"I remember two officers talking down the butts one day. You know what the butts are? It's where you stay below the targets on the rifle range so that you don't get shot. Anyway, them officers was talking about a new weapon we was getting. Seems that it'd been designed to fire over a distance no one could believe. One of them said it was to kill Hitler from miles away. Being young, I didn't pay much attention at the time. I seem to remember I was having women troubles at the time." Bert gave a sly grin that suggested to Steve this old boy had been a character in his day.

Bert sat back a little and closed his eyes again. Just as Steve was about to wake him, he started again, "Then one day a lorry arrived with three large green wooden cases, two of them were unloaded outside our workshop. The third one was taken to the stores. The driver came back and just pushed an envelope in me hand and said, 'Sign here.' In them days, although we all knew about security, things were still a bit civvy street. You know what I mean?"

"Yes, I think I do." This to appease the old man. Steve had no idea what he meant.

"Anyway, it was late afternoon I remember. I was all on me own. Every other bugger had skipped off early. I opened the envelope and took out some papers and there it was. TOP SECRET. I didn't know what to do so I read it." Bert gave a conspiratorial laugh. "Heh! I was a right devil in them days, but I thought if I were caught, I might be done as a spy. You know, reading top-secret papers. I can't rightly remember what they said except it was a weapon to match the War Department's request for a weapon to be used by snipers and capable of firing over a distance of up to four miles." Bert paused for effect. "Not bad for an old memory like mine. Eh! I've always remembered them words."

He pointed his claw-like index finger to the left side of his head. "See, it's in here. I were so scared of getting caught, I suppose fear ingrained it inside me head."

Just as Bert was set to carry on, Mabel arrived pushing a small trolley. Tea, not forgetting the biscuits, had arrived. After a few pleasantries exchanged with Mabel and over his cup of tea, Steve began to realise this was a waste of time.

Old Bert was at the camp at the right time but listening to a 94-year-old man reminiscing wasn't moving his case forwards, especially when the DCI was sure this wasn't the weapon he was looking for. How could it be?

"Drink up your tea. Mabel don't like it if we leave any!" Bert chuckled more to himself. "Where was I?"

Steve decided to humour the old man. "You had just read the top-secret papers."

"Oh! Yeah, that's right. So, I put everything back in the envelope. Next morning, me gaffer got me to open the boxes. He didn't know I'd peeked at the papers. Kind of James Bond like, eh!" Bert was enjoying his trip down memory lane. "He said it was secret and not to tell anyone what we was doing. We pulled these wonderful shining pieces of metal from the boxes. There was instructions on how to put them together. You know, sort of assembly instructions. Anyway, as the apprentice, all I did was fetch and carry tools, but the machines were built. Wonderful looking things. One was taken to the range and the main man in the school—I think his name was Senior Warrant Officer Clive Taylor—set it up. We all went to watch even though it was secret. They set a target up so far away I couldn't see it. The SWO spent an age fiddling with it and reading an instruction book but eventually, he fired it. It made a thud rather than a bang. The thing about it was that it wasn't a rifle. At the time I didn't know but after, I realised it was more like a navy gun but only a lot smaller."

"Did it hit the target?" Steve wanted to move the story along.

"They brought the target back from the butts and it was untouched. I remember they brought the range down by half a mile. The second time it fired, it didn't hit anything either. Bloody useless."

Bert put his cup down. "They brought it back to the workshop so that the armourers and us could look it over. It was a thing of beauty. Breech loaded, it even had sleeves you could put inside the barrel if you wanted to fire different calibre rounds. Lovely piece of engineering." Bert drifted off again, staring into the distance. He returned in a split second. "I remember it had a box on the side. It was all dials and switches and there were a telescope on top of this box. My gaffer told me this was the future. A weapon where you dialled in the target parameters and you got a hit every time. I didn't believe it. Lot of rubbish. The boffins from Browning came and went for weeks but the trial weapon was never fired again."

Bert was clearly getting tired now. His voice was getting weaker. "Then a lad came from one of them engineering universities. Don't know which one. He set up in our workshop and started fiddling with the gun. I don't know how or why but after about a month or so, he got the army to take the first weapon out again. I think the target was set up again at four miles, just like the first time.

"The SWO fiddled with it along with the young bloke from the university.

"Eventually, they fired at the target. I couldn't see it 'cause it was so far away. Bugger me. When they brought the target back, it was a hit. Right in the bull's eye." Bert smacked his lips and raised a clenched fist. "That young lad must have known his stuff."

"Hold on, Bert. Are you saying it worked?"

"Oh yeah! They fired it a dozen times and it hit the target every time. The thing I couldn't get me head around were the bullets. They was using frozen water. This young scientist engineer bloke was using stuff that smoked but froze his bullets rock hard. I don't know how or why but they worked."

Suddenly, Steve felt his journey was perhaps not such a waste of time after all. Maybe he had his answer to the riddle of the gun. "So, this machine fired frozen water bullets accurately over a four-mile distance? Is that what you're saying, Bert?" Steve was almost speechless.

"That's about it. We pulled it apart to clean it and it were a marvel. Did I tell you it was a magnificent piece of engineering?"

"Yes, you did, Bert. Did you ever see it fired close up?"

"Only once. It was the SWO what fired it. He saw me one day looking at it out on the range. I think he liked me and was a pal of me dad's. He tried to explain how it worked but I didn't take a lot of it in. I can't rightly remember but as near as I can, he set the dials and lined the barrel up with the target. I remember he explained about the sight. He said it was incredible. All you had to do was line up the target through the scope. Dial in some numbers you saw down the scope and bang. You couldn't miss. Bloody marvellous." Bert was obviously a big fan.

"The SWO took the frozen water shell from a flask just like the university bloke. I think he said if I were to put me hand inside the flask, it would burn me hand off. He were wearing big heavy gloves. Did I tell you it were breech loaded?

"Just like a Navy gun but a bit smaller."

"Yes, Bert. You told me. Are you able to carry on with your story?"

Bert wasn't looking too healthy but Steve thought at his age, who would?

Bert ignored Steve's question. "The SWO stuck the shell in the breech and put something like a cap in after it. The shell were a bit bigger in diameter than a .303 round and a bit longer. I know now that the cap were a cordite charge that fired the shell. Strange but I can clearly remember he kept adjusting the dials on the box. Then he pushed a white button on the side of the box and that were that. They brought the target back to us and it scored right in the middle."

Steve could see Bert was beginning to nod off. He was drifting in and out of consciousness. When he came to, he just staring into the distance. Probably living in 1943. Steve had to keep this old man talking. It was likely he held the key to two murders.

Steve whispered, "Bert! Are you OK?"

Bert gave a shudder and in a low voice said, "Yeah, I'm just a bit tired."

"Bert, this is very important. What happened to the three guns?"

Bert shook himself and bravely carried on. "Well, there was a demonstration for the bigwigs from London. One machine was set up and worked. I'm not sure but afterwards, they said that one of them London people asked if the SWO could take the same shot from 50 yards further right. Well! The thing were so heavy it seems it took the SWO half an hour to split it down, then he had to drag it to the new firing point and another half an hour to assemble and test it again before he could fire it. The word were that it were supposed to be a sniper weapon. Light and easy to move. This thing had to be split into three parts just so you could move it and each part was heavy enough on its own. I think we heard later that because it were too heavy and cumbersome, it weren't going to be used. So, it were to be scrapped. It were only the weight of the thing them experts from London didn't like. Not the fact it didn't work. We thought it were probably over-engineered. That's why it were so heavy."

The DCI was beside himself. Everything this 94-year-old man was telling him supported what they knew about the shootings. The facts pointed to a 78-year-old gun being the murder weapon today. But how?

"Bert. We're almost done. What happened to the three guns?"

"It were a long time ago so I'm not sure. But I remember the two we used for trials were put on a lorry and sent to the foundry in Chatham. I know that much. It were me that had to crate the bloody things up. The third weapon were never used so were never taken out of its box. I suppose it were just left in stores. I don't rightly remember. What I do remember were that the soldier in charge of the stores were a right wide boy. If it wasn't screwed down, it were his. A real black-market dealer. He could get anything, and he'd nick anything."

"Is it possible he kept the third gun?" The DCI was looking for evidence that the third gun might have survived.

"Anything's possible. He used to drive an old Ford lorry. He didn't stay in the camp. I think he were billeted in Hythe. I didn't have a lot to do with him. From his reputation, it's possible he kept it but I'm sure he would've had it away for scrap. Remember, there was a fair weight of metal in the gun."

Bert was now seriously beginning to doze off. His head seemed to be getting heavier until it dropped to his chest and a weak sound came from him. Not sure what to do, Steve left the old man gently snoring in his chair. He'd told the DCI everything he could remember. There was just one more question Steve wanted to ask but it could wait.

He went to find Mabel. She was in the main hallway talking to another women dressed in civilian clothes rather than a nurse's uniform. She had a stethoscope around her neck. As a detective, Steve took a bet with himself that this second woman could be a doctor. Mabel saw Steve approaching and stood away from the other woman to welcome Steve. "Ah! Detective Inspector, was Bert helpful?"

"More than he will ever know." Steve was still on a high and trying to digest Bert's information.

"Dr Mills, this is DCI Burt. He's been to see our Albert Spinks."

Steve put out his hand to greet Dr Mills. As they shook hands, they exchanged first names. "Please, it's Steve."

"Likewise, it's Alison. Pleased to meet you."

Despite the excitement Steve felt about his meeting with Bert, he felt equally excited about meeting Alison Mills. She was about five foot ten inches tall, with light blonde hair and a pretty but not beautiful face. He noticed her nose was small and turned up at the end. She obviously shopped at the same stores as Miss Hawkins, PA to the head of HR for the Metropolitan Police. The difference was Alison Mills filled the clothes better and was a lot more sophisticated looking than the ultra-thin Miss Hawkins.

"Mabel, could I ask you a favour?"

"You can ask."

"Well, Bert nodded off before I could ask him one last question. Would you mind asking him if he can remember the name of the storeman at the Small Arms School when they were testing the gun? I'm sure Bert will know what you're talking about."

Before Steve could produce a business card, Mabel said she was off shift and going home and had a week's holiday starting now.

Alison Mills asked if the answer was important.

"Probably not but it could tie up a loose end."

"Give me your card. I have to give Bert his monthly check-up later this afternoon. He usually manages to stay awake for that." Steve was not surprised. Even a 94-year-old man would enjoy being examined by this doctor.

Steve handed over the card. He felt awkward in the doctor's presence. He didn't know why. "It's probably not vital but if you could, I'd be very grateful. My landline and mobile are on the card."

"Leave it with me." She placed the card in the pocket of her skirt. "Well, I must get on if I'm going to get out of here tonight. Patients to see and no doubt tales to listen to, sometimes for the second and third time." Dr Mills waved and walked away. Mabel said goodbye and she followed the doctor towards the back of the hallway.

Steve was very impressed with Alison Mills and wondered what her story was. As a detective, he had spotted she wasn't wearing a wedding ring. He hoped he might meet her again but didn't know why. There was something to like in the good doctor. He set off for his hotel to do a lot of thinking and to enjoy an evening away from London.

In his room, the DCI lay on the very comfortable bed and thought about what Bert had told him. His subconscious was screaming something at him but he couldn't bring it to the surface. He told himself this piece of ancient weaponry had actually worked. It was the only thing he'd found that could shoot at the distances that were stumping the current experts. Bert said the weapon had to be split in three to be moved. The statement from the first killing spoke of three cases. The CCTV from the hotel showed the killer bringing in and leaving with three large suitcases. It all seemed to fit but something was missing. Could a museum piece really be the murder weapon? How was it the killer had it after all this time? Steve felt the pieces were slowly falling into place but there was something he wasn't seeing. He would get Twiggy and the Cap looking for connections to the camp at Hythe on Monday. The list of nine names would be the starting point.

All this thinking lulled Steve into sleep mode. He dozed off and woke just before 6 o'clock. Showered and refreshed, he headed for the bar and the dining room at 7pm.

In the bar, he ordered a tonic water, thinking Twiggy would be proud of him. He was given the dinner menu to look at and settled into a comfortable armchair. A waiter approached him as he was finishing his drink to say his table was ready. He followed the waiter into the same large elegant room he'd had his lunch in. This evening, it was set up with tables of various sizes with starched white tablecloths covered with sparkling glasses and highly polished cutlery. The waiter guided Steve to a table set for two people. They didn't do tables that were only set for one. The waiter would remove the second-place setting once Steve had ordered.

As Steve was considering his choices, he was aware someone was standing behind and to one side of him. A delicate cough caught his attention. "Good evening, Chief Inspector." It was Dr Alison Mills.

Steve was a bit taken aback at the sight of Alison Mills standing beside him. The doctor agreed to join Steve for dinner. He was glad he had taken the trouble to dress in his new Primark best. Alison Mills was elegantly dressed in a pink-coloured dress that shouted quality and class. They passed the evening in small talk pleasantly, enjoying the food and touching on their personal lives where it was appropriate. Steve asked why the doctor was working at the care home.

"My mother died a few years ago. She was staying at The View and they looked after her right up till the end. I thought it would be nice to give something

183

back, so I volunteered and now I do one or two Saturdays a month. Nothing official. I just help out with any medical queries. There's not much to do but the staff and the residents like to have a doctor in the place, and I like hearing the old folks' stories."

Steve explained about his current issues with the police and that he was only here to meet Bert to learn about an old gun. He explained about Hector and talked about his two colleagues. "So, in six months or so, I'll be looking for my third career. No idea what I'll do but something always crops up."

Steve enjoyed the evening and talking to Alison Mills. He now knew she was single, had no current boyfriend or serious other, she lived in Kensington and was a consultant with her own private medical practice. Steve offered to pay the total bill the waiter had delicately placed on the table by Steve. Alison smiled sweetly and said with a cheeky grin, "Thank you but my mother told me not to accept gifts from strangers. Let me pay for mine. Please?" Reluctantly, Steve agreed. He felt he couldn't refuse this woman anything. He felt like an adolescent schoolboy.

As they finished their coffee, Steve thought this doctor was someone he wanted to get to know better.

They stood opposite each other in the foyer of the hotel. Alison fished inside her handbag and produced her business card and handed it to Steve. "You gave me yours so it's only fair I give you mine," she said with a smile.

Steve took it willingly. "Maybe I could call you. We could have dinner in London one evening?"

"Yes. I'd like that. My mobile number is on the back." The doctor leaned forwards and pecked the DCI on the cheek. She set off up the grand staircase that led to the bedrooms. Halfway up, she stopped and turned, looking down at Steve. "Oh! I almost forgot. I asked Bert that question about the storeman at the army camp. He couldn't remember his name but apparently everybody called him Nobby; hope that helps." With a wave and a charming smile, she turned back and carried on climbing the staircase.

The DCI wouldn't get much sleep tonight. This piece of information given so casually by Alison Mills would bring the DCI even closer to the killer, but he didn't know it yet.

Chapter Twenty-Nine

Sunday, 19 April

Steve was down early for his breakfast hoping to meet the good doctor again.

He was disappointed.

Sunday's drive back was uneventful. Steve's head was full of the case and, he admitted, Alison Mills. There was something eating away at his subconscious. No matter how hard he concentrated, it wouldn't come to him. He worried away at the problem.

He decided to return the pool car early and visit the office. It was a good place to think.

When he got to the corridor on the second floor of New Scotland Yard, he noticed the office door was ajar. Cautiously, he approached the office and heard voices inside. He recognised them as Twiggy and the Cap.

"What are you two doing here on a Sunday?"

"Well," said Twiggy, "my yoga class was cancelled and I'd nothing better to do," she lied with a smile on her face. The DCI didn't take the bait.

"No really, the Cap and I've been going over the nine names from the list. Neither of us could let it go so we agreed to try and impress our boss and solve the case before he came in." That cheeky Twiggy grin again. "But what're you doing here?"

"I'm not sure. There's something I learned yesterday but I just can't get to it. I thought a peaceful afternoon in the office might bring it to the surface. But now that I find you two here, I suppose that idea's out of the window."

"Twiggy and I've been through the nine names. It's not good news."

"Well, I suppose as we're all here, we might as well get to it. What've you got?"

"Twiggy, you better start. Boss, before she starts, this is nothing to do with me."

"Intriguing; let's hear it, Twiggy. They say confession's good for the soul and it is a Sunday."

Twiggy put on what she thought was her most pious expression. "Well, you remember you asked me to follow up on the military history of our nine suspects but that balloon at the MOD wasn't helpful?"

"Yes."

"Well, I got my friend Tom to hack into the MOD personnel database." Twiggy was prepared to have the world come down on her. When the DCI just sat and stared, she rushed on, "Steve, it was the only way to get ahead of this. Tom says he didn't leave any footprints and no one will ever know."

"Twiggy. You continue to amaze me. Full marks for initiative but you haven't half taken a chance."

"Yeah, well. Who dares wins, eh, sir?" That cheeky smile again.

The Cap butted in, "With Twiggy's military information on our nine names sorted, it was easy for me to track them down as civilians. Like I said, Steve, it's not good."

"Let's hear it."

"Of the nine, four are dead, all-natural causes. That leaves five."

Twiggy took over. "None of the nine were ever in the military. Of the five still alive, two live abroad and one's in a care home suffering from dementia."

The Cap now took over. It was the double act in operation again. Just like in the beginning. Steve was impressed with his team. "One lives in Scotland and runs a fish farm. He doesn't have a record, not even a speeding ticket. Seems to have a successful business and hasn't been to London for years."

Twiggy was back. "The last guy owns a string of downmarket seaside boarding houses. Seems he's almost bust. We were told he has a lot of debts and has taken to the bottle. He doesn't seem like a candidate for a shooter."

"Sorry, Steve, that's it, another dead end. All nine accounted for and, we think, ruled out."

"You're sure the last guy couldn't be our killer?"

"Well, anything's possible. But a down at heel drunk doesn't look likely. I think you need a steady hand to take the shots our man's making." Twiggy nodded.

"Besides, he hasn't any military training."

"Good point, Cap. Not sure where we are but good work, you two. We seem to be good at finding dead ends just now. Let's look at it fresh in the morning."

186

All three were slightly deflated as they left and went their separate ways.

Sunday at 9pm, it all changed. In a subconscious moment, something flashed into the DCI's brain. He had a moment of clarity when everything made sense and he could join the dots. The DCI had the answer. He'd found the piece of the puzzle his subconscious had been trying to force him to accept. He knew the identity of the killer.

Chapter Thirty

Monday, 20 April

It was after 10 o'clock when the DCI arrived at the office. The Cap and Twiggy were trying hard to look busy. To Steve's eyes, they were failing. After the usual pleasantries, Steve sat at his desk and studied his colleagues. He sat for a few minutes in silence.

"Twiggy, do you have that knocked off database Tom got for you? The one with army personnel records?"

"Yes."

"Check and see whether a Private Arthur Clark was on strength at the Small Arms School, Hythe, in 1942. If he was, what was his date of birth?"

"OK. Any reason?"

"No. Not now. Just get the information." Steve was on his feet ready to leave the office. "Cap, can you get us coffees? I'm off up to the eleventh floor. Should be back in a few minutes." Twiggy and the Cap looked at each other. The DCI obviously had a bee in his bonnet this morning. Both detectives wondered what was happening. Their boss seemed unusually serious.

When he returned, Steve took his coffee to his desk instead of his normal position around the table with his team. His team knew something was up. But what?

"Can you listen up please?" Steve's tone was firm and sharp. Even official. It sounded as though an important announcement was about to be made.

"I want to talk us through a few details to confirm what we know or think we know. If we get it right, then I think we can identify our killer today. But we can't afford to be wrong. So, bear with me."

Both Twiggy and the Cap sat up, giving Steve their full attention.

"Most of this you already know. If we strip out all the financial smokescreen stuff, we're left with two murders. We know both victims were shot from long range and that the killer doesn't appear to be using conventional bullets. We have a witness statement from the first murder and CCTV from the second that say the killer had three large suitcases or cases at the kill sites. The witness at the first kill site said he saw a uniformed police sergeant on the day before and again on the same day of the first murder. But was this our killer and was he a cop?" Steve paused to make sure his colleagues were listening.

"He certainly wore a police sergeant's uniform." Steve stopped again but this time for effect. "I hope we all agree so far?" Without waiting for confirmation, he carried on, "We assumed the killer had to be an ex-client of TPPP. We have a list of nine potential suspects we extracted from the client list Twiggy found on one of the laptops. Both victims were partners in TPPP and seem to have been involved in a rip-off scheme that took people's money with no intention of ever paying it back. Are we still agreed so far?" This time, Steve waited.

Both nodded. "Yes, I think that sums things up," said the Cap, wondering where Steve was going by re-hashing old news. Twiggy just listened.

"You remember I visited Major Hector Simms at the War Museum. Hector could suggest only one gun that might have the range to have been used in our murders, but it was WW2 vintage and he said it was scrapped early on. The assumption was it was because the thing didn't work. Hector gave me a contact who was at the trials of this gun in 1943. I went to see him over the weekend." The DCI was being deliberately slow in telling his story.

"Well, it turns out that the gun did work and did fire accurately over long distances. It seems it was too heavy to be used as a sniper rifle and that's the only reason it was scrapped. My old guy told me it was accurate and the only reason it was scrapped was that it had to be transported in three parts because it was so heavy."

Steve stopped again but this time to let this new information sink in.

"Remember we have evidence that three large cases were involved at each kill site." Silence as the significance seeped in.

"Are you saying this is the murder weapon? An old WW2 gun?" Twiggy was taken aback.

"Hear me out." Steve sipped his now cold coffee. "There were three prototypes of the weapon delivered to Hythe in 1942. Two were definitely destroyed during 1943 but the third is unaccounted for. It turns out they only experimented with two of the weapons and the third was a spare. According to my old guy, it was never even taken out of its box. We don't know what happened to this third gun, but I'm prepared to bet it's our murder weapon."

The Cap sat back and took a deep breath. "Steve, that's one gigantic leap. I see where you get it from and sure, we have coincidences with the three boxes, but how do we prove it?"

"All in good time." The DCI was smiling just a bit. "Twiggy, did you get the info from the MOD file?"

"Arthur Clark, Private, born 25 February 1922. Served in the Kent Regiment from 1940 till 1946. Never rose higher than Private. He had what they called a spotted record, but just an ordinary conscripted bloke."

"Thanks, Twiggy. There's a suggestion that this Private Clark was known as a bit of a wide boy. He was said to have been into the black market and shady deals. Remember, it was wartime." Steve again paused. "Suppose he took the third gun? He had it in his stores. No one went near it. I was told he lived off camp and drove a Ford open-back lorry. He could easily have had it away. My contact at the care home said it would have fetched a fair price in scrap but what if he couldn't sell it? Selling a gun to a private scrapyard in wartime maybe wasn't too easy. But if he didn't scrap it, maybe he kept it?"

Twiggy raised a hand from the table to catch Steve's attention. "Suppose all this is true. Where does it take us? There's a lot of speculation in what you're saying."

"Just bear with me. It'll become clear. I want you both to follow and hopefully confirm my logic."

Steve paused and composed himself. "We've been assuming the killer is on our list of 35 and then 9. Correct?" He paused for confirmation. Nods all around. "Suppose a name on our list is the reason for the killings but that name is not our actual killer?" Again, a pause. The Cap and Twiggy felt like school kids hearing a story.

"The old chap I saw at the weekend couldn't remember the name of the storeman. All he remembered was that he was called Nobby, as a nickname. If our storeman called Nobby did steal the weapon and didn't or couldn't get rid of it, then it stands to reason he and his family must still have it or at least know what happened to it." Another pause. "Do we agree?"

"I suppose so."

"Twiggy, get the list of 35 names out. Is there a Mr Arthur Clark on the list?"

Twiggy set to searching her papers until she found the list. She scanned it.

"Yes. He was one of the serial investors. In 2007, he reinvested his entire pot of £194,000. According to the list, he didn't get any of it back."

"Did he live in Walthamstow?"

"Yes." Twiggy knew Steve didn't have a copy of the list. This was getting interesting. "But how did you know?"

"You said the list gave the ages of the investors. When this Mr Clark reinvested in 2007, how old was he?"

Twiggy jotted down some numbers. "He's shown as being 85 years old."

"So, he was born in 1922?"

"Is it likely this Arthur Clark, the ripped off investor, could be the same Arthur Clark we think nicked the gun in 1943?" The Cap was thinking hard but said nothing.

"You have to admit it's possible. Agreed?"

Steve moved on. "In the army, no matter what your Christian name is, if your surname is Clark, you automatically get Nobby from all your mates. Our storeman at Hythe was called Nobby and there was one Private Arthur Clark stationed there in 1943. I was at Somerset House this morning. That's why I was a bit late. Arthur Clark, born 25 February 1922. Died 25 December 2009. He married Ethel Burton on 11 August 1955. They had one son, born 6 January 1958. The boy was called Malcolm." There was a stunned silence in the room. The atmosphere was electric. No one spoke.

"When I went out just now, I went to HR on the 11th floor. I made up a story about doing something for the commander's birthday. After a lot of nudge nudge, wink wink, Miss Hawkins confirmed that Commander Malcolm Clark was born 6 January 1958. There's no doubt that our commander is the son of Private Nobby Clark late, of the Kent Regiment. The Private Clark who lost a small fortune to a scam run by two people who are now dead and the same Private Clark who probably nicked the only gun capable of firing at long ranges."

The room was silent. No one spoke and there was not much breathing going on either. Eventually, Steve started again, "On 25 December 2009, Mr Arthur Clark committed suicide by hanging himself. The coroner's inquest confirmed he left a note. It said he'd lost all his money and couldn't provide for his family. His wife died three months later on 1 March 2010."

Steve looked at his officers. "So, there you have it. What I'm thinking is our Malcolm Clark has the weapon from 1943 that his father probably stole but couldn't sell. That's how it survived. I'm betting something happened recently that reminded our Clark of his father's suicide and the reasons for it. And there's another thing. I've been wondering why the commander gave us this case and effectively told us to do nothing with it. If he's our killer, that might explain it." Steve waited to see if either of his colleagues had anything to add.

They didn't.

"If we're right and the son of Private Arthur Clark is in fact our murderer, it starts to make sense. He didn't think the three of us, with only months left in the police, would be bothered to look into it. He'd planned to get away with murder."

The Cap sighed heavily. "It all fits. The motive, the weapon, the opportunity. No one could have seen this. The commander must've thought he'd get away with it and be able to control the investigation. The perfect crime. But why wait so long?"

"That's something we'll have to ask."

"Boss, are we really saying that a police commander is a serial killer?"

"Looks that way, Twiggy. I think we've enough to push this up to higher authority and pull the commander in for questioning. But…it's all circumstantial." Steve broke off. "Are we agreed it's at least possible? I value your input and opinions."

"Steve, what you've pulled together looks convincing. If you're right, then we've solved it. If you're wrong, then we're out on our ear anyway."

"I agree with the Cap. We've nothing to lose."

"OK. There's one slight problem. He's signed out on a week's leave and we still have Peter Randall out there. If we're right, then Randall's his next target." You could feel the expectation in the room.

"I'd prefer it if we could finish this off ourselves. Get definite proof that Commander Clark is our killer. The only way is to catch him in the act." Everyone agreed.

"If Clark's on a week's leave, then the chances are he's going to go after Randall in the next few days. He could even be setting up the weapon now. We'd better get over to 'The Pines' and warn Randall. Cap get us a pool car double quick. Twiggy, call Randall and tell him we're coming over and not to go outside under any circumstances. That gun can fire from four miles."

With a flurry of activity, all three detectives were gone.

It was 11.18 when they left the police garage.

Chapter Thirty-One

Monday, 20 April

As the DCI and his team were on their way from Scotland Yard, a police sergeant drove up to the security barrier in Esher. It was 11.47. This time, he didn't get out of the car. He noted the CCTV cameras and reminded himself to take the tapes after he had killed the guard.

"You back again?" The guard ambled out of his hut.

"Yes, I have to revisit some sites. It seems we missed something first time. Sorry to be a pest but I have to get around eight different places today. Can you open the gate, I'll only be a few minutes?"

Reluctantly, the guard opened the gate and the killer was inside. He drove straight to 'The Pines'.

11.53. The killer rang the front doorbell of 'The Pines'. The same maid answered and again showed the police sergeant into the vast circular hallway. "I wonder if I might have a word with Mr Randall? Nothing too important but I do need to speak to him."

"I'm sorry, Mr Randall's in his study and never sees anyone while he's working."

"Are there any other people in the house or anyone in the gardens?"

"No, sir, only me and Mr Randall."

"Is Mr Randall working from his study down that corridor?" The sergeant pointed. He just needed to check. It was all in the planning.

"Yes, sir. Just down there, but like I said, he won't see anybody."

"I think Mr Randall will see me when he hears why I'm here."

"Well, maybe, sir, but as—"

11.59. The unnamed maid lay dead in the middle of the circular hallway. The killer had strangled her just as he had strangled Mrs Boyd those few weeks earlier when all this had begun. He felt the same revulsion just as he had before. For a second, he stood, unable to move, hit by the realisation he had taken yet another life. More collateral damage.

The killer silently walked down the corridor that led to the study of Peter Randall. Once he had killed this greedy excuse for a human being, his revenge would be complete. He felt the excitement rising.

12.03. The killer stood outside the only door that opened from the corridor. Behind this door was his target. He took out a revolver. It was the one his father had said he'd 'found' during his time in the army. The killer dwelt on this, fondly remembering his father. Under his breath, he murmured, "Almost finished now, Dad."

12.07. The killer opened the door and stood inside. He saw a handsome well-groomed man sitting behind an expensive-looking desk. He seemed to be typing on the keyboard of a computer. At first, the handsome guy didn't notice he had company.

"Good afternoon, Mr Randall."

"What! Who the hell are you! What'd you want! Get the hell out of here!" He reached for the internal telephone on his desk and dialled.

"Put the phone down, nobody's coming."

For the first time, Peter Randall saw the gun.

11.27. Steve and his team were racing across London with blues and twos blazing. Twiggy said she was getting no reply from Randall. The call was going straight to the answer phone. "That's no problem maybe. Remember, we were told he spent all day locked away in his study. Maybe he doesn't take calls. Let's hope so."

12.05. The three detectives arrived at the barrier of the estate where Peter Randall lived. The Cap was driving and braked sharply, just avoiding hitting the gate. The guard almost ran from his office. "What's going on? One of your lot went in over 20 minutes ago. Said he'd only be a couple of minutes. I'm ready to call in the mobile patrol to get him out. It's more—"

"What do you mean?" demanded the DCI.

"One of your lot. The same sergeant that was here the other day."

The DCI looked at his colleagues. "He's here?" Steve got out of the car. "Do you have a key for Mr Randall's house?"

"Yes. I have keys for all the houses, but I'm not allowed—"

Steve cut him off. "Look, this is official police business." He produced his warrant card. Anger and frustration were mixing together in Steve. This by the book, lookalike American cop was annoying him. "There's a serious incident going on at 'The Pines' and I want the keys and I want them now." With a final shout— "Do you understand?"

Whether the guard understood or not, he was scared enough to get the keys and hand them over. Steve got back in the front seat of the car.

From the inside of the car, he shouted, "Now open the gates and phone 999. Tell them DCI Burt needs backup here now. Have you got that? And tell them to send armed response." Before the guard could reply, the Cap had the car in gear and was moving. He almost caught the gates in his hurry to be off. He'd set the rear wheels spinning, leaving black marks on the road behind the car.

12.09. The Cap drew up outside 'The Pines'. All three detectives got out and headed for the front door. Steve tried the handle, but it was locked. He tried various keys from the bunch the guard had handed him. He found one that fitted. Carefully, he eased the door open. There was no sound from inside the house. He pushed the door further and saw the body of the maid lying more or less in the centre of the circle. The thought that it looked like some kind of ritual killing flashed through Steve's mind. In a barely audible whisper, he said, "Twiggy, you stay out here. The Cap and I'll go in."

"You're leaving me out here because I'm a woman?" Twiggy wasn't happy.

"Twiggy, this isn't the time." Still in his forced whisper and with just a bit of annoyance. "I need you here in case somebody tries to leave around the side of the house or through the front door. Now don't argue."

Leaving a peeved detective constable behind, the two detectives crossed the threshold. Steve deliberately left the door ajar for the backup team he hoped was on its way. The house was silent. They remembered the study was to the back of the house. The Cap pointed to a corridor and copying Steve's whisper, said, "I think it's probably down there." Both officers advanced.

12.14. From outside what he hoped was the study, Steve slowly pulled the handle of the door down and gently pushed. He heard voices and opened the door further. He saw Peter Randall still alive and sitting at a desk. His face was covered in blood. He also saw Malcolm Clark standing behind Randall, holding what looked like an army issue revolver.

Malcolm saw the door open and the two detectives entering. Steve took the lead and the Cap held back.

"Well, well, look who's here. I didn't expect to see you here. What're you doing? Come to see the grand finale?" The commander looked somehow different to Steve. His eyes were wild and his speech was more aggressive than Steve had ever heard. "It'll make no difference you being here. This is the end anyway. I thought I might get away with it if I could live with myself when it was all finished. You see, I had it all planned." The commander was talking fast but seemed somehow tired. His eyes were bulging and his upper lip was wet with sweat. It was almost as though he were talking to himself.

"Kill this piece of garbage, take the CCTV from the house, kill that overweight cop-lookalike of a guard, take his CCTV and be on my way. All done. Neat and tidy. No witnesses, no forensics. No clues." The commander shook his head.

"But here you are. Ready to spoil everything. Well, Detective Chief Inspector Burt, I can't allow that." The commander gave a sigh and shook his shoulders. "This scum's been begging for his life ever since I got here. You should hear the garbage he's been spouting. He thinks he's a victim." The commander gave a loud sound that was supposed to be a laugh but was more like a cry.

Peter Randall was a frightened man. "Please. Take anything you want, money, this house even, only don't hurt me," he screamed. There was a smell in the room. Steve thought the victim had soiled himself.

"Inspector do something. This mad man wants to kill me. I've done nothing wrong. My wife and my kids. Oh! Please. Stop him!" The third name on the list was screaming and in floods of tears.

"Shut up," the commander screamed. "If you say another word, I'll kill you slowly. Stay quiet and it'll be quick. But your death is coming." It was as though the commander were taunting his victim. Steve had never seen Malcolm Clark like this; clearly, he was ill.

Steve took in the scene. It was time to get involved. "Why, Malcolm; you've killed four people but for what?" Steve remembered from a course he'd been on that if you could get a perpetrator to talk, it was possible to defuse the situation.

The commander flew into a rage. Pointing the gun at Steve, he launched into a demented rage, shouting, "For what? For what? You're asking for what? I'll tell you. Revenge. Justice. The kind of justice the courts don't understand." The commander's eyes were wide and spit was coming from his mouth. "This turd here and his mates robbed old folks out of their pensions and life savings. You ask, 'For what?'" The killer was getting more excited and louder. He seemed to be out of control. "For what? So that they could have more money than anybody else. So that they could have flash cars, overseas holidays, villas in the sun and mansions like this to rattle around in. Kids at expensive private schools. They wanted it all but who paid for it?" Without waiting, Malcolm carried on but he was getting louder and crazier by the second.

"I'll tell you. My dad and people like him. My dad paid for this house and all the other things this piece of crap thinks he needs." Tears began to appear in the commander's eyes.

"When my dad topped himself and I learned why, I knew then all those years ago, I'd have to do something." Malcolm calmed down and started to speak in a softer voice. "My old man was a great guy. Not always straight but no one got the better of him. If he'd been younger, he would've had these guys up against the wall and beaten them until they gave him his money back, and then some." Malcolm was almost talking to himself. He appeared calmer. "He worked right up till he was in his late 80s. He dealt in anything. He even had a big second-hand car lot on the Mile End Road. He knew how to deal. Then along came these sharks. Bloody vultures. My mum told me after Dad's funeral. Some smooth-talking sales guy promising the earth if only he would put his money into their property company. What they didn't say was when things went tits up, it was sod you, we're all right."

The commander was slowly working himself up again. "My father was robbed of his nest egg and his will to live. I swore after my mum died that I'd get the scumbags." The commander was clearly not a well man. Steve thought he must be having some form of mental breakdown. But then he remembered the precision of the first two killings. This was no madman but a coldblooded killer. Then, with a sudden flash, the commander looked at Steve as he raised the revolver to Peter Randall's head. "This one was the worst. I saved him till last. It's the feeling of getting even. You see, I'm the avenging angel. I wanted this piece of human muck to know what was coming. To be scared. Retribution. Justice. Payback. Revenge. Everything I want and the death he deserves. The first two I got cleanly from long range, but this coward doesn't leave this place. So, I had to come in. It's more satisfying than I thought seeing him squirm and beg."

As the commander looked like he might pull the trigger, Peter Randall—who had been sitting silent and lifeless more or less since the DCI had arrived—cried out, "For Christ's sake, do something. He's a madman!" This cry was directed at Steve, but it was the commander who answered.

"Your Christ isn't going to help you now."

"Please. I have a wife. Children. For pity's sake, think of them." The victim was crying and pleading again.

The commander got very close to Randall's face. His face was red with rage. "And I had a family. A father, a mother. You took them from me. Ruined my life by your greed."

12.29. Peter Randall died. The shot fired at point-blank range took the top part of his skull off and deposited it in pieces on the French doors leading out to the garden.

There was nothing Steve or the Cap could have done.

The commander now pointed the revolver at Steve, but Steve got in first with a question in an attempt to divert the attention of this killer he'd once respected and admired. Holding up his arms in surrender— "How did you get the big gun, Malcolm?"

Malcolm was once again angry but more under control. "It's not a gun. It's a weapon!" he bellowed. "It's a fine piece of engineering. It said so in the instruction manual." Malcolm paused and lowered the gun slightly. His eyes were out of focus. "My dad used to tell me stories about his time in the army. One day he said he had a great secret tucked away in his lock up. He said it was a killing machine that couldn't miss." Malcolm sat down on the chair in front of the desk. The almost headless body of Peter Randall was slumped in the big chair behind the desk. The revolver dropped a bit more.

"When I was clearing Dad's things out after he and Mum died, I found a box in his lock up. It was the killing machine he'd told me about years before. I don't know when it happened, but I knew I had to avenge him. The thought must have come slowly because I knew there was poetic justice in killing the scum that had killed my dad with the weapon my dad had nicked from the army all those years ago. It would be like he was getting his own revenge. I found vengeance and revenge to be slow-burning emotions, certainly in me."

"Why wait so long before taking this vengeance and revenge? It's over ten years since your father died."

Steve was feeling some sympathy for Malcolm Clark. Maybe he had flipped? Maybe he was mentally ill? If he was, he was still a mentally ill man with a gun in his hand. The same gun that was still just about pointed at the DCI. He had to humour his old boss to keep him calm. Steve noticed the Cap had started edging around the outside of the room, keeping hard against the wall.

Malcolm was calm and seemed happy to tell his story.

"I don't know. I kept the machine. Left it untouched in the lock up. I suppose I knew one day I'd use it. One day I'd get even for my dad. I think it was last month when I visited my parents' grave. Something inside me just snapped, I suppose. I got really angry inside. I realised these crooks had taken my parents from me. It seemed logical to let their families know what it feels like. My dad had a few good comfortable years left in him. He didn't have to top himself and wouldn't have if these crooks had left him alone. I realised I owed my dad a lot, so I had to avenge him. You do see that, Steve?" The commander was rambling. Not a good sign but the DCI had to keep him talking.

"Yes, Malcolm. I see that."

"I used Dad's old van he kept in the lock up. The weapon is a big bugger, but I got it to fit into three suitcases. I'd practiced with it a few times years ago in Epping Forest. Only the odd Sunday or two each year. I didn't want to be seen. Once I understood the directing computer, it was easy to use. The box of tricks turned the weapon into the killing machine. The science was way ahead of its time. Today, we'd call it a computer and take what it could do for granted. But back in the war years, it must have been a miracle."

"How did you get the liquid nitrogen?"

"Easy. A lab tech in St Bart's Hospital got it for me. My dad had lifted one of the moulds to make the water shell so even that was in the box. The charge was the hardest but the Internet's a great thing."

The commander almost looked as though he might fall asleep. His eyes were heavy and moist. Telling his story seemed to have exhausted him. His chin was resting on his chest. The Cap, who had been moving slowly into the room by hugging the wall, now moved more quickly but quietly to get nearer the back of the desk to try and take the commander down.

"Stop right there, sergeant." The commander was maybe exhausted, but he wasn't asleep. "Move back to your boss. I want both of you where I can see you."

Steve had taken a few small steps nearer the commander.

"Where's the killing machine now, Malcolm?"

"It's in the back of my dad's van in his lock up in Walthamstow." The commander looked defeated. His eyes were still wide and wild, but he seemed calmer. "I wanted to use it on this one." He pointed with his revolver at the almost headless corpse of Peter Randall. "If I had, you'd never have found me. But there it is. We can't undo things, can we, Steve?"

Steve had what he wanted. He had the evidence, the motive, the proof and the weapon. It was time to bring this to an end. "Come on, Malcolm. Give me the gun. You've avenged your father. Let's have no more killing. Eh!" Steve took a pace towards the commander.

"You must think I'm simple. Granted I am probably a bit nuts but I'm not stupid. I've seen this on those TV shows. You talk me out of shooting anyone else. Probably you. I hand over the gun. I start crying, saying I'm sorry, and you lead me off into the sunset. Everybody keeps on living. Well, not this time, my friend. The killing only stops when I say it does."

Before Steve could say anything or take another step forward, a uniformed inspector appeared in the doorway to the study.

"We had a call for back—"

12.47. Commander Malcolm Clark died by his own hand. He put the revolver into his mouth and pulled the trigger. His brain matter mixed instantly with that of his last victim. Both brains' shards merged onto the glass of the French doors and formed a surreal abstract shape, slowly sliding down the glass.

Twiggy appeared at the door and stepped inside. She looked around and ran out to be violently sick on the front lawn of 'The Pines'.

Steve and the Cap were in shock. They stood motionless for a long time in silence. Eventually, the DCI recovered and shook himself. There were procedures to be followed. He was still the SIO.

Steve asked the uniformed inspector to sort out the after-incident teams. The inspector didn't look too happy. He might have wanted to follow Twiggy outside but bravely swallowed whatever was trying to escape from his throat.

"Yes, sir. Forensics, scene of crime, pathologist and undertaker."

"That's it. Keep everyone out of here until scene of crime and forensics are done. Understand?" The inspector nodded. Steve also made sure the inspector cordoned off the house and grounds. He said he wanted a family liaison officer to be sent for. Mrs Randall and her daughters didn't need to see this and would need support. Steve handed his card to the inspector and said he and his DS would make their statements back at the office.

Twiggy was looking a bit pale and was leaning her back against the wall of 'The Pines'. "Bloody hell. I don't want to see that again. It was horrible." She had recovered from the initial shock, but only just.

As the three detectives left the scene in their pool car, the Cap tried humour to lift the mood. "We won't be short of anything to do for a while. The paperwork on this will last for months. We'll still be at it when they kick us out."

This only got a grunt from Steve and a "phew" from Twiggy.

12.59. Only 50 minutes after entering the upmarket Esher estate, three people were dead and an impossible case had been solved. None of the three detectives felt like celebrating.

Chapter Thirty-Two

Monday, 26 April

The three drove through the gate and left the guard behind. He would never know how lucky he'd been. If things had gone differently, he would now be dead.

The atmosphere in the car was solemn. The Cap, driving again, tried to lighten the mood. "Seriously though, the paperwork on this'll take forever and I bet we have to fill everything out in triplicate. We could really still be at it when we get the boot." He smiled at his own joke. Steve just grunted again, although he suspected the Cap was right.

From the backseat, Twiggy just sighed. "At least it'll only be paper. We won't have to deal with bits of brain." She still didn't feel fully recovered.

The Cap was right about the paperwork. The three gave their statements separately when they got back. These were only initial summaries. Their full and official comments would come later.

Chapter Thirty-Three

After Monday, 26 April

There seemed a lot of activity that didn't appear to be joined up somehow. Steve felt all at sea. He wasn't sure what he was supposed to do. After the excitement of the chase, he seemed to be at every senior officer's beck and call. Answering questions and explaining himself. He was fed up recreating the events of Commander Clark's suicide. Suddenly, he felt adrift again. Not fully in control of his own destiny. He was becoming reactive to events.

The Metropolitan Police were quick to convene an inquiry. Three days after the death of Commander Malcolm Clark, Steve, the Cap and Twiggy gave their evidence and official statements to the internal inquiry.

Steve phoned Alison Mills and cancelled their dinner date, explaining that he would call and rearrange an evening once things settled down. He told her a little of the events over the previous few days.

He phoned Major Hector Simms. He thanked him for his help and told him what he could about the conclusion of the case and how the Major's information had helped solve it. They agreed to meet up for dinner and 'a jolly good chin wag' within the next few weeks. Steve asked if the Museum might like to have the Mk 1 LRSR killing machine? The Major thought it a good idea but would have to seek higher authority before accepting what was now a murder weapon.

The requests for more detailed explanations of events never seemed to end. Then, about a week later, everything stopped. There was silence. No meetings. No interrogations. No requests for filled out forms. Just silence from above.

The three detectives were in their office sitting around the square table made up of three separate tables with nothing to do except drink their coffee. To fill in time, the Cap asked Steve, "How did you make the connection between the killings and Malcolm Clark? It seemed to come from nowhere."

Steve allowed his mind to go back. "I suppose it did. From the witness statement at the first shooting, our man, if he was our man, was wearing a copper's uniform. Didn't mean he was a cop, but our witness was sure he was. So, I thought of a police connection. The laptop from our second victim was nicked from my desk. Only somebody with access could've taken it. Again, a cop. Then I learned the only machine that Major Hector, and indeed anyone, thought might be capable of making the two long-range shots could have been stolen years ago from the army by a guy called Nobby. Like I said, in the army almost everyone called Nobby was a Clark. That put the surname Clark in the frame. So, I started to think about cops called Clark who work in this building and could have stolen the laptop from the office. Then the name Clark was on the list of TPPP clients and one of them had seriously been ripped off. But he was dead. Then I was curious as to why we were put together as a team and given a high-profile murder case. None of us had worked murder before. We were expendable as far as the Force was concerned. Washed up. Our careers finished. So why give us the case unless we were certain to fail? The guy who gave us the first case was Malcolm Clark with instructions to effectively do nothing. There was the Clark connection again." Steve paused to think.

"So, we had a possible weapon stolen by an Arthur Clark in 1943. From Births and Deaths, we saw this Arthur Clark had a son christened Malcolm born 6 January 1958. Miss Hawkins confirmed our Commander Clark was also born on 6 January 1958. Malcolm Clark lived in Walthamstow when I first worked for him. Clark senior's address on the TPPP list was Walthamstow. Our Commander Clark was Arthur Clark's son."

"Go on, your mind must have worked overtime to figure this out." Twiggy was full of admiration for her DCI.

"Clark senior died by committing suicide after the three charlatans at TPPP effectively stole his money. I thought about a father and son connection. That led to motive. Add the fact that the weapon was almost fool-proof and didn't need a marksman to fire it then you come to the conclusion anyone could have fired the shots. I never knew Malcolm Clark as a great shot. He was clever. We all thought we were looking for a great marksman. We never thought the weapon more or less locked onto the victims by itself and couldn't miss. He would have gotten away with it without you two giving me a kick up the bum and forcing me to take the case seriously. So there you have it. We all three solved an impossible multiple murder. Six people dead in the space of 20 days and five murders solved at the same time." The DCI pondered. "I wonder if that's a record?"

"Even if it's not, it's still great work, boss. At least we're leaving with our heads held high. I'm not sure the murder squad with all their teams couldn't have done a better job. Come on. Let's go to the pub. We haven't celebrated and I think it's time our DCI had a pint. I'll buy the first of many rounds!" Twiggy stood up and they all went to the other office.

Chief Inspector Steven Burt was summoned to the office of the Assistant Chief Constable (Admin) Metropolitan Police exactly 11 days after the death of the commander. He was smartly dressed and had forsaken Primark for Moss Bros. He had a lady to impress but not the one who had summoned him. When he entered the large and well-furnished room on the 12th floor, he was greeted by the ACC seated at her large uncluttered desk and to her left, the Chief Superintendent from Human Resources. To her right stood a man Steve didn't know but was dressed in civilian clothes. Steve had spoken to the ACC a few times and remembered that he liked her.

He wasn't invited to sit. He stood more or less to attention. Without any preamble, the ACC started reading from a pre-prepared script. "DCI Steven Burt, you have been called here today to be commended on your work in the Clark case. You exhibited exceptional leadership skills and in solving five murders and a suicide, you have proven yourself to be an outstanding police officer. On behalf of the police service, we wish to thank you for your discretion in the handling of the fallout from what could have been a very unfortunate public relations crisis. Further, your resolve and tenacity in seeing the case through showed outstanding deductive skills. You are to be congratulated on the leadership of your team and upholding the high standards of the police service." The ACC stopped talking.

She now looked up at Steve who was still almost standing to attention. The ACC gave Steve a pleasant smile. "Sit down, Steve. That's the formal bit on the record." She pointed to a high-backed chair to the side of her desk.

The ACC was a largish lady of about fifty. Steve thought maybe fifty-five. Her uniform was tailored to try and disguise some of her bulk. "We've been looking into Malcolm Clark. It's obvious he had some sort of mental breakdown. We think he created your department not as a help to you, but so that he could put someone in charge who wouldn't pursue his crimes. We think he thought all three of you were all washed up and would just put in your six months extension without doing anything. I think it's to your credit that you carried on and saw this through."

The ACC was playing with her pen. She seemed to have more to say. The DCI sat in silence with his hands on his lap.

"Of course, there'll be no trial so no media coverage. A senior police officer having a mental breakdown and running amuck isn't good publicity."

The ACC seemed to come to a decision that pleased her. "So, Steve, your record has been cleaned up. No mention of your recent disciplinary problems will be in your file. You're also reinstated fully back to duty and you keep your DCI rank. We both know the establishment of Special Resolutions as a department was a sham to satisfy our budget demands?"

Steve nodded.

"Well, we're formally establishing your department just as Malcolm Clark set it up. He did it for the wrong reasons but it's a good idea. You'll stay in charge of the Special Resolutions Unit on a permanent basis. You'll sit in on major crime reviews and select the cases you want to pursue. You'll have access to additional resources as you need them. You'll also spearhead our outside requests. When any Force asks the Mets to help with a specific serious case, then you'll be first on the scene. We normally get about six a year. Mostly difficult murder cases, so you should be in your element. Is that clear?"

"Yes, Ma'am."

"Chief Superintendent Charles here will draw up your job description and reporting guidelines. How does that sound?"

"Thank you, Ma'am. It sounds fine but what about DS Ishmal and DC Rough?"

"Chief Superintendent Charles here has letters for them confirming their return to permanent staff status." The ACC for the first time acknowledged the head of HR standing next to her.

The Chief Superintendent produced two sealed envelopes and handed them to Steve. "We thought you'd prefer to give them the good news yourself." The voice was still high-pitched and nerdy but somehow softer. The DCI remembered the last time this Chief Superintendent was about to hand him a letter. How things had changed.

"Can I ask a favour, Ma'am?"

"You can ask." The ACC looked a bit sceptical.

"Well, DS Ishmal has explained how his disciplinary and reduction in rank happened. I believe he was, in part, set up. I'd like him reinstated to Inspector. He's been invaluable and has learned his lesson."

The ACC looked at Chief Superintendent Charles. "Steve, we don't think it's a good idea for you to keep your DS and DC going forward."

Steve was about to interrupt when the ACC held up a hand. "Just hear us out. Chief Superintendent Charles, any comments on DS Ishmal?"

"Yes, Ma'am. Of course, we feel he should be recognised for his contribution in solving the case. However, we don't think it's a good idea to reinstate him in his previous rank within CID. It would be easier if he spent, say, a year in uniform, and then was quietly posted back to plainclothes. We have several vacancies for uniformed inspectors. He could be in post as of the first of the month." Looking at the ACC, the head of HR continued, "If you agree, I could arrange something this afternoon, Ma'am?"

"Yes, I think that's a good idea." She didn't consult Steve but gave him a look that said do not comment. "Now, I suppose you want something for DC Rough?" The ACC held up her hand once more before Steve could speak. The ACC turned to her right. "This is Patrick Mallow from the Treasury."

The man in plainclothes walked around the ACC's desk. Steve stood and shook Mr Mallow's hand. "It seems the work you and your team did in getting to the bottom of the financial arrangements of these companies you came across has led to our Financial Crimes Division tracking down millions of pounds in illegal activities. Just for your information, both Squires and Booker were laundering funds for Far Eastern gangs involved in drugs, prostitution, gambling and God knows what else. That bank in Monaco was at the centre of the entire operation. The work you and your team did and the information you passed on has been invaluable. I can also tell you that Interpol is looking into the death of the fourth partner in this TPPP outfit. Once the gang connection was established, it seems possible the death of Mr Philip Du Bois was not accidental. The people in control of San Soto Bank are currently helping with inquiries. So, a good result all round, well done."

"Thank you, sir, but it was mainly down to Miss Rough."

"We thought that was the case, especially when she was making a nuisance of herself with financial crimes."

"Yes, absolutely, she ferreted away at it. Doesn't like to let things beat her. But what do you mean by your Financial Crimes Division?"

"The world of high finance is not always black and white, Steve. We have to be aware that many legitimate organisations, not just organised crime, are always finding new ways to hide their earnings. We can't always be one step ahead. We usually get a sniff or a rumour of something and then financial crimes has to start their detective work. It's not glamorous but it's vital work and it's hard. The work of financial crimes has been responsible for bringing some of Europe's worst crime lords to justice. The Treasury holds a watching brief over the Met's financial section. You could say we run it and the head of department reports to me, not a senior police officer. Some of the people working downstairs now are in fact civil servants."

Steve was taken slightly aback. He had no idea the government had any control, except the obvious, over police matters. "Well, Mr Mallow, that's all very interesting, but why are you telling me?"

The ACC spoke up, "The Treasury has requested that DC Rough be transferred to them. The work you and your team did has impressed everyone who counts around here. You said DC Rough had been key to sifting the data. Her work on the files she passed over was exceptional considering she's had no formal training. We think she would be an asset to financial crimes. As Mr Mallow has said, we've already made progress into the money laundering she picked up on, going back to 2006, plus there's the ongoing issue of her weight. Although you have a letter for her confirming her return to police duty, we feel she still has issues. Who knows where her weight will finish up. We could be back considering her for a medical discharge in a few months' time."

Mr Mallow scratched the top of his balding head and carried on, "We think she might be better suited to working for the government. We're proposing to transfer her after a period of intense training to the Treasury as a senior investigative officer. She'd work from here with financial crimes and carry the rank of Inspector. The training she'll get will be second to none. If she works at it—and from what I've heard, I'm sure she will—then with time she could easily become one of the top 100 forensic accountants in the UK. What do you say?"

"Obviously, it's up to her. It sounds a great opportunity. I'll be sorry to see her go, especially if DS Ishmal is being transferred to uniform, but I have to agree, this could be exactly what she needs."

"DCI Burt, the question was rhetorical." The ACC was firmly in charge. "We know you would like to keep her, but her talents lie elsewhere. This is a tremendous opportunity for her. Given her weight and size issues, we frankly believe she's more suited to an analytical role instead of frontline police work. HR will interview her next week, so for now, say nothing. If she turns it down, which I think is unlikely, then she can stay in Special Resources until her weight becomes a problem."

"Right, that's us done here except, Steve, you have a new suite of offices on the 8th floor."

The DCI had been in a bit of a daze for the past few minutes trying to digest what was happening. All he could do was stand, nod to the three people who would be left in the room, say a hurried "thank you" and leave the ACC's office.

DCI Steve Burt felt a sense of relief. Both Twiggy and the Cap's jobs were safe. Both were being promoted and would be looked after. His second career was now back on track. He had a dinner date with Dr Alison Mills and he had his new Moss Bros suit. Suddenly, the world looked a much better place than it had four weeks ago.

The End